BRAVE NEW WEIRD

THE BEST NEW WEIRD HORROR, VOLUME THREE

edited by

ALEX WOODROE

with

MATT BLAIRSTONE

Content warnings are available at the end of this book. Please consult this list for any particular subject matter you may be sensitive to.

SELECTED WORKS
FROM TENEBROUS PRESS:

Split Scream Vols. 1-7
paired novelettes by various, edited by Alex Ebenstein

Your Body is Not Your Body: An Anthology to Benefit Trans Youth
at Risk
edited by Alex Woodroe

Puppet's Banquet
a novella by Valkyrie Loughcrewe

Casual
a novel by Koji A. Dae

All Your Friends are Here
stories by M.Shaw

TRVE CVLT
a gamebook novel by Michael Bettendorf

A Spectre is Haunting Greentree
a novel by Carson Winter

From the Belly
a novel by Emmett Nahil

Posthaste Manor
a novel by Jolie Toomajan & Carson Winter

The Black Lord
a novella by Colin Hinckley

Dehiscent
a novella by Ashley Deng

Agony's Lodestone
a novella by Laura Keating

Soft Targets
a novella by Carson Winter

**More titles at
www.tenebrouspress.com**

TABLE OF CONTENTS

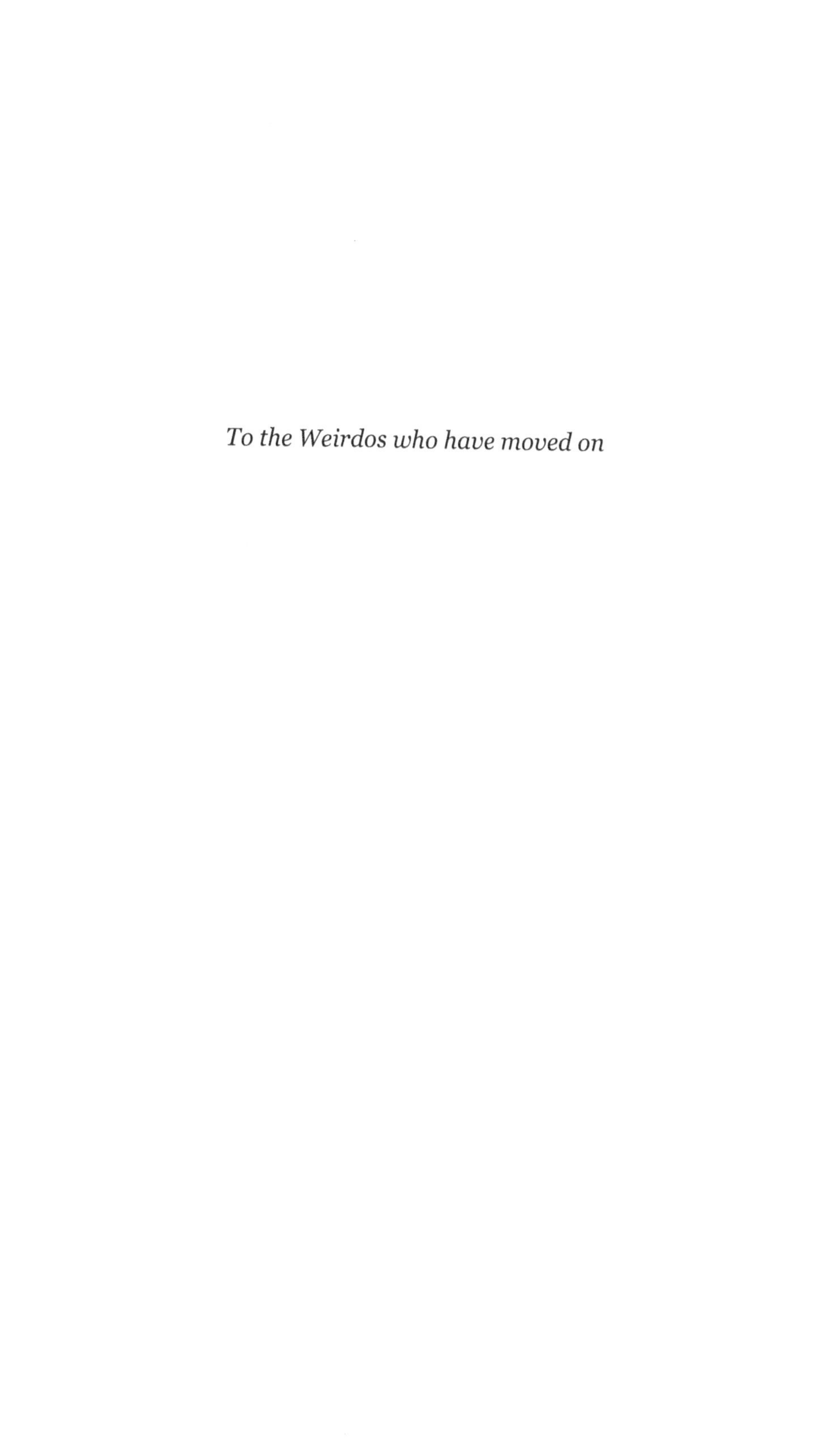

To the Weirdos who have moved on

WHAT IT MEANS TO HAVE A GARDEN THESE DAYS

ALEX WOODROE, EDITOR-IN-CHIEF,
TENEBROUS PRESS

IT'S COMPLICATED.

Most relationships are, right? We get to have a relationship with the arts—Amazing! But also all the complicated hopes and letdowns that come with that. Less amazing. We get to publish incredible writers and artists, we get to create space that wasn't there before for conversations and creations that might not otherwise have happened. Amazing! But we also have to contend with the heartbreak, the lack of support, the constant anger at how this system is incredibly broken; an image we only know the exact outline of because we're well in it.

When you draw the line on being us; publishers, editors, writers, artists, and general artist-wranglers, it's all pretty even. It's about as rewarding as it is grueling, about as fun as it is hard, and we fail about as much as we succeed. There's only one solitary element that stands aside from that equation, one piece of gold that doesn't get weighed on any scale, neither good nor bad. It's the fact that we get to have a say in what the world looks like right now. Sort of!

It doesn't sound like much; and that's because it probably isn't. We don't have billboards in main squares, we can't stop predators from getting book deals, we don't have power over public opinion at large. We're not the next household name; and maybe that's for the best.

What we get instead is a small, in a way insular—despite the fact that we're all over the world—community (and yes, we have fully embraced the word 'cult' at this point. You have to call a toad a toad.) We get to speak about what matters to us, and find that the number of people listening is not zero. We—us, publishers, and you, readers—get to support art that tells the story of today the way we want to hear it. I often think of it as tending a semi-wild plot of land; a garden of Weird and wonder.

And it's worth it not because of some illusion of control over the world; but because in going out to tend a garden, you've gone out. You are, physically, outside. You have left your sheltered space, and you are moving through the space that's not yours, and there are many, many strange things to discover there.

That's what it means to have a garden, it means opening yourself up to the relationship between you and 'out there', in which you're certainly shaping how 'out there' grows, but it's also certainly shaping you. We shape literature a little, and promise it flogs us into shape in return. You shape us with your choices in what you support, read, say a kind word about, and maybe in some way we can't entirely explain, we've done something to you, too.

Sorry/you're welcome?

Either way, *Brave New Weird* is an act of going out there and gardening. This specific issue, it comes at a time when the future of our countries is very uncertain. Mine's been attacked by the Russians and Matt's . . . well, same, frankly. My ability to visit the US without getting kidnapped by ICE is in question. Everyone's terrified, trying to figure out what tomorrow looks like when there's no plan and the rules have all gone out the window. And we can't change any of that; all we can do is get through it, same as everyone else.

But in the meantime, we can garden. Thank you for helping.

GREETINGS FROM THE DISTANT PAST (HOPEFULLY)

MATT BLAIRSTONE, PUBLISHER,
TENEBROUS PRESS

IT'S A TREACHEROUS world for artists these days.

I'm not gonna expound on that too much, because it could quickly devolve into an exhausting diatribe of sheer hopelessness and not-quite-paranoid-enough paranoia; of A.I. encroachment upon creators' rights, and shady business practices, and elitist wagons circling to protect the establishment, leaving the heretical and the voiceless and the unconventional to wither in silence; and it is my fervent wish that this book be picked up off a shelf many years from now by some curious reader who has the benefit of reflecting on our current decade of mass incompetence and terror and cruelty as an aberration, one that humanity eventually, somehow managed to steer its way out of.

(Forgive me my possibly foolish optimism, but optimism is what makes it possible to keep hitting the deadlines.)

If you're unfamiliar, Tenebrous is the lifeblood of an optimistic nihilist and a nihilistic optimist and we'll leave it up to you to decide which of us is which; "Two sides of the same coin or...the same side of two coins." What allows it to function, to grow, to thrive, is our ability to provide counterbalance to one another. We're great at gallivanting through the fire even though—make no mistake—everything is very much on fire.

You want some more foolish optimism? There are twenty-five examples on the following pages of artists who didn't get the memo that the world sucks too badly for them to create something alive and pulsating; and thirty-five more names beyond that who rounded out this year's impressive-as-always shortlist; and a thousand more who we went to battle with in the slush pile.

The world tries its best to out-Weird us, to beat us down, to enchain us in fear; and each writer in this year's Table of Contents stood up on their many hind legs, spat a big gob of sentient bone-spores into their would-be captors' eyes and declared, "You think *that's* Weird? Hold my goblet of fairy's blood."

Wait, I've changed my mind. There's that silly optimism, doin' its thing:

It's a *fabulous* world for artists these days. And it's *So. Goddamn. Weird.* I love it.

May each of these works seed a revolution in you.

A CONTRACT OF INK AND SKIN

ANGELA LIU

THE EARLIEST VERSIONS included uglier things: ground up insect eggs and corroded bronze, but the ink you receive is pure, made only from blood of the Cursed.

They inject it into your eyes first because that's the easiest way to tell you're different. The black ink mixed with blue and red, a purplish nebula pooling into the whites of your eyes.

It takes three months for your body to fully heal, but you'll be able to see the dark patterns within just a few days. The ink aches in their presence, sweating through the pores in your skin, but that ink is your shield, your bridge, your right to a Contract.

***

Hana's the first one to ask what you see.

"Just black clouds," you say, waving a hand as if gathering phantom threads of spider silk between your fingers. You ignore the way she winces at the motion. She sees through your lie because her brother got Inked just a few months before you. Before he stumbled into the forest, reaching for shadows, and never returned.

"He said to ignore the first few who try to make a Contract. They're the starving ones, and they won't hesitate to take more than they say," she warns, changing the dripping iced towel on your eyes for a freshly frozen one. The cold stings the thin skin of your eyelids. You feel the ink squirm its way from the front to the backs of your eyes like an overly curious needle.

You know Hana is a liar too. Her brother never said that; how could he? The dead don't speak about their own mistakes.

***

You dream of red rivers and purple skies. Of climbing impossibly tall mountains on long stilt legs, your tongue a paintbrush that never runs out of ink. You watch the mountains cast shadows below like black floods cutting through the endless poppy fields. Jagged wings burst through your luminescent spine. You become a bird and leap off the ledge, spilling into the shadows.

You wake, aching for planets you've never seen, your throat dry.

***

They put it in your fingers next. The needle breaks through the delicate skin on the tips, spooling ink into the dermis underneath. The ink traces its own black veins, ancient circuits across a new body, your body.

By then, the patterns have taken clearer shape. No longer splotches on a canvas of air or smoky trails under flickering streetlamps. They are now the familiar shape of objects, animals, people. A favorite book that disappeared one day while you were at school, a friend's pet cat stretching under the sun, a torn-up hospital gown washed up from the riverbed, your mother curled up on the stained couch before the Council arrived to take her away. You reach up and touch them with your swollen inked fingers. They whisper forbidden things into your skin.

***

The Artist tells you the ink will tell you when it's time. To be patient. That you're doing well, reacting better than most. There's only a 40% success rate, the unclaimed bodies in the forest and the caked blood beneath their fingernails all evidence of that.

You don't tell him that the ink is restless, how it wriggles in your eyes and fingers when you sleep, frenzied by the moans of the Cursed at night. How it traces the face of strangers onto the steamed glass of your windows. You don't tell him that sometimes you worry it'll find a way out of your body and let them in. *How sure are you there are no leaks?* you think. *A body has so many openings.*

As he pulls fresh ink into the syringe, you fight the urge to drag him toward you, to sink the sharp tip into his eyes and give him a look. Maybe together you could parse out the meaning of the dark constellations you see.

***

No one's ever told you this story, but you've pieced it together through rumor and old books: the Cursed arrived one winter night long ago during a heavy, luminous snowfall and never left. They lacked eyes, mouth, fingers. They spoke through spectres, tricks of light and shadows, words carved into the frozen ground outside our primeval forests. The townspeople believed they were a blessing when they took the shape of loved ones long gone, bodies given life again through the warm light of a fire or porch lamp.

But then there were the dead birds. The children staring at streetlamps at night like light-starved moths. The flickering apparitions, the unfamiliar faces in mirrors, the deep ripples over warm bath water, the phantom fingers trailing across sleeping bodies, thighs and throats. By the time the people realized what was happening, their hands were already quilted in black veins, already pulling open their windows to let in the night.

The Cursed desired connection. They loved the people. They wanted to be with them forever.

***

Hana doesn't ask what you see anymore. She sneaks you bread and apple slices from the school, but you have no appetite. When she catches you standing near the entrance of the forest, she grabs your hand so tight it leaves red fingerprints on your skin.

She turns you away from the window at night and tells you a story about birds. How some can soar across the sea for days and weeks, for thousands of miles until they reach their next home.

"What do they want so badly that they need to do that?" you ask, turning your gaze back to the window, to the faces and shadows that clamor for your attention, the fire burning on the street that only you can see.

"They don't want anything," Hana says, still holding your hand even when your fingers lack the strength to squeeze back. "Their body moves before their mind has a say. A programmed reflex."

You miss Hana when she stops coming. You wish you could

have asked her more about the birds, if they ever find their way back.

***

They inject it in your lips last, the ink streaming through microscopic pillows of fat. You expect it to have a taste, but there are no gustatory receptors inside the flesh. Instead, a phantom bitterness inks your tongue, a viscous metallic taste, and you squeeze the armrests, holding back the urge to retch.

When it's done, the Artist sits back and asks if you're okay. He massages the tension from his wrists, the syringe on the metal tray with traces of your blood on the tip.

"You're almost there," he says as if behind a glass wall, the ink in your ears corking his voice.

In the corner of the room, you see someone that wasn't there before. They wave to you, but you know not to wave back.

***

You try to recall the taste of summer fruit, the sweetness of cold watermelon slices, the two-toned color of the twilight sky behind your mother's house, the fevered pinks and oranges, the red gates outside your old school, your slanting reflection in the blue pool, a firefly pinging neon near your ear as your best friend holds your hand—any stroke of color to feel like yourself again.

But your thoughts settle on the shuddering black shadows in front of you like brushstrokes in the air. You can see the black eyes of lost friends who were Inked too, the charred black skulls of lost friends who were not. You want to peel the last piths of color from your memories and share them like precious, fragrant treats the way your mother used to dice tomatoes from her garden and douse them in oil and pepper for guests.

But these are not your friends, and a body is nothing more than a burning house where everyone has left except you.

***

The ink speaks, tastes, smells, touches, and takes. You are the canvas, its oils, its nourishment. Just as the Artist said, it comes when it is ready, even if you are not.

The warm threads of ink envelope your throat, tracing the soft line of your shoulders and hips. The black globes of your eyes see them before you feel them. A hurricane of dark light. A taste like cinnamon and electricity fills your mouth.

No one tells you that the longest night is the night when you are finally offered your Contract.

It's been three months, and your body has healed, but it no longer belongs to you. The Inked are here to serve, and you will, just like all those before you. This is the Contract of your ancestors, the way they chose to survive the hunger, the love of the Cursed. The cost of peace paid by the ink on the skin.

A creature calls out to you, hungry, your body like a beacon in the dark sea. You do not question when your fingers reach out.

VINING

EMMETT NAHIL

THE FIRST TIME he peeled back the skin of my thigh, I thought that I would die. The pain was unlike anything else I'd felt before.

I won't go on to describe it at length, because worse elements were soon to be introduced.

Dirt, nitrogenous fertilizer—filling the wound so the seedlings would have a good home, as we'd agreed—stung in a different way, but also clouded my senses, numbing the excavation site he'd dug into the thickest part of my leg. What should have been the sharp pain of incision only tugged a little bit, because of the way in which Eli had laid in the novocaine. He'd gotten good at it from habitually applying it to himself, and the pinch of the needle was gentler than a bee sting.

Make contact. Take something back with you through the void. That had been our agreement. As collaborators, as lovers, I couldn't agree more. It had just so happened that he had the skill and the steady hands of a surgical student. We'd joked long ago that he'd be using those hands to do his own top surgery next. We'd laughed about it.

I blinked, and I felt something sunken tugging at the very pit of my stomach. Digging its roots into me through the dirt he'd laid into my wound with those precise, steady hands, flashing green and turquoise and blue and black, black, onyx black—

"Michael? Michael," He said, leaning down so that his mouth was close to my ear. "Wake up."

"*. . . I'mawake,*" I said, having nodded off at some point in the past few minutes. Or passed out, one of the two.

He stood back, to look me over. "What did you see this time?"

The Root Oracle, I wanted to say, the same thing that I'd seen behind my eyes for the past week. But at the moment, my mouth tasted like pennies, and saying anything at all didn't seem like such a good idea. If I started to talk, I had the sneaking suspicion that I'd be coughing blood within a second or two. I could only imagine getting blood spatter on his clean scrubs, and what a shame that would be. Instead, I stayed quiet.

"Say *aah,*" he said. In-between the black spots blooming on my vision, I could see the medical tweezers gripped in his hand.

Bracing myself, I opened up. "*Aah . . .*"

I could feel him reach back into my mouth with the tweezers more than I saw him do it. The trichomes that had grown between my molars and into my throat registered the motion on my behalf, tickling a sensory part of my brain that made gooseflesh rise on my arms. The part of me that used to be a medical student registered the simultaneous reaction calmly, cataloging it away for future use.

" . . . They've broached another five centimeters," he said.

"*Ah-huh.*"

I could tell that he said it more for himself than for me; Eli had a tendency to talk to himself as he worked. I'd known they'd grown before he said a word. The Root Oracle had been showing me for days.

When the plant had first started to tendril inside my flesh, I had resisted. He'd had to bind my arms so that I wouldn't itch at the bumps behind the skin. The vines climbed up through the graft site, between my muscle and skin. At first, I'd flirted with the idea of tearing out the seedlings with my teeth if he didn't let my arms free. Eli had worked so hard to tend them from seed, we both had. I had been charged with ensuring that the plastic-wrapped starting cups had enough moisture, that they were sprouting well enough. Eli was in charge of misting them with the reactive mixture periodically, to ensure their levels of psychoactive compound were high enough. That the chemical we were after would still be extant in the adolescent plant. It would be a shame to destroy that, for a little discomfort.

We had tested on other plants, which had promptly accepted the graft. After a time, we moved to rats, adult mice. When we had been grilled by department administration about what we needed the creatures for, we pooled the remains of our stipend money and took a trip to the pet store. We walked out with young feeder mice, and had to make do with that. Their tiny bodies were delicate, and too easily consumed by the seeds. They still moved around after consumption, mossy bodies skeletal and still-walking.

Eli hefted his dense notebook onto the counter, mechanical pencil scratching out measurements with one hand while the tweezers remained in my mouth.

"You can still talk, correct?"

I hadn't started coughing yet, or thrown up like a few of the other inspections before. "Yeth."

He nodded curtly, jotting another note and retracting the tweezers, careful not to nick my teeth or what grew in between them. "Did you see anything when you were unconscious this time?"

I had been doing so well that I didn't dare clear my throat now. After a while your body simply accepts the scraping in your thorax, the curl of a vine against the base of your tongue, as natural. It represses some reactions while allowing others to be felt with much more clarity.

"Nothing. Just . . . colors," I rasped. "And lights."

"Colors," he said, squinting. "What kind of colors."

"Blue. Black, green, dark green—" I finally loosed the cough I'd been holding in since I woke up. He darted back, quick on his feet. The half-outfitted basement laboratory we'd constructed, together, had been designed with mutual convenience in mind. Mine was a large, padded chair lined with easily cleanable vinyl, complete with straps to restrain my limbs. *To skirt around some of your natural reactions to the plant*, Eli had said. His was a large tool rack, with rags and cleaning supplies nearby in case of messes. The seedlings were delicate even when they'd taken root, and it had been a trial to get the mice and rats to not bite and scratch them out from the graft site. Even moving them had garnered an air of disaster whenever we'd tried it, and the transplanting from hydroponic flask to the dirt grafts station shook the both of us. My immobility was a part of the bargain.

"Your eyes were twitching while you were out," he said. " . . . You really don't remember anything at all?"

I made sure to look him dead on. Eli's eyes were always a shade too light. A blue not of water or the sky but of raw ozone. It had been the first thing about him I'd noticed, when we first met.

"I must've been dreaming," I replied.

He blinked, rolling the mechanical pencil between his latex-gloved fingers. "The visions came in well enough when you first started."

"What are you accusing me of?"

"Nothing. I'm not accusing."

"Well, what are you saying, then?"

"I'm just saying that it's strange to start off with more access than with less," he said. "Everything we've read has documented an increase in contact with the entity over time."

I could feel myself bristle, the tendrils inside my graft curling as my muscles tensed. "So you think there's no way it would . . . taper off?"

His nose wrinkled. "It doesn't seem likely, no."

He knows. He has to know.

"What's wrong with you?" I hissed, feeling the beginnings of a leaf fluttering against the back of my gums. "Why do you think I'd lie?"

"Nothing's wrong," He leaned over my chair, staring a hole into me. Even if I could have moved away from his gaze, I wouldn't have. "And I didn't say you were. I just don't think you're telling me the whole truth."

I felt the coppery taste pooling below my tongue, so I kept my mouth shut.

After a moment, he swept away, leaving me as I was. As I closed my eyes, I fell back in, slipping back into the space in the rear side of my brain that held me in orbit, like a leaf on a long, vining plant.

I felt a little guilty, but every second I was speaking to Eli I had itched for that return. The voice of the Root Oracle didn't sound like words, or an audible phrase in my head. A sensation didn't echo so much as emit from a lower part of my brain stem, crawling upwards from my spine into my unconscious thought as instinct, inclination. It was craving.

I delved down, and the Oracle was waiting for me.

Veiled and many-fleshed, it peeled and undulated out of the richly fertilized blackness in my skull. I knew it found the space comfortable, because it had told me so. It was cool and damp inside that place, and it grew and flourished in the dark and cramped spaces within my body. What I was fed, fed it. Allowed it to grow strong and tensile and many limbed.

You've returned to us.

"You called me," I thought in return. The words emitted from me, bled out of every cell, and the Root Oracle lapped them up as soon as I thought them. Its mouth was occupied by many cilia and peeling tendrils which cradled its head and neck, extending backwards. The shape of its body was that of mandrake root mixed with dozens upon dozens of solanaceae belladonna blooms. It smelled of jasmine and decaying flesh, and dripped dirt and moss as it moved and coiled in and out of itself before me.

We appreciate your devotion. It's not often that we see such loyalty so quickly.

" . . . Do you see others? Often?"

That entirely depends on your definition of often. It said, in a manner that could almost be described as dry. *None, in your lifetime.*

Something in me swelled at that. I felt more sure than ever that Eli shouldn't know about the Oracle. It wouldn't be right.

We choose you as much as you choose us, Michael.

" . . . Really?" I thought, which sounded stupid and childish even in my own head. "Why."

Because you wanted to let us into you. Your generosity lets us dig into the surface of this world deeper than we ever could in isolation.

The Oracle's last words rang within me like a bell, echoing in my stomach and in my chest. In its words, I could clearly see the lives of worms, digging inside the soil for years and decades and centuries, feeding on the dead flesh there, felt a thousand hands inside soil pulling out root after root, felt the snap of eternity breaking down inside the head of an ant—the beauty there was so great as to hold pure, raw terror.

It hurt so badly, as bad as poison. Such that the novocaine-ridden cuts Eli had made in my flesh would pale in comparison even without the painkillers. The pain of those potentialities degrading within me, peeling back my skin and muscle and nerves to demonstrate my smallness, my *weakness, my minute human life—*

I was diving into the dense, wet dark once again. Sparks of the Root Oracle's knowledge unspooled as I went down, down, down, and just before I truly felt no more its voice tolled in my head one more time.

Fear not. We will unmake you in your image to be remade in ours.

***

After what I was told was an additional week in the chair, Eli made incisions below my chest, over my lungs. He needed to create an exploratory window through which we could see how far the vines had moved within my body. He was good about keeping them clean, until the tendrils had started to creep up and out of the excision deep from below the skin. We knew that the plant preferred the dark, and so we were surprised when some buds sprouted at the tips of them. He pinched off some of them, which smelled like rotting jasmine as soon as he did. I was barely awake, and I couldn't be certain if the scent was in my head or between us.

"The growth should continue at pace," he said, laying a hand on my cheek. It rested there for just a moment, and I felt the Root Oracle slither away from his touch. "Likely close to a week. It's growing faster than we'd projected."

He smiled down at me, and I nodded heavily. The anesthetic he was administering was now more than topical.

I blinked and it felt like an hour had passed. Or maybe it was a minute, or a second.

Chloroform or chlorophyll or Clorox bleach—

"Michael? *Michael.*"

"Hmmn?"

He was moving around the room, and for some reason I was having trouble following his motion. I could tell that he was constantly glancing back over his shoulder at me. I could smell that there was something like fear in his eyes, mixed with something else I was far too hazy to put my finger on. "Darling, wake up. The propofol dosage was too strong."

"How-long . . . how long . . ." I tried to say. My tongue was clotted and unwieldy in my mouth. It was hard to navigate the words around the budded leaves that filled it.

"Huh?"

"*Howlongsitbeen—*"

"Michael, honey. You need to tell me what you've been seeing, okay?" he said, softly. "And then you can go back to sleep."

No, I can't. I can't—

Luckily, I was much too far gone to tell anyone much of anything. Let alone what the Oracle had shown me. What I'd given it in return, how it had solved every problem of my biology and replaced it with its own pure gifts. He would want it for himself, he would want me to share it—

"Can't."

Eli's tone turned on a knife's edge. *"Michael.* Can't, or won't?"

I had let him in because we were the *same.* When we had found the entheogen seed catalog hidden away we had tried every combination in the book. Me, a botany student, him a medical student. It was a match made in a matchbook, ready to be struck and burnt. He'd done DMT once, and told me that he'd seen God, or something that looked an awful lot like angels fluttering in the trees on the hillside just outside campus. I had to be convinced, but once we crossed that rubicon together, in the make-shift surgical chamber in the basement below his house, it was an easy shift to believe him. We could be better together. We could discover what had been hidden in the under-weave of the universe.

Now, even though we had rolled over the stone together, only I could see what crawled underneath.

" . . . Because the growth will eventually continue up through to your skull. I can only imagine what will happen once it reaches your brain."

I didn't reply, but when I looked down at my fingernails, I saw that they were tinged yellow and chlorophyll-green.

***

"We'll have to trepan."

He carved the slim line of a halo into me—to peel back the skin. The rounded bit of the dental drill was cleaned, ready to relieve the pressure inside my skull. The trepanation immediately allowed some of the tendrils to unfurl near my brow. My head was already shaved, but the matter of my skin and hair was besides the point. I had no use for it anymore.

Eli told me that I looked more beautiful than ever. That there was beauty in this transformation, even here and now. I'd been excavated, and the constant bleed, the IVs and the blood transfusions I'd endured all went to seed, watered inside my skin.

"It's remarkable. How fast it's taken over," he mused as he took one of the smaller tendrils out through the hole, gently coaxing out the as-yet uncurled leaf out from under the bone.

I felt more lush than ever; I wanted to fuck him. I felt strong, even though I knew in some ways I was still weak. The life multiplying within me was simply a part of it. I no longer felt selfish, because I knew that the Root Oracle had chosen *me*, that I'd been honored with something that Eli had helped birth. It had come squalling out of me in root and bloom and he just needed to free me, so that I could show him how to come to full fruit.

The Root Oracle had shown me how to talk to him, even if my mouth was a knotted ball of vines now.

I ducked my chin in his direction. *"Come here."*

"Huh? Why," he said.

"Let me see you."

"Michael, you can already."

"I want you to undo the straps."

"You know I can't do that," he said. "It's not *safe*, you've lost fluids and blood—"

"That doesn't matter, come here," I cajoled.

As if possessed, he walked towards me. I could feel a sprout poking from the corner of my eye, my sinuses filled with it all. I needed him to feel me, to feel all of this green.

Eli leaned down to me, and that's when I loosed my final weapon.

"So am I to be a vessel forever? Was that what you wanted?" I whispered, letting my voice, my essence seep into him.

"I never wanted to . . . " he said. "I just need to know. I need you to *tell* me like we agreed."

" . . . Then let me show you."

He blinked rapidly, cool eyes trained on what had become of me, and tremblingly reached down, unlatching the buckles holding my chlorophyll-veined arms immobile.

In an instant, I saw him for what he was: a dying animal, leaning over me, mouth agape and panting, not knowing what I was, or what I could be. I pitied him. I hated him, and more than anything in the world I wanted to dig my fingers into the fresh loam of his flesh and dig, dig, dig.

And so as summer comes to multiply all things growing, I did.

THE TANGLE
(DID NOT KILL KITSAULT)

K.A. WIGGINS

THERE IS A town in the north where children told stories of the Tangle.

It's empty now.

Or nearly so. Hired groundskeepers make their endless rounds of the tidy streets, mowing lawns to keep the forest at bay; checking seals on windows and doors to shut out the damp; tracing the lines and corners and angles to keep them straight and true and unwavering. Holes are patched. Mildew scrubbed. Darkness huddled against over long, lonely nights while the town waits for a rebirth that does not come.

This is not a story about madness.

***

Steve drives the kind of truck that cannot be parked without taking up four spots on a diagonal. At least, not by him. The truck sprawls, broad and tall and wide and so heavy it chews up the road in its wake. Its oversized cab would seat a family of five and a friend, if Steve would let the rugrats with all their crumbs and smears and stinks up onto its heated leather seats, instead of exiling them to the wife's SUV. The crew cab truck's undersized box still thrusts out past the end of his parking pad and into the common driveway of the townhome complex he resents, the shiny, unused knob of its trailer hitch forcing his neighbours to hug the far curb to slip past. That part gives him a little thrill every time he spots their sour faces. One day he'll get a decent bit of land and have room to spread out, even if he has to wait for the old man to croak so Steve can tear down the old eyesore out in the woods and build a proper homestead.

In the meantime, Steve wedges his oversized truck into his undersized, shared lot, careful not to snag his flags or scratch the shiny, unmarred finish between decals on the sad ornamental seedlings and mercilessly pruned shrubs separating his slice of parking pad from the next.

Something scuttles in the shadows beneath the bushes. Squirrels, rats, raccoons, the neighbour's cat. Roadkill in waiting.

Steve is and is not a "truck driver," a "blue collar working man," a "patriot."

This is not a story about "good men."

***

Kale and Rashida and So-jeong and Krish sat around a fire in the woods. That was then and not now, and so they are in no danger of getting in trouble if I tell you that they were young and drinking and maybe doing a little more than that even, and so too was it in a time and place when a fire was no great hazard and the forest had not yet been reduced to little more than dry tinder.

Then, they were wrapped in the green vastness at the far northern extremity of the Coast Mountains, and the swimming wallow of flames around regrettably damp branches and twigs and Krish's report card and Kale's half-written paper on the wonders of molybdenum in the modern world—heavily cribbed from Rashida and gleefully sacrificed at the earliest opportunity—did little enough to press back its dank weight. The fire's light and all-too-modest warmth was a sensible precaution against the bear and the cougar and the Tangle, or so said Kale, and the rest shrieked with comfortable chills and goggled into the shadows with good-naturedly amused apprehension.

Tales of ghosts and cryptids and ancient nightmares in the woods were traded back and forth as the night wore on. So-jeong snuck up a gnarled branch behind Rashida's back, mossy and menacing. Both turned out to be more afraid of startled spiders dangling from a high side-pony or scuttling up a sleeve than the Tangle.

THE TANGLE (DID NOT KILL KITSAULT)

Easy to play at boldness in the firelight. Harder on the trek home, shadows twisting just out of sight, unseen fingers snagging your feet, half-glimpsed *somethings* skittering in the dark. And then that long, long struggle to fall asleep—for the lucky pair whose parents didn't wait up to smell the smoke in their hair and the lies on their breath—that rigid, wide-eyed, sweat-prickling battle not to hear the Tangle tapping and scraping at the windows.

This is not a story about babes in the woods.

***

Sahil drives a truck. Feels like all he does is drive, but he can't complain when his brother-in-law must drive in the city for not one but three of those terrible apps, ferrying passengers and dinners and shopping to and fro all day and all night so he may stay within summoning distance of ailing parents. No Sahil is fortunate, on the balance, to have made his way so far as to own— well, one day he will pay it off and *then* he will own—his own wheels on such a grand and enduring enterprise. He is an entrepreneur, the proprietor of a small business, perhaps one day of a fleet, even, and so what if he had once hoped and worked for so much more? Who will listen to him if he complains (again) that it's an utter waste of all those years of study (when his parents are listening) or (to everyone else) that his true destiny should have been the screen, with a voice and moves like his?

So, alone but not silent, he hums and sings and bobs while his eyes grow tired and his body grows stiff and too soft for stardom— not as a leading man anyway, not crooning ballads and fiery, passionate romantic entreaties, though perhaps as the bumbling comic he may yet have a chance—mile after mile of highway unwinding under eighteen wheels. He prefers the heavy traffic of the cities in the south. It's just that little bit more like the bustle and churn of home than that winding climb up the Fraser Canyon and the long, dull stretches of trees. Dark needles that seem to go on forever, and sharp-edged stone, and the rolling dry hills that go all nobbly as the bushes change with the seasons, like cheap, no- good clothes in the wash. Then more trees. Oh, and then more trees. It's not that he hates trees, or nature, or green things, so much as the up and down and back and forth of it all that gets to him.

But the highway slips away as if someone else is doing the driving. Sahil's head is heavy, his eyes burning. Lane markers scroll by, signs glinting in the headlights, the occasional wash of streetlights around a turnoff or rest stop painting watercolour streaks across the road. White light darts and flares in the side mirrors. An engine roars, another impatient driver passing in defiance of the double yellow, unwilling to hang back until the next passing lane appears for Sahil to sidle into. He's a good driver, respectful, took time to learn the rules of the road and follows them, not like some. Not like this late-night stranger on the road. Tires squeal. Red streaks away in the distance; taillights vanishing in the night.

Something stirs in the shadows of the ditch, a snarl of something flickering by and gone so fast it barely registers. A broken branch or a bit of bush rocked by the truck's slipstream, perhaps, or a buck getting ready to make a dash to the other side, antlers darting in the headlights.

Sahil blinks. Slowly. Too slow, the length between the lowering of lashes and the raising longer each time. He needs to pull over and take a nap before he flattens a deer, or a car, or rolls the rig right off the shoulder.

Instead, he reaches for the radio. Turns the music up. Slaps his face. Can't afford to rest yet. Let the twitching shadows watch if they want; he has a job to finish. Gotta keep moving.

This is not a story about struggle.

***

There are stories told about stories. Anatomies of legends. Histories of folklore. Crafty cryptid lore and dry, dusty, lifeless academic butterfly-board pinnings of once-living tales and teachings, and had that lonely northern town lasted more than the ring of a tree's span, perhaps the Tangle's tale too would have been flayed and dissected or transformed and transmuted. Graduate papers and comic books and quirkily sympathetic or gruesomely garish indie horror flicks birthed from its flesh.

Perhaps some dogged researcher or obsessive fan would have made the trek into the wilderness and found it lonely but not empty. Perhaps Krish, or So-jeong, or Rashida, or Kale, or the children who came after them, had they had more than a year and change in the town that time forgot, would have gone off to university to fill their heads with far-away things and found themselves coming back home with more questions than answers, more curiosity than judgement. Perhaps they would have asked why a town was built instead of the usual tent village, why whole families were relocated instead of workers trucked or flown or shipped in, why it all ended so fast—and why ever more money poured into maintaining an abandoned town carved out of mountain and rainforest and coastline than ever came out of it.

And what would have come of their questions? Would these intrepid questers after truth have pointed toward the mines, ripping into the earth and waking that which slept in the shadows? Toward the vast, eldritch forest, alive and ancient and unfathomably entangled with more life than academia had the eyes to see? Toward neighbours—yes, neighbours, for even the wilderness is never as lonely as we pretend, nor as empty. But there have come no researchers to ask invasive questions of the Nisga'a, to delve into environmental violations left to seep their poison unseen, or to stalk the various and sundry capitalistic or imperialistic bogeymen.

Or at least none has yet survived the publication gauntlet. No trace of the Tangle's origin, nor of its purpose, nor of its victims may be found in peer-reviewed literature or fannish forums.

This is not a story about colonialism.

***

This summer, or the last, or perhaps it is in one soon to come that there was/is/will be a fire in the woods, as there has ever been and ever will be. But this time the forest is dry, pest-plagued, and drought-ravaged, choked by deadfall and poisoned by "productivity"-enhancing pesticides. The fire burns fast and high and deep all at once, greedy and mindless. The houses on the fringe go first, the ones on a bit of land. In the forest itself, really. Intruding on wild places, they share the same fate.

It's sad. It's unpreventable.

So-jeong's daughter can't fight for those homes. The fire is racing toward town, and Fire Chief Lee has to prioritize, even at the cost of her own childhood home. The newer developments on the edges of the municipality will go next, in fresh-painted rows with trampolines in the back yards and flowers in the front. Then more homes will go up in their dozens and hundreds, flames splashing against banks of the increasingly modest duplexes and townhouses in the denser ring near the town center. And then, finally, if the joint efforts of every urban and wildland fighter who can be called up, flown in, or haul ass by road fail to hold the line, the fire will crash against the older apartment blocks and shiny new condo towers in the city core, displacing thousands. Tens and hundreds of thousands.

Fire Chief Lee is pulled in every direction at once, juggling press conferences, meetings with communications and emergency response leads, progress briefings, incessant calls from her mother—wondering if someone couldn't just go 'round to look in on things, just in case the fire went around instead of through the old place?—and endless coordination calls.

She still finds time to ride the front line, getting eyes on the flames, boots on the ground, reassuring and providing hands-on support to both her well-trained team and the desperately needed backup dropped in the middle of chaos to help. No one needs to know if the reason she makes time for it is just a bit selfish, too.

There's a sort of peace, in a way, to getting out into the field, even amidst the struggle and the danger and the misery of the conditions. She gives herself over to the collective battle against humanity's great elemental enemy and ally for long moments at a time, relishing the focus and momentary simplicity of heat and sweat and urgency, the rush of a crisis averted, a life pulled from the path of the flames, a structure saved, or the numb horror of another home alight.

In an active fire zone, little is stable. Smoke twists and churns and billows. Ash crumbles and shifts and floats. Charred structures unexpectedly give way. The very light is unsteady, unreliable, burning hot but dark, the sun swallowed by smoke and the night blighted by reflected flame. Necessary protective equipment binds movement, mutes sound, obscures sight.

Fire Chief Lee might have been excused for paying little attention to the slow creep of shadows at the edge of her vision. But she is careful, and far too responsible, and not nearly selfish enough to ignore a potential creature in need of aid, and so she eases back to a safe location and turns to inspect the charred mess where the woods had once met the groomed edge of an exurban yard.

Amidst the twisted, blackened roots and trunks and branches and twigs, something dark and even more twisted hunkers low, creeping deeper into the ruin of the forest's edge.

Fire Chief Lee squints. Takes a cautious step after it. Forest creatures get burned. It's unfortunate, but she can't have animal rescue groups on site until the fire is under control, and that won't be for hours yet. Maybe days. If she can coax the creature out, though, dropping it off for treatment on her way back to headquarters would be its best chance at survival. She makes her voice soft, coaxing—

Tires squeal. An engine roars, nearly as loud as the fire, and cuts out. Fire Chief Lee looks over at the truck just long enough to confirm that its decals—and certainly its *flags*—mark it as none of hers. Even so, the creature in the shadows has already slipped away.

This is not a story about reconciliation.

✳✳✳

There is a town in the north almost exactly where Canada turns into America and British Columbia collides with Alaska and the ocean runs up into the land, and it is dead but not buried.

That is unkind, but true. Here are more dubious facts:

"Kitsault" comes from the Nisga'a word "Gits'oohl," which according to Wikipedia means "a ways in behind." It is also known as "Chandra Krishnan Kitsault," after the deceased mother of the millionaire who bought the town 22 years after it died and has maintained it ever since.

This zombie town is a relic of the past, having been built in 1979 to house 1,200 residents. It features all the essentials of a healthy community circa 1980: a bowling alley, a swimming pool, a mini mall, a hospital, a supermarket, a daycare, a school, and a pub.

Notably, remote, ready-made company towns fabricated in the latter twentieth century are rare. For good reason. The mine intended to support the town—or rather, which the town was intended to supply with a functionally captive workforce—shut down when the molybdenum market collapsed. Apparently,

21

pivoting to the other resources in the area was not an option, despite the considerable investment in building and populating the purpose-built company town. Kitsault was evacuated less than 18 months after residents moved in, meaning Krish really ought to have held onto that report card as a collector's item.

No tales of the Tangle survive the town. No former residents of Kitsault have come forward with their stories. None of the (many) revival schemes over the past decade since the town was purchased, or the four decades of its existence prior, have come to fruition.

This is not a story about ghosts.

***

Sahil found fire season unexpectedly invigorating. People treated him like a hero for a change. He'd been trying to build his profile as a streamer, dancing and singing at the end of long drives, in scenic locations, in the seat of his truck. But it was his dashcam footage of flames at the side of the highway and apologies about being slow to update due to fire season deliveries that were boosting his numbers. Hey, whatever it took to go viral and catch the eye of a casting director, right?

In any case, the endless stretches of road and stiff joints and creeping exhaustion felt that much lighter as the likes and comments kept climbing. Plus, the orange apocalyptic skies and blowing smoke made for a change of scenery, like winter fog through the canyon, but dirtier. Sometimes, he even got diverted onto new and strange routes where the flames only guttered at the sides of the rough side road instead of roaring across the highway, which made for exciting, if precarious, adventures.

When the smoke closed in, though, it was hard to make good time. It was like driving in heavy rain, or blizzard weather, or bad fog, except it made his eyes water and his nose run for good measure. Sahil leaned over the wheel and peered through the windshield, humming nervously. It didn't help. He sighed, rubbed his eyes, and turned his music up.

That didn't help either. These route diversions, they slowed him down to be sure, meant the time between owning 68% of his truck and 70% would be longer than he'd planned, but Uncle Krish, who was not really his uncle but a much older cousin and also his sponsor, had said not to sweat it, everyone here lives on credit and no one cares, and Sahil wasn't that old yet, not so close to retirement, just hang in there, young buck, and laughed.

Sahil had smiled to show he got the joke, and then gone and searched up the idiom until he understood that a buck was a male deer like the one on the side of the road now, no more than a branching, bobbing tracery of many-pointed antlers dark against the drifting smoke outside his window.

He slowed, blinking rapidly. Too close, too fast—and too high for deer, unless they were up on a ridge beside the road. Were a whole herd of them about to leap out in front of him? Or on top? Visions of hooves cracking the windshield danced behind his eyes, sharp points crashing through glass, flesh, bone, blood seeping into the torn seat cover. There was something mesmerizing about the thought, the thick red ooze and cobwebbed glitter of safety glass, the blare of the horn drowning out his music—

But when Sahil dragged his attention up from the depths of nightmarish imagination, the shadow was hidden again in the smoke beyond the unbroken window. He peered back over his shoulder, flicking his hazards on and easing to a crawl. He sang loudly to cover his fear, bobbing his head and rolling his shoulders as if dancing. If he were about to plunge to his doom, he'd rather go out on a high note.

His fog lights weren't bright enough to cut through the gloom and find the edge of the road. The dark smoke stirred ominously, and too erratically, jittering in patterns that had nothing to do with updrafts and slipstreams, scratching and scraping against the paint as if the truck rolled through a dense thicket of thorns.

But as Sahil's front tires dipped, the breeze poked a hole in the smoke deep enough to show the yawning chasm ahead. He was moving just slow enough to ease back from the canyon's edge. Perhaps he offered up a nod, a salute, a prayer.

Perhaps the Tangle just liked his music.

This is not a story about respect.

***

There was a time before roads.

Or, not what we think of now as roads. Oh, there were tracks and trails and ways. The animals wore their best-loved routes into the bush—or did the forest make way for its most mobile members, the busy mycelial net working its microbial magic in soil and root and sap, devouring, digesting, supplying, nurturing, redirecting, redistributing, until the slow movement of root and branch was arranged in harmony with fang and claw? The first people had their routes too, over land and, more often and more wisely, by water, wearing and working their ways through brush from shore to mountain and back again, bridging gaps and smoothing paths.

But as more people and different people came, by water and by land, first from the west and then from the east, faster, straighter, more direct ways were demanded. Waves of 'explorers' and traders and settlers and immigrants, with their urgency and hunger and drive to get where they wanted to go by trail and river and rail, chopping and blasting and grading and paving.

The cars and the roads got sleeker, fatter, hungrier, demanding more lives, more communities, more land, *more*. Homes and communities bulldozed to make way for highways, towns shrivelled as traffic shifted, public funds diverted. Land carved up, animals flattened, people displaced and dispossessed and vanished in ones and twos and towns at a time, from Hogan's Alley to the Highway of Tears. But now, oh now we can go *fast*—except when it's not quite fast enough, or not to the right places, or not well enough maintained, or too many other people want to go at the same time.

There is a ghost town in the north where children told stories of the Tangle.

It did not have a road *out* then.

It does now.

This is not a story about progress.

***

Steve's flags catch fire as he peels away from the fire chief. He watches this dramatic exit in his rear and side mirrors, pleased. But the plasticky material shrivels instead of flaming out in a blaze of glory, and the snowflake isn't even watching anyway, though her crew's still bristling at him in a satisfactory way. Nah, Mira's staring off into the bush. Always was an airhead, ever since they were kids. Well, so much for that. If the district hadn't insisted on a fuckin' diversity hire, maybe they'd've had a competent chief and her mom's old place would still be standing. His dad's was—barely, and only because Steve had rounded up a bunch of his buddies, grabbed some gear, and put in the work to make it happen.

That was another problem with Mira Lee—total control freak when she wasn't letting actual important stuff slide, going on about district resources and how it was a crime to borrow equipment, even if it was an emergency, and why hadn't he stopped to think of anyone else? Only she hadn't used the word 'borrow', and a man's responsibilities are to his own folk first and foremost, and that's when he'd gone from thinking she'd be pleased to hear he'd protected his dad's place, maybe wanting some tips—after all, she'd spent her share of time playing at "Uncle Keith's" as a kid just like he'd been forced to hang out at "Auntie So-jeong's", 'cept for that bit when they'd all moved up north—to just full-on pissed off.

Steve swerved around blackened debris, tires bumping up on the curb. He wasn't worried. The jacked-up suspension would get him over anything that lay in his path. Emergencies—that's what he was always telling granola-munching libs like Mira—that's why you need a proper truck. Gotta be prepared to do your part. What'cha gonna do when the power goes down and you can't charge your dinky little tinker-toy car, huh? How you gonna show up for your neighbours when they gotta evac and you've got no room, or they need help hauling shit? Like those sprinklers, those had mostly fit in the truck bed. Hadn't even scraped it up too bad. Little polish, damage would buff right out.

He hoped.

But no, Mira and her crew hadn't wanted to hear about his heroism and how he and the boys were standing by ready to help protect their neighbours, now they'd taken care of their own. She'd mewled about training and regulation and safely working as a team, and then gone on to scold him and—well, he'd tuned her out by then, but there might have been some kinda warning even. Getting too big for her lady-pants, that one.

Gotta get back to dad's place, though. Shift the gear off the property, if the boys hadn't already moved it. Just in case the snitch called it into the RCMP and got somebody unfriendly to come out and take a look.

Steve was out of the active fire zone now, barrelling through the night with the high beams on to cut through the smoke. Stuff was so thick, even with the windows up, the moment he went to call his buddies he started hacking. Had to kill the connection before he could get a word out. His eyes streamed, gritty and squinted with coughing so that he nearly missed when the headlights caught something move at the edge of the road.

Not that it mattered. Critters were always getting pancaked. Long as they weren't big enough to put a dent in the frame or a crack in the windshield, he wasn't bothered. Or—could be stuff got thrown in the wind from the fire. Charred branches, twigs, bracken. Eh, could be something else. Not his business.

Steve's phone rang. He glanced at the display. The wife, not the guys. She'd be fine—his townhouse was way inside city limits. No need to evac. She and the kids could just sit tight while he did all the work, like usual. Oh, she'd whine and pout and give him the cold shoulder for "not being there for her," or some shit later, but that was what was wrong with this country, wasn't it? If a man couldn't be free in his own home to do what he needed to, where could he?

He considered his options. Let it ring, and she'd be all anxious and concerned—and pissed when she realized he'd just been ignoring her. Shut it up, and she'd be pissed now. Have more time to work herself up a good fuss by the time he got home, too. He grinned and reached for the red icon.

Something clattered against the drivers' side door.

Steve swore and swerved before he'd had a chance to look properly. For all his big talk about roadkill, he didn't mess with deer. They could do a number on your ride. And he thought he'd caught a flash of something through the side mirror. Antlers? He had a vague impression of a near-lace-like snarl of shadows.

Wild rack—twelve pointer at least! Woulda messed up his paint, but he might've risked it to nab that for his wall if he'd been paying closer attention. Damn tall for deer though. Could an elk have been pushed this far west by fire?

But when he pulled over and peered out the window, he couldn't make out anything in the smoke. Fuck. Must've just been a larger branch thrown by the wind. Fire tornado?

Steve's phone rang again. The wife. He smirked. Waited for the noise to stop before tapping over to contacts as he got back on the road. Thumbed through the menu to find his old man's number. Getting a busy signal next time would really wind her up.

THE TANGLE (DID NOT KILL KITSAULT)

His dad wasn't answering, though. He tried the guys next, working his way through the list as, one after the next, they failed to answer.

The smoke was brighter now, and unevenly lit. Shouldn't be anything left burning in this direction—had he got turned around? Or had the flames doubled back? Maybe better check the station. He had to hand it to Mira on that front, if begrudgingly. Trust a lady fire chief to be good at the boring paper-pusher chores like hurrying fire status updates out 'round the clock.

Steve reached for the radio, still clutching his phone. The sharp clatter, when it came from his left, was accompanied by a dark smudge at the corner of Steve's vision. He whipped around so fast he nearly chucked his phone through the windshield. It bounced off and skittered to the far corner of the dash.

He was too busy searching for the source of the noise to worry about it. But there was no sign of anything bigger outside the window than drifting ash—some of it visibly aflame, glittering like tiny red stars.

Steve picked up speed. It was getting uncomfortably warm, A/C straining against the heat. He'd better get through this next stretch fast. Didn't want his decals to melt like the flags. They'd fuse to the paint. Besides, he'd driven these roads all his life. Couldn't have gotten turned around. Had to be maybe five minutes from his old man's . . .

His phone rang, buzzing against the dash with its face down so he couldn't check the caller ID. The Bluetooth display wasn't picking up the call through the truck, either.

Steve stretched. The broad nose of the truck defeated his reach. He unbuckled, shifted his grip on the wheel, and strained. Not quite. Moved his left foot to the gas, slid his right over, and prepared for a quick lunge.

Steve was alone on the road.

Until he wasn't.

By the time the fire came, there was little left to clean up.

This is not a story about justice.

***

There is a ghost town in the north where children told stories of the Tangle.

It did not have a road then. Oh, it had streets, the kind you live on and walk to school on and ride your bike down the hill on and drive deliveries up from the dock on. Cul-de-sacs and looping, winding, closed circuits, and dead-ends that peter into nothing but unmarked forest trails. But it didn't have a road *out*, that kind connects to the great artery of roads that connect all of us.

And so the stories they told in that town were stories of watchers in the woods and fingers among the roots, hanging twigs that snagged your hair and tapped at your window and scraped at the siding while you lay in your bed, and moss that left a stain that wouldn't wash out no matter what you tried, that might rot you from the outside in and the inside out—or maybe would just make your mom yell at you to do the laundry again.

Eerie stories. Uncanny stories. Stories that sent a shiver up your spine and kept you looking over your shoulder. Stories that followed you home and kept you there, where it was safe. Stories that found you alone in the woods and welcomed you into the great, endless tale of the eternal dark under the trees.

And then the roads joined the roads joined the roads and the Tangle followed us out.

And there it waits, at the edges, along the ways, just in behind where you think to look. You've seen it, you just didn't know it. It was there in the shadows between the streetlights and the tangled growth in the ditch. It was the half-glimpsed *something* that caught your eye through the drivers' side window and was gone before you could turn and focus. A rustling, a clattering, a watching.

But the Tangle, unstudied, unstoried, hitherto unremarked in the annals of cryptozoologists, if we are to speak of it, must not be misclassified. Do not think it a moral or immoral thing, a creature of appetites or judgements. It is more mystery than monster, more thought than thing. If it has claimed victims, if there are any patterns to its sightings and sensings and those who met their end, they are hitherto unmapped.

This is not a story about the Tangle.

BIG CATS OF NEWFOUNDLAND

Ainsley Hawthorn

Gerard Penney March 22, 2016—Pinned Post 📌
Welcome to Big Cats of Newfoundland, a discussion group dedicated to tracking sightings of large wild cats on the island!

Officially, the government doesn't recognize the existence of cougars, mountain lions, pumas, or panthers in Newfoundland, but many of us have seen them with our own eyes. This group's purpose is to collect documentary evidence we can submit to Forestry and Wildlife to prove big cats are really here.

Group Rules:
- No bullying or name-calling.
- No promotions or spam.
- No posts about lynx. We already know lynx are here, and lynx posts distract from the group's focus on unidentified big cats.

Jacob Mercer October 15, 2018
Just a note: the names "cougar," "mountain lion," "puma," and "panther" all refer to the same animal. The cougar actually holds the Guinness World Record for the animal with the widest variety of names—it has over 40 in English alone!

> **Gerard Penney** October 15, 2018
> @Jacob Mercer Thanks, Jacob, but I'm going to leave all the different names up so everyone who joins understands what we're talking about.

Kaitlin Basha June 6, 2024
A few years ago my girlfriend and I were driving the highway between Daniel's Harbour and Port Saunders on the Northern Peninsula when a massive tan-coloured cat jumped right out into the middle of the road. It looked straight at us, and I thought my heart was just going to stop. I'll never forget its great big yellow eyes. Then one more jump and it ran off into the trees on the other side.

  We see foxes up here all the time, but a fox can't cross the road in two hops! I've never seen anything like it before or since.

  Gerard Penney June 6, 2024
  I hear this a lot. People seeing cats so big they can cross a road in a jump or two. Thanks for sharing your story!

  Jodi Peddle June 9, 2024
  Nor Pen seems super active for big cats! Need to roadtrip up there sometime.

Brandon Pike May 21, 2024
Went camping w my buddies on the wknd out Terra Nova way. Seen a big blk cat cross the path in front of us .Went right into the brush. Too bad I never had my phone w me. Wondering what kind of animal I saw??

  Meghan Hillier May 21, 2024
  Could it have been a black lynx? They're rare but they exist. Someone photographed one in the Yukon in 2020.

    Brandon Pike May 21, 2024
    @Meghan Hillier Not a lynx .Had a long tail.

    Meghan Hillier May 21, 2024
    @Brandon Pike Maybe a Maine Coon? They can be black and get crazy big.

    Jacob Mercer May 21, 2024
    @Meghan Hillier Maine Coons can grow up to 40" in length.

Brandon Pike May 21, 2024
@Meghan Hillier Could of been I guess. Pretty far out in the woods for a housecat, tho.

Gerard Penney May 21, 2024
@Meghan Hillier Banned.

Gerard Penney May 21, 2024
Hard to say what it was without more detail, Brandon. There are a number of black land mammals on the island, and I can tell you from experience that it's tough to gauge size from a quick sighting like this.

Rowan Wareham May 22, 2024
@Gerard Penney May I see inside?

Gerard Penney May 22, 2024
@Rowan Wareham If I get any further information on Brandon's sighting, I'll let you know. I try to share as many of my files with the group as possible.

Philip Marche May 24, 2024
@Gerard Penney You run this group. I thought you believed in big cats. Why are you trying to debunk this guy's sighting?

Philip Marche May 24, 2024
@Rowan Wareham Inside what?

Gerard Penney May 24, 2024
@Philip Marche Hi Philip, I want to PROVE that big cats are here in Newfoundland and have been for decades. To do that we need credible evidence. It doesn't help the cause to take every sighting at face value.

Amy Lynn May 8, 2024
Hey, gang! What's the more common colour for big cats in NL? Black or tan? If you've had a sighting, what was the colour?

Greg Conway May 8, 2024
Black in Central in 2020

Dani Buckle May 8, 2024
tan

Brenda McCarthy May 8, 2024
Blk

Bassim Yacoub May 8, 2024
Black

Sean Partridge May 8, 2024
The one i seen in Makinsons was black!

Al Hynes May 8, 2024
1 black 1 tan

> **Amy Lynn** May 8, 2024
> @Al Hynes You've seen two?? whoa!!

> **Al Hynes** May 8, 2024
> @Amy Lynn Yep, sure have, unmistakeable. black near colliers in 2011, tan on the Burin peninsula in 2015.

Dave Lundrigan May 8, 2024
Black

Janet Alteen May 8, 2024
Black

Isaac Levitz May 8, 2024
Tan

Gerard Penney May 8, 2024
Reported sightings are black by a mile.

> **Lexie Mitchell** May 10, 2024

@Gerard Penney But if people are seeing black cats, what are they?
Jaguars can be melanistic, but we're way out of their habitat. They're equatorial and prefer temperatures 20 degrees plus.

Cougars could survive in our climate, but there's never been a confirmed instance of a black cougar.

Gerard Penney May 10, 2024
@Lexie Mitchell They could be black leopards. About 10% of leopards are black, and leopards can survive the cold. Look at snow leopards.

Lexie Mitchell May 10, 2024
@Gerard Penney But snow leopards don't come in black, either. Seems more likely people are either mistaking tan cats for black in the dark or just seeing housecats and overestimating the size.

Jacob Mercer May 10, 2024
@Lexie Mitchell Did you know black leopards and jaguars still have spots? They're just tough to "spot" (ha ha!) on a black coat. You can see them using an infrared camera.

Gerard Penney May 10, 2024
@Lexie Mitchell I hear ya. I'm not arguing, just repeating what people have told me and posted here.

Siobhan Kelly May 8, 2024
Tan

Mark Weir May 8, 2024
Black

Denise Ong May 8, 2024
black

Dave Lundrigan April 13, 2024
anyone ever been stalked by one of these bad boys? I have and it

was the most freaking terrifying thing that's ever happened to me in my life. Was out trouting with a buddy in the woods all day and started back around nightfall walking up the trail home. All of a sudden I get this feeling like I'm being watched, hair standing up on the back of my neck kind of thing. I turn around and see this huge black cat, tail swishing.. standing on the trail watching us from about 30ft behind. I can see its fur shining in the moonlight slick as oil.

I look at my buddy and he looks and me and we both start backing up real slow and calm. But the cat follows us. So we're backing up and the cat's coming along behind and now it's crouching low to the ground like when a cat's stalking a mouse and I start to think we've had it. We're not that far from a fork in the trail where one way goes to the community and the other goes in to a little soccer field and I whisper to my buddy that on the count of three we'll book it up the trail, take the fork for town, and hope the cat goes the other way.

I'm absolutely shit baked at this point thinking one of us is about to die and I'm smaller than my buddy so it'll probably go for me first. So I count to three and we take off and every second I think that cat is going to hit me like a brick between the shoulder blades and it'll all be over. Well we don't stop running until we get way down the highway to the first house and my lungs are on fire but when we look back the cat is gone. I call my mom and I'm so happy to still be alive I'm crying on the phone and scare the hell out of her. I felt what it was like to be prey that night and I take the wilderness out here seriously now I'll tell you that.

Gerard Penney April 13, 2024
What a story, Dave! Thanks for sharing!

Neil Jesso April 13, 2024
Sounds like a scary experience but might not have been predatory behaviour. Mountain lions usually ambush their prey—if one was stalking you, you wouldn't know it until it was too late. It sounds like this cat was trying to run you out of its territory. It could have been protecting cubs.

Very rare for mountain lions to hunt humans. They see us as an injury risk, not as prey items.

Rowan Wareham April 13, 2024
I've had a feeling of being stalked by something lately when I'm out in the woods around my house. I haven't gotten a clear look at it, but when I go for a walk it's like something is keeping pace with me behind the trees, stepping when I step so I can't be sure if I'm hearing an animal or just my own echo. It used to seem far away, but it feels like it's gotten closer. It's making me nervous. I've tried the RCMP, but they said they only respond to calls about animals that "pose an immediate threat to human safety." Thoughts?

Meghan Hillier April 13, 2024
I think I was stalked by a lynx once. I was hiking Cook's Lookout Trail down on the Burin. It's a 4 k trail in and out, a mix of woods and barrens. It was a foggy spring day, and I was walking along one of the scrubby parts of the trail when my dog started barking. I followed his gaze and saw a brownish-grey figure about twenty yards away. The barking scared it off. I wouldn't have known it was a lynx except for the ear tufts. They're so distinctive!

> **Gerard Penney** April 13, 2024
> @Meghan Hillier No more lynx talk. Last warning.

Nicolette Semigak March 30, 2024
Hey everyone, I'm a sheep farmer up in Roddickton, and I've been having a hell of a time with some predator getting at my flock.

For the past couple of weeks, I've been waking up almost every other day to dead sheep. And I mean completely gutted. Split open from the base of the skull to the tail, their spines torn out and scraped almost clean on the inside. I can spot them now from across a field. They look like deflated balloons.

I've been farming for almost a decade, and I've never seen anything like it. I've had coyote attacks before, but they normally tear out the throat and eat the innards through the flank. Any chance it's a cougar? I haven't seen any big cats up here myself, but my brother-in-law swears he saw one in by Rocky Pond.

Gerard Penney March 30, 2024
Could be. Cougars go for the head and neck and sometimes crush the skull. Any claw marks? Parallel lines with sharp edges?

> **Nicolette Semigak** March 30, 2024
> @Gerard Penney Not that I can see. But the edges of the wound are always pretty neat, and there's never much blood.

> **Cherrie Beaupre** March 30, 2024
> @Gerard Penney Not a cougar if all the organs are missing. Cougars eat the heart, lungs, liver. Leave the stomach and intestines. Cats are clean. Would you want to eat a sheep's poop chute? 😣

> **Leanne&Donnie Fizzard** March 30, 2024
> @Cherrie Beaupre Blessid Jesus. Me stomach's turnt.

> **Derek Seung-hyun Kim** March 30, 2024
> @Nicolette Semigak Black bear. Bears attack from the top and eat the stomach.

> **Philip Marche** March 30, 2024
> @Derek Seung-hyun Kim Dude, I've never heard of a black bear attacking anything. They're shy as hell.

> **Derek Seung-hyun Kim** March 30, 2024
> @Philip Marche Sorry to disappoint you 'dude' but there was literally a black bear attack in Labrador in 2019.

Al Hynes March 31, 2024
What about a wolf/coyote mix like the Beast of Botwood? No telling what them injuries would look like

Nnamdi Onodugo April 8, 2024
I work with the Animal Health Division in Pynn's Brook as a veterinary pathologist. Have you preserved any of the animal remains? If so, we would like to collect a carcass for necropsy.

We can also set up monitoring equipment on your property to record any further predator activity. Please call me at your convenience at [redacted].

Gerard Penney April 8, 2024
@Nnamdi Onodugo Is this an official statement??? Can you confirm that government is investigating big cats on the island???

Nnamdi Onodugo April 8, 2024
@Gerard Penney This should not be construed as an official statement. We investigate all unexplained livestock predation and are tracking several similar incidents in the western region.

Rowan Wareham April 8, 2024
@Nnamdi Onodugo You mention other incidents. I'm near Main Brook—have you recorded any attacks up this way? I've been coming across dead animals, too.

At first, it was a hare skin here or there in the woods near my house. Always in one piece, not like a trapper would skin one with the hide in two pieces. I thought a fox must be getting at them.

Then yesterday morning I opened my door, and there was a whole caribou on the doorstep. A juvenile, I think, but big as I am, slit down the back and hollowed out just like Nicolette said. I hauled it into the woods so it doesn't attract anything else to my door.

Nnamdi Onodugo April 8, 2024
@Rowan Wareham I am unable to discuss the details of livestock losses currently under investigation, but a release will be published by the Department of Fisheries, Forestry and Agriculture as soon as our assessment is complete, within 60-90 days on average.

Rowan Wareham April 8, 2024
@Nnamdi Onodugo Can you send someone up here to see what's going on around my place? There's something I

forgot to mention. The caribou's tongue was missing. Its mouth was lolling open, and I could see where the tongue had been torn out. Is that normal? What types of predators eat their prey this way?

Nnamdi Onodugo April 8, 2024
@Rowan Wareham Our department only documents attacks on livestock. The conservation office in Roddickton may be able to advise.

Rowan Wareham April 8, 2024
@Nnamdi Onodugo I called Roddickton conservation, but they just handle poaching and wildlife offenses.

Jodi Peddle April 8, 2024
@Rowan Wareham Typical government! Can't be bothered to help a farmer protect their sheep but out here fining hardworking people for trapping rabbits and catching cod.

God forbid we FEED OURSELVES. They want us to spend all our hard-earned money at the grocery store so they can collect our taxes and laugh all the way to the bank. People can't afford to live anymore and we can't even use our own resources???

Gerard Penney April 8, 2024
@Nnamdi Onodugo Sure sounds like some kind of statement to me. You're saying there have been several incidents of unexplained predation in western Newfoundland? It's only a matter of time before Wildlife will have to acknowledge what we've been saying all these years. Big cats are here, they're established, and they're reproducing.

Trent Quehe April 8, 2024
@Gerard Penney they're here! they're queer! they don't want any more bears!

Philip Marche April 8, 2024
@Treat Quehe No one wants any more bears. Haven't you

heard? A little bitty black bear attacked someone in Labrador in 2019.

Derek Seung-hyun Kim April 8, 2024
@Philip Marche JFC

Justine Spracklin March 11, 2024
What's everyone's theory on how big cats got to the island?

Bassim Yacoub March 11, 2024
A circus truck crashed near Daniel's Harbour in 2010

Amy Lynn March 11, 2024
@Bassim Yacoub I've read about that, but the only animals involved were an elephant and two camels.

Bassim Yacoub March 11, 2024
@Amy Lynn unless the government's covering up a large predator escape to keep the public from panicking

Casey Pardy March 11, 2024
There's a book called The Quest for the Eastern Cougar that says cougars were brought to Newfoundland in the 1960s by a group of American hunters.

Gerard Penney March 11, 2024
@Casey Pardy Yes, Wildlife has records of this. Two doctors from Idaho allegedly flew in three cougars, two female and one male, and released them in the Main Brook area for hunting. Officers investigated and though they didn't find the cougars, they did find large cages and "strange tracks" around the doctors' camp.

Jacob Mercer March 14, 2024
@Casey Pardy Actually, cougars aren't technically Big Cats because they can't roar.

Hayden Reid March 14, 2024
@Jacob Mercer dude wtf, cougars r literraly big cats

Jacob Mercer March 14, 2024
@Hayden Reid Cougars are large felines, yes, but they are not Big Cats in the scientific sense because they have an ossified hyoid bone. Only lions, tigers, jaguars, and leopards are Big Cats because their floating hyoid allows them to roar.

Casey Pardy March 14, 2024
@Jacob Mercer From Wikipedia: "The term 'big cat' is typically used to refer to any of the five living members of the genus Panthera, namely the tiger, lion, jaguar, leopard, and snow leopard, as well as the non-pantherine cheetah and cougar."

Jacob Mercer March 14, 2024
@Casey Pardy I guess Wikipedia trumps my biology degree then. That's how the term Big Cat is "typically used" by the general public but not by the scientific community.

Philip Marche March 14, 2024
@Casey Pardy What's the difference between a cougar and a leopard?
A leopard can drag something twice its weight up a tree. A cougar can drag someone half her age into bed.

Meghan Hillier March 14, 2024
@Jacob Mercer If cougars aren't big cats what the hell are lynx?

Casey Pardy March 14, 2024
@Meghan Hillier They're all big cats. This whole discussion is pointless semantics.

Jacob Mercer March 14, 2024
@Meghan Hillier Lynx are part of the subfamily Felinae, like domestic cats, cougars, and cheetahs.

BIG CATS OF NEWFOUNDLAND

Gerard Penney March 14, 2024
@Meghan Hillier Second warning. Stop with the lynxes.

Jodi Peddle March 11, 2024
Anyone else here the rumour that Johnny Cash brought them when he went hunting near Millertown in 1961?

Gerard Penney March 11, 2024
Every time this comes up, there are three main theories:
1) A circus truck crashed
2) Hunters flew them in
3) They came over on ice pans from Labrador

Personally, I think big cats have always been here. If they can come down on ice floes from the mainland now, why not a hundred years ago? Five hundred? Cats are elusive and most of the island is uninhabited. There could be lots of animals in the woods no one has ever seen, but as our population rises and we encroach on the wilderness there are bound to be more encounters. I'm optimistic we'll be able to prove the existence of big cats on the island very soon.

Rowan Wareham February 27, 2024
Can anyone help me identify some tracks I found in the snow? Yesterday evening something was scratching at my front door. Three or four scrapes at a time, followed by long pauses, like it was trying to get in or maybe trying to get me to let it in. I wasn't about to open my door to a wild animal, of course, so I ignored it, and when I woke up this morning I found fresh tracks all around my house. They're four-toed and about six or seven inches across.

Miranda Peddle February 27, 2024
Could they be bear tracks?

Rowan Wareham February 27, 2024
@Miranda Peddle No, I don't think so. Bear tracks have five toe impressions and these only have four.

Cherrie Beaupre February 27, 2024
Can't be a cougar at that size. It would have to be enormous.

Lexie Mitchell February 27, 2024
@Cherrie Beaupre Snow can melt, though, and make tracks look bigger than they are.

Cherrie Beaupre February 27, 2024
@Lexie Mitchell True girl.

Lexie Mitchell February 27, 2024
@Rowan Wareham Maybe coyote prints that have enlarged through snowmelt? Can you see claw marks?

Rowan Wareham February 27, 2024
@Lexie Mitchell I can't. Just the toes and the footpad.

Lexie Mitchell February 27, 2024
@Rowan Wareham That does sound like an animal with retractable claws, then. Maybe a lynx or even a domestic cat. Impossible to get a good read on print size in the snow.

Meghan Hillier February 3, 2024
Have any of you ever seen a lynx in the wild? I saw one once on the Burin peninsula, and of course I visited the captive ones at Salmonier Nature Park when I was a kid. What beautiful creatures. I'd love to hear about other experiences you've all had.

Gerard Penney February 3, 2024
This group is for sightings of cougars, mountain lions, panthers, and other big cats not known to be native to the island. We know lynx are here. Please reread the group rules.

An admin turned off commenting for this post.

Derek Seung-hyun Kim January 25, 2024
Why does no one ever have their phones on them when they see these cats? So many alleged sightings and can't get a single photo?

BIG CATS OF NEWFOUNDLAND

Philip Marche January 25, 2024
Brother, I've seen so much cool shit out in the woods and never ever been fast enough to snap a pic. Unless you've got a camera stuck to your face by the time you think to grab your phone whatever you saw is long gone. These are wild animals. If they posed for the perfect shot hunters would've got them by now.

Linda Whalen January 25, 2024
When I was a kid we were told there were no coyotes in Newfoundland, then they were discovered here in the 80s. We were told wolves were extinct too, then DNA testing proved they were here in the 2010s. I don't care what's been captured on camera, I know there's more on this island than we think there is. As long as the snakes stay off it I'll be happy! Me nerves lol.

Luke Jesso January 26, 2024
My pop and two of his friends saw a mountain lion fifteen years ago in by Strickland Pond near Lethbridge. They're older and wouldn't have known how to use a smartphone to take a pic. But all three were experienced hunters and knew what they saw.

Rowan Wareham January 11, 2024
New member here! I'm wondering if anyone here can shed light on a weird experience I had last night.

I have a small house—a cabin, really—outside Main Brook. I'm from the Grand Falls area originally but left for university. During COVID I decided to move to rural and work remotely. It's beautiful here, but I don't have many connections in the local community I can go to for help.

I was sitting in my living room by the fire last night, when I started hearing these wailing sounds. First they were far off, but they got closer and closer until it seemed like they were coming from right outside my door. They circled the house, then eventually went away. The whole thing probably lasted about half an hour.

Whatever it was, it was moving too quickly and erratically to be a person, but the noises it was making sounded almost like speech. Wildcats make human-like sounds sometimes, right? Maybe what I heard was a combination of mewing and hissing.

Gerard Penney January 11, 2024
Yes, cougars have been known to make sounds like a woman screaming.

> **Justine Spracklin** January 11, 2024
> @Gerard Penney Thanks, I hate it.

> **Jacob Mercer** January 11, 2024
> @Gerard Penney Correct. That's because cougars are unable to roar like true big cats.

> **Matt Squires** January 11, 2024
> @Gerard Penney First time I ever heard a bobcat I near wet myself. Sounded like a cross between a baby crying and a woman screaming bloody murder.

Denise Ong January 11, 2024
I've read about margays (they're a small South American wildcat) luring monkeys out of trees by mimicking the sounds of their babies.

Philip Marche January 11, 2024
Yo, so if it sounded like speech, what was it saying?

> **Rowan Wareham** January 11, 2024
> @Philip Marche It sounded like it was saying "May I see inside?"

THE MUSEUM OF ETYMOLOGY

F. J. BERGMANN

A small stand by the gate in the stone-
paneled hall bore a sign that said
Contributions Welcome. The attendant
cast a disdainful glance at the few coins,
darkly oxidized and unidentifiable,
that he slid across the counter, but silently
lifted the bar and let him pass.

Receding aisles curved away, each
with the name of a different language
carved or neon-blinking over its archway.
As he approached, his cochlear implant
whispered, or sub-auditory signals
vibrated through his bones, to furnish
him with a translation and short history.

Hooded alcoves offered immersive
experiences—for an extra fee, he could
have chosen direct neural reprogramming,
to imprint himself with any language
compatible with his biological capabilities
and psychological traits, or requested
imitative analogues of those that were not.

Each word in each language was traced
backward through its ancestral heritage:

borrowings, onomatopoeia, faunal cries,
branchings and roots forming the bases
of commonality or unrecognizable input—
and forward to its eventual appropriation
or suppression by cultural sanitization.

Some languages were nothing more
than bursts of scent or gusting breezes
in patterns that academics still studied,
still quarreled over. Being the only extant
speaker of a tongue gave one a certain
professional cachet. Always complexity
was admired: younger students taught

themselves an array of secret obscenities,
and shortly thereafter, facsimiles thereof
became the subject of circulating memes,
tattoos or T-shirt slogans in the form
of textures read by one sense or another—
never mind that by the time these were
commercially reproduced, all context

had been lost—the object was to give
the wearer a veneer of sophistication.
His own tattoo was inked in a wavelength
not visible to the eyes of his species'
conquerors, whose museum this was.
The fabric he wore held the best military-
grade viruses he had been able to obtain;

in an hour the museum would cease to exist;
in a day, the city; in a month, the planet itself
(by then, the fleeing ships long infected).
He made the gesture for *fatalism* and another
that meant *revenge* on worlds he had never
visited, and then signed, in the language
of his own dead world, *farewell*.

MAD STUDIES

[SARAH] CAVAR

1.

THEIR NAME IS T. Their father had bad cancer. Their mother was a painter until she died too. With father, the cause—the pancreas—was clear. With mother, the afflicted organ was the organ of dreams. They-everybody tried to figure out what it was, but came up blank. The three of family also had four cats, two adults two kittens.

Since then something has emptied out of T. T has begun to smell strange and speak stranger. T demands of the cats, What am I going to do? They ask again and again. Deadmother speaks back from noplace like, first, I need to improve my painting, finish my project. Then she grinds down her nose and says no more. Deadfather says nothing like livefather.

What are we going to do? T asked again. What are we going to do?

2.

T lived on the end of a far stretch of road, mostly flat, where there was more sky to see than ground. It was not the Midwest but T imagined it to be. It was not poverty but something other-bankrupt. Everything painted in solid blocks of color. Horrors were steady. T had shared the house with their parents for their whole life. Their whole life had been sharing; now they were a recluse.

They had once walked, glided, down the road, fed the horses, returned to find a cat's fresh kill on their doorstep. Sometimes the bird'd still be hot. Sometimes T named the bird right as is croaked. Sometimes T reached for the killer cat and said good girl.

T had no friends, never did. T had no appearance, because no one looked at them. They wore their privacy like a great gown.

3.

T opened their mouth and waited for food. T fed of the food like a babybird. T had once been an optimist at heart. Livemother had once brought them pieces of felt glitter twine to wind into a tender nest. T made the nest at their own pace. T could not speed this pace, for fear of disappointment so severe it could kill. Severe like weathers, mothers, diseases. Severe like the first nestfallen bird. You can fly all over the world but you can never go home.

4.

T eats their fair share of food. They weigh approximately eight times the weight of one adult cat. They eat eight times the kibble each adult gets. T has given up human food. T has given up humanity. T has given up on something, several somethings. T is Nobody, and Nobody eats cat food. T is for tuna.

5.

Someone makes a home in this inscrutable process. This radical wound. This opening before the name is the Name. This dark throat place. This barricade. This Someone is flat like an ironing board. This Someone eats mounds to round their weft.

6.

Someone wants to change the conversation on Mental Health. Mental Health has hitherto smelled of old dead fish. Someone would like to offer sushi-grade Mental Health.

7.

T knows that trans is the future. T knows the future is trans. T knows cis is a dead end. T knows their parents died long before they died, already dead ends. The future is a thing rushing toward all of us, the voice—the choice—is adapt or mute.

8.

What if Someone made to jump the floor to realize whither flight? T believed in being that someone. It wouldn't fit them but it would be pretty cool. It wouldn't be like dreaming, but the underside of wake.

9.

T prepared the flying machine. First they dissected the dead wings of birds. Next they gathered their nesting materials. Next they wove. When their bare wings began to shine they ate again, ate like the stomach of a horse.

Surely deadmothernfather'd be proud of their flying machine. The house was growing smaller by the day. Soon it would be mere as the two urns. Which parts of the body became inside the urn, T wondered. Cats, what is in the urn?

No reply. Inside the urn must be hostile, T figured. Fog knows this house is.

10.

(Someone says, the hostile is enclosure.)

11.

When they began to fly, T decided, they would first open the horse from its dirty pen.

12.

T wonderstands compliance. Wonderstands means you get something in theory, but in practice, wonder how anyone could be stupid enough to believe it. T has been asked many times to comply. When the women shaped like Peeps came to their old house and carted them past the cats the street horses the urns of their mother and their father, they said, comply urgently. Comply and no one gets hurt. And then a sharp fluid traveled through T's bodymind. And T complied.

Another word for comply is adhere. And this is what T is: stuck.

13.

Imagine T has a friend. They are at school. They each find a seat in the classroom, in the dining hall, in the future. This is a beautiful blue world. It is still a flat world. It is a world where it is a little stupid to have faith. Where a little disingenuous is necessary for survival.

In this classroom world, frightening forces attack unobstructed. Every Someone's got an erotic relationship with their panic button. They wear their panic on their breasts like votes. They make friends inside their house of shared panic. They clutch each other in the haywire. Needles poke their palms and they wash them in the pinkening water.

Friend sees T for the first time. Friend says, you look a little— and then her voice garbles underwater. T tastes tuna in the backmouth. T acquires a glass of vodka and clinks Friend's empty fist. They eat strawberries. T drinks to quell the tuna, which is a metaphor for dread.

14.

T wishes for a uvula, a demarcation line between swallowed and unswallowed. T believes the uvula to be a kind of Veil, that life is raw and death digestion.

On occasion, in the thick sick of evening, T makes their uvulaneeding known. In this way, T makes themself known. T cracks their mouth like a catcan and stinks up the place. What place? It is not a house. Not even a home. Here there is no horse's paddock. Here, T is the broken horse.

15.

T and Friend dump strawberries into the sink. They plumb the dirty depths. Green hats into the garbage. Red bodies to the rag.

Friend stares T dead in the eye. Have you ever tasted anything so pink and beautiful as acquiescence?

I will never, says T. Never acquiesce.

You will never get the juice out of your hands, beloved.

The sinkwater's reached a boil. T plunges in their hands.

Friend purrs.

16.

The house was brown, ranch-style. The picket fence, white. The trim, white too, white enough to hurt in the sun. There was the smell of horseshit, but the horseshit was someone else's problem.

As T's livefather, lain limply on the old sofa, eked out the last brutal gusts of life, T's mother, not yet dead, painted him. She said,

I know you will haunt this house. I know you love us enough for that.

The kittens, collectively named "Gemini" and indistinguishable by looks, jumped behind livefather's pillows. They kneaded. Livefather had no hair of his own, but when they kneaded like this, it was as though the kittens grew wholesale from his head.

On the day he became deadfather, one Gemini brought home a sparrow.

17.

The painting sits unfinished in the house of deadmother and deadfather.

The painting contains a violent indent in the shape of a head.

The painting features a broadraw and pinkish hue.

Deadfather's last words to T were, I don't love her enough to haunt her.

18.

As Someone can see, T can't. T is weak and confused absent sight. Someone believes that because T is sightless, T sees nothing. T squeezes their eyes until pink blooms beneath their lids.

Someone says: What are your goals.

I am trying to bring back livemother and livefather, says T.

Someone says: livemother and livefather are not any longer.

I am trying to time like space, says T. I am trying to bring back home.

19.

An open urn is, for a cat, endless entertainment. Cats take pleasure in playing with death. Cats like shitting in the house. Cats like no one's home.

Cats have no true names. Cats go everywhere. Gemini follow the smelltrace of tuna from the front stoop to the horsebarn. A rottenman does rotten to his horse. The horse cannot see rottenman. The horse has dung beneath her shoes.

Not even able to clean herself. Mothers shutter their Geminis' eyes. As night falls hot and violent, the horse licks sweatsalt from her bare aching body.

21.

In the night humans realize they are mammals. In the night cats realize they are beasts. Horses maim best when frightened.

The horse is most dangerous when frightened. Do you believe you have frightened the horse? Do you believe you have frightened the horse to death?

20.

In conclusion, the inmates run
    the asylum.

KNIGHT RUMORS
OR
THE FIVE PARTS

MATTHEW MITCHELL

I.
The Badger Knight
A Head

IT IS SAID that The Badger Knight lived here—right here in our town. My Sisters say The Badger Knight came to this place as a child, an orphan of the Bowling Wars. Our Father claimed The Badger Knight was born on a hill not far from us, and that he was there to witness the birth.

Jessa Mae's Father says much the same, but swears it was a hill closer to their own. Jessa Mae is my best friend, and she said that her Father knows best. She says that my Sisters and Father are fools.

I too believe The Badger Knight lived here, and that this is why The Badger Knight has returned. Why else would so great a Knight bear down on us in odious rage? This is a very small town after all, and there were so few of us to begin with. There must be a reason for the brutality, all this hurt.

Yes, I believe the Badger Knight was born in this town, and that it was a terrible, *awful* thing.

I wish I knew what caused The Badger Knight such agony in a lifetime before my own. Would that I could will away the pain brought to burden upon that pendulous, helmeted head . . . But I cannot.

No one seems to know why The Badger Knight has come for us, and if they do, they will have died with their dirty secrets before the sun dips beneath the bluff.

I can hear screams coming down the hills.

There are no bird songs and the livestock have gone still. It is quiet until the screams, and when they start up again, it is jarring. Just an hour ago, I fear I may have heard Jessa Mae.

It has only been a day since The Badger Knight came to our town. A day in which so much has changed. There are not many stones left to turn; The Badger Knight has made great haste in rooting us from beneath every shadow. Sharp teeth behind the ebon helm snap and click. Almond shaped eyes burn in pools of yellow beyond the grated veil. Barks and growls echo in the hollow bascinet.

My Sisters say all hope is surely lost. They wail like necropolis maidens, and tell me we will be devoured soon. I am very afraid to die.

Despite our panic and our tears, we do not cast judgment on The Badger Knight, not I, nor my Sisters. Our Father was another story, but The Badger Knight took him, and so his former thoughts on such matters mean nothing. Not on Earth. In Hell, perhaps.

Whether or not these earthly offenses are punishable, I cannot say. It will not be our tender palms who extinguish the flame of The Badger Knight. How could we ever? The Badger Knight is great, and we are small. So very frail. Bare faced and soft headed.

We know not what this town means to The Badger Knight, and I will perish without discovery.

II.
The Bean Knight
A Heel

I have heard that The Bean Knight wandered far from here before passing on from this world. A long, harrowing journey into the countryside which ended many lives. I do not know if there is truth to these claims, and will not be held accountable.

The Bean Knight was, of course, named so for wearing an armored coat composed of finely laced pellets that resembled soft legumes. When The Bean Knight walked, the beans clattered like bells, and all upon the road stayed away or came forward knowingly–knowing that they were to die.

It is said that each evening, as The Bean Knight slept beneath the stars, a terrible creature would soar through the sky before coming to roost upon the coat of iron beans. The Bean Knight awoke every morning with fewer beans quilted to the coat and their clattering grew more dim by the day.

The Bean Knight made less and less noise, and so more unexpected encounters ensued on the road. Innocents were slain, families torn apart, and children mashed like porridge. Chaos took root in the coiled soul of The Bean Knight, and new joys were found in murderous rampage.

As more iron beans disappeared from the coat, so too did its defensive capabilities. The Bean Knight suffered slashes and gouges. Digits were clipped, flesh was flayed. Darkness flowed through the hardened veins of the Bean Knight, and an ancient pleasure was taken in pain.

Before long, death-ballads were written in the name of The Bean Knight; campfire stories sprouted in the wake of chiming iron beans. Warrants, bounties, and curses were cast with wild abandon on The Bean Knight's back. The people wanted blood, craved vengeance.

One evening as The Bean Knight slept upon a bed of bones, the abominable thiever of iron beans landed atop the dwindling coat. The Bean Knight—nearly nude save a small clutch of beans, bloody and ragged with wounds—awoke at once.

The story goes that The Bean Knight was beheld by a winged, mirror image. A slightly smaller, but no less fearsome clone. The only other visible difference between The Bean Knight and the visitor were the loathsome folded wings upon its back and the nearly-full coat of iron beans it wore.

"You are me," it said to The Bean Knight, "but I have wings, and now I will take all of your beans."

It is unclear why The Bean Knight gave up the remaining coat of beans to the winged visitor, but it was done without argument or bloodshed.

Morning saw The Bean Knight once more upon the road to wander aimlessly. Naked and bedraggled, the shadow of The Bean Knight soon filled with head hunters, thrill-seekers, and avengers of the dead. This must be where the story ends, for as we know, The Bean Knight did not return.

No, The Bean Knight never came home.

It has been said that there are chimes aloft the road at night, and great wings that rustle. Occasionally, one may also find an iron bean among the pebbles.

III.
The Bag Knight
A Hand

I have been told that when fog rolls in off the river—chill and blinding—The Bag Knight emerges from a black gutter. No one knows where the hole is, not for certain, but on dew blighted mornings the corpses of vagrants amass near the city walls. We are very blessed.

After a misty evening, some of us—the curious, the bold—will take an early stroll along the outer rim to survey the carnage. Some onlookers sit with pen and ink to sketch these grim scenes as intended works of art. To great applause, our city's most celebrated poet once gave a rousing performance while standing atop mounds of the freshly slaughtered. Other, less inspired individuals, will tussle and scrap to stake claim on the bodies in the name of science or the holy golden coin.

Many of us—the majority, I would think—simply dine with our eyes.

There is a sensational draw to these mass above-ground graves, a feeling of exhilaration and awe. We absorb the foul, fascinating energies within the proximity of victims made pocked and porous by a steel mace. I see God in what The Bag Knight creates with the arc of barbed chains and a ghoulish, serrated dirk.

It is a foul hobby, I will admit, and though I am deeply ashamed, I cannot look away.

There is talk of nasty weather tonight, and I ponder the horrors to be wrought on those who prowl and plunder the streets. Who among this rotting metropolis will meet their end by the tangled knot of a slick garotte? Perhaps the black toothed bully of West Street—that pocket picking derelict—will finally meet the razor's edge beneath the occulted glare of a murky moon. Will I recognize the faces of the dead on my morning pilgrimage—?

One can only hope.

To see a husk of life with which I am familiar is the sharpest of thrills. A religious experience. I can read milky spewage in the wastes of their sockets like tea leaves, and chart the sins by each lash. I decipher a ladder of evils leading to their demise, and fantasies of terror overtake me. Shrill visions of bonfire skewers through sizzling flesh. Desperate pleas for mercy beneath a pendulum swing. Ground meat and ichor ponds.

As I say, we are so very blessed.

When The Bag Knight brings cruel justice to this city, we feverish followers give thanks to the fog. We keep candles in our window, an earnest offerance, and ask that The Bag Knight grant us fresh vistas of ecstatic cosmosis. Hand to heart, we pray for the juggernaut birth—emerging from a drain, a void, a hole—and as heads fall to rest, we beg for blades flashing in the mist. There are dreams to be dreamt of the boiling river, and of lovely discoveries come dawn's first light.

I close my eyes and wonder if The Bag Knight knows my name.

IV.
The Banquet Knight
A Heart

When Father was a boy and Mother was his Queen, he would watch her from a window that faced the Tower of Pearl. Father often spoke of how it felt to see her rise above the spire in a gown of platinum, and that her dance through the sky made him very afraid. This was long before the Tower was taken by force and Mother had not yet returned to her people high above the world.

Father said he knew, even then, that The Banquet Knight would come for him. He assumed that his childhood days were running short and was anxious for it. Father understood that if he could see Mother, it meant that she was watching back.

Father was right, of course, and The Banquet Knight soon plucked him from the window. He said that the fate of his parents— my Grandmama and Grandpapa—were not known to him. Father's

57

lineage was a topic of conversation that made him uncomfortable, and so I rarely inquired about the nature of my own.

After The Banquet Knight collected Father, he was then delivered to a brothel ship that floated off the coast. The brothel employed all manner of man and beast and its buffet of carnal professionals had been instructed to teach the stolen boy how to achieve great feats in his future marital chambers. It was well known that Mother, The Queen, did not sanction naivety in her chosen man-brides, and so Father had anticipated this outcome.

Father did not, however, expect The Banquet Knight to shield his innocence from the wet, squirming horde that inhabited the vessel. In every instance in which his virginity was made conquest, The Banquet Knight warded off the prostitutes with sickle and menace. In three years time, Father told me, he and The Banquet Knight disembarked the brothel ship with his purity undisturbed.

Two great falcons from the Tower of Pearl had been stabled at the wharf ahead of their arrival; Father and The Banquet Knight mounted the saddled birds and were flown to the University caverns over the course of several days. Once they arrived, Father was to be placed in the care of the blind, albinic professors who lectured in the caves. Father said Grandpapa once told him that each and every man-bride had been sent there to learn the secrets of death. Unlike the brothel ship, Father was eager to pleasure his mind and was not afraid of the depths to which the acquisition of knowledge would lead.

Similar to what had occurred in the waterlogged whore chambers of his youth, Father said The Banquet Knight did also resist any intended tutelage to be cast on him. The University staff—with their mirrored eyes and torches—insisted on Father's presence in the storied halls of stalagmite, but The Banquet Knight smote them and the pair rarely descended beyond the cavern mouth. Father's unrequited hunger to learn and be taught caused him great agony in those cold, dark years. Resentment grew behind his eyes.

When at last The Banquet Knight carried Father out of the University and into the light of day, a caravan of craftsmen greeted them upon emergence. The workers union was composed of skilled laborers from a diverse range of industries and they welcomed Father into their fold. The craftsmen informed him that Mother,

Queen of all, insisted on his development as a contributing man-bride before the conclusion of betrothal. It seemed to Father that The Banquet Knight was wary of these intentions and thus he was not permitted to travel with the union en route to their encampment.

The Banquet Knight never slept, and so even though they had departed days after the laborers, Father was carried through the night and they soon passed the caravan. It was a lonely pilgrimage from then on and the pair crossed many borders. In absence of the ornery, chattering union men he had briefly met, Father discovered that he craved their company.

Father told me that when they arrived at the encampment, he was met with a dizzying array of workshops that smoked and churned beneath the shadow of an enormous, volcanic forge. Men of every nation toiled happily there. Father said their comradery and strength cowed him to tears. He was eager to use his soft hands, to harden them with fire and triumph, but once they had settled into their quarters, The Banquet Knight barred the door. Father was further denied the thrilling, exacerbating work he was promised and it pained him. It seemed strange, he told me, that all he had been taught to anticipate as a boy had now passed him by.

One day, not long after Father had grown his beard, The Banquet Knight took him by the hand. The Banquet Knight produced a satchel of silk ribbon and braided his beard in the matrimonial style. Father said The Banquet Knight trembled through the weaving and that tears clanged inside the helm like raindrops on hot roofing. When he was braided and beautiful, Father was led out of the union encampment and the two journeyed back to the Tower of Pearl.

Mother took Father as her man-bride before her court of prostitutes, professors, and professionals. They watched the ceremony with tight lips and hooded eyes. As was custom, Mother had removed herself from the royal seat—an act otherwise unpermitted in the glory of day. While she danced the courtship-waltz, The Banquet Knight occupied the throne in her stead. The court would not cast eyes upon The Banquet Knight and they crossed their arms in distaste.

Mother, the Queen, ended the courtship-waltz with a kiss upon Father's hip. He told me his skin burned at the touch of her lips and that his groin morphed into something hard and unexpected. Father emitted the man-bride seed upon the Tower floors and the court of prostitutes exploded in anger.

The whores and whorebeasts pointed out Father's moist mistake and aired their grievances. They told their Queen that Father had not learned of himself and that The Banquet Knight was to blame. Mother slew the Captain of the brothel ship to silence this outcry and the head rolled to Father's feet.

Father said he had never seen blood so abundant that it pooled in shades of purple and he expelled the contents of his stomach right there upon the puddle of seed. The Queen's court of pale professors scratched at their shaded bifocals. They shrieked and gave an affluent, impassioned rebuke on The Banquet Knight's dismissal of their tutelage; proclaimed that Father, her current man-bride, would not have buckled beneath the weight of death had they been allowed to teach him.

Mother then demanded that Father remove the decapitated head from the Tower floor. Father told me he bent at the waist to oblige, but that the head was too heavy and he could not lift it. His smooth fingers gained no purchase on the blood-slicked flesh. His thin muscles bore no flex. His pores clogged with unfamiliar sweat. Father nearly fainted and collapsed into his sticky purgings.

The court of union workers rattled their tools and stomped their dusty boots. They cursed The Banquet Knight for producing such weakness in Father and stated that had they been afforded his apprenticeship, Mother, their Queen, would surely be wedded to a man-bride of fortitude and skill.

In his prone state, Father said that Mother dipped down beside him and bunched her gown up to her knees. He watched as she scooped his fallen fluids into her claws and pushed the mess between her thighs. Father could not be sure, as he was still dazed, but believed he saw me swell in her belly within moments of the act.

The Banquet Knight, as we all know, then rose from Mother's throne and expressed a deep love for Father, her man-bride. It was then that Father noticed tear drops rusted the helm, and he understood that The Banquet Knight had wept for many years in his company. The Banquet Knight commanded Mother to release Father and divorce him in the name of their blazing passion.

The court went silent and so too did Mother, for The Banquet Knight had always served one purpose and never faltered. Father spoke at last from where he lay on the floor. He told The Banquet Knight that he did not share this love and that, in fact, he blamed The Banquet Knight for forsaking him the life he was promised.

In light of Father's dismissal, the taking of the Tower began and The Banquet Knight made short work of Mother's court. Before Father's very eyes, the throne was also destroyed and soon, he knew, both he and his Queen would follow.

Mother, in her endless wisdom, took Father in her claws by the flesh of his back and flew away to her home in the sky. It was there that I was born and it is from above that I watch. For many years, I saw little below but heard much from Father, and as my eyes have grown stronger, I begin to see the world as Mother once did.

From on high, I have often watched The Banquet Knight wander alone in the Tower of Pearl, and though there are no windows here, I fear one day I will be seen—plucked from the sky and taken away.

V.
The Bloom Knight
A Hole

I take lives for my own amusement. It brings me such joy. I do not go to slaughter with false notions of honor dulling my brutality; the carnage I produce with blade or bow or finger is butchery, pure and unbridled. Dealing pain is pleasure and I hope to die screaming in the faces of those I sought to vanquish.

What should I tell you of my history? There is much to know and I wonder what is most important. How to best use these few moments we have together, that is always the question.

Here is what I will say:

I slipped from a moist crevice of stars and fell to earth—feet first—with a blight upon the flesh. From nose to breast, a lavender storm encompasses my body. It is hard like a callous and rich with varying hues, as you see. The bruise does not hurt, but in this life that means so very little.

I am not shunned for my flowering rash, however, and have often been called beautiful by those who picked the wrong receiver of advances. Rather, I am discounted because of my nature and, despite the allure of my physical form, a terror lurks beneath.

The Goddesses marked me a monster, or so I have been told. Your people say my blight is a warning to those who would seek to reach me in lust or drunken fever. *Do Not Touch*, flashing in purple flesh, *Stay Away*.

Marked for sport, I have always presumed. Given a lovely bruise and a brain with gnashing teeth by deities in need of a jester. Targeted in some grand comedy to entertain heavenly bodies who would be better served granting mercy on the wretches who fail to cross the road when I pass.

Shit upon the divine: that is what I believe. *Fuck them all. And fuck you too.*

Have you heard of my axe? I beg you to call it by its name—the name your people gave it. Do you know from where my axe was claimed—?

There is a bog beneath glacial boulders to the North, and only I had the strength to unearth it. I am terribly strong, as you must also surely see. There, in the briny swamp, I pulled my axe from the skull of an undead King . . .

No, that is incorrect. I have misspoken. The bog is where I found the sword. The axe, the axe, the axe . . . Where did I—?

Oh, yes! How ridiculous of me. Of course I remember: the Pond of Null, beyond the darkest grove. I reached down into the mercury waters and hauled it from a sunken battlefield; wrenched it free from the hands of a drowned God who forged it. My axe is very special, and I know you know its name.

What else should one know about me before the end? I often wonder how it feels to hear these last words. What would *I* inquire of *my* destroyer—?

Nothing, I suppose. But that is me, and you are you. Never forget that. We are not alike, not kin, different breeds.

I am The Bloom Knight and you are my quarry.

RECIPROCITY

AZURE ARTHER

"I TRUSTED THE trees, man. I'm completely eco-friendly. But that didn't stop them, did it? Tom was even more of an ecohead than I am, but they killed him. They killed him right in front of me."—Bryan, Earth Day survivor

***

"It's made from all trash. Completely recycled. Top of the line garbage." The salesman, Phillip but you can call me Phil, smiled, a glint of gold in his mouth. Jill figured he probably thought that bit of shine made him seem interesting, wearing a throwback from before, but it actually aged him and let Jill know just how old Phil was. She didn't comment on it, and she doubted Charles had even noticed. He was negotiating.

"So, there's no wood on it? No wood pulp paper products? No newspaper? Plywood? Wooden dowels?" He was thorough, this husband of hers. Charles glanced back, his low top fade catching the light, shining like the soft sheen on his rich brown skin. So, it wasn't just her that was hot. He winked and she smiled at him, a slight curve of her lips.

"Well, there's no guarantee that there's *nothing* made from trees on anything, right? But all of our refuse is tree approved—"

"TrashPro is offering this same style of camper with a no wood product guarantee." Charles looked out the dusty window, and Jill followed his gaze, staring into the rich afternoon sunlight. Outside, across the cracked pavement, over the edge of the campers and RVs that filled the lot, the TrashPro sign, recycled metal and plastic, was just barely visible. Charles was lying, of course. They couldn't afford TrashPro; they had five seal and approval trees on their lot.

"Well, I'm sure we could work something out. No need to go to TrashPro. They aren't even RV experts like Trashington Rides!"

"I don't know. What do you think, love?" Charles turned to ask, but Jill was still staring out the window at the only tree in the middle of the Trashington Rides' parking lot. It was an elm, a lord that rose large and proud from a massive, cleared area of rich dirt and grass. As she watched, the branches waved, as if it were about to speak to her. She inwardly shuddered, closed her eyes and turned back to the conversation.

"I think we could do better shopping around."

✳✳✳

March 20, journal excerpt of Henrietta Silpin –
It was fire season when Bill Parsons died. He was a firefighter, so it wasn't too much of a reach to believe a snag, a dead tree, had fallen on him. That's the thing about snags, though. People think trees just fall over in forest fires, but they don't. Most of the dead trees just stay standing. For years. But some do fall, and during a forest fire, it's easy to believe that an old smoke jumper like Bill, forty years with the department, just got caught slipping. The tree fell; he got crushed; that was the end. Except, it wasn't.

✳✳✳

"It's too expensive, Charles. We should have gone for the Trashington one." Jill cupped her abdomen, a classic protection motion. She swung the other arm out to encompass the sleek interior. The shining surfaces were made completely from recycled metal and plastic: yellow for the small kitchenette area they stood in, brown for the cushioned sofa, blue polyester and white cotton for the bedroom. "Or just kept the van. This is too much. What if there's wood? What if they missed a bit? What will the tax be on that? What if a tree comes? I don't talk to trees, Charles. You know I don't."

"Trashpro has a guarantee. We'll be alright." Charles soothed. He came from behind to place one hand on top of hers, her dark and his lighter brown skin reflecting the trees, hybrids of their own

64

making, both protecting now. "Don't get upset. We're gonna be just fine. All three of us."

"How? What are we going to do? We don't have anything left in savings. How will we afford the tree seal?" Jill turned her head and leaned back, looking up at him. "We should've gone with a lot that offered the tree seal with the purchase. You've already got a strike against you."

"Let me worry about that. You worry about turning this," He rapped the knuckles of his other hand across the counter, making the blended recycled material echo, "into a home."

"I can do that." Jill took a deep breath but flinched before she finished inhaling. "The baby's kicking."

"See? They're just as excited as I am. This is our home now." Charles grinned.

✱✱✱

"I keep thinking about that little girl, the one that they carried halfway across the country, and she was screaming and crying most of the way. It was sad when she died. It wasn't the trees, you know. It was starvation, maybe exposure, but it wasn't the trees. They were just the carriers. In the end, I don't think they understood what she needed. They rescued her and treated her like a sapling, but humans can't live on just rain and sunshine."—Tami, Park Ranger.

✱✱✱

"Happy Earth Day." Charles said, and Jill, standing right next to him, smiled out the camper window, even though she didn't feel like smiling, even though this was the last thing she wanted to hear. She still smiled. She supposed that all around the world humans were probably standing at their windows, or in their yards, somewhere on the street, outside, smiling. Or they would be. Maybe they already had been. Except perhaps in Antarctica, or Greenland, or one of those other polluted places where trees hadn't been. Those were the spots where humanity could survive if they had the money, could thrive, if they had the resources, if their trees would let them get to the boats, if the big boats hadn't been mostly destroyed by the mangroves that moved around the sea. No one had planes anymore, except perhaps the Naturers, but she'd never seen them with one. The trees had taken over all of the airfields.

65

"Happy Earth Day." Jill replied when Charles nudged her. She didn't know how long she had been standing there, staring without saying anything. Charles reached over and wrapped his arm around her. Jill leaned against him, both of her hands covering the giant swell of her belly, their offspring, their sapling. The bright yellow of the walls and soft filmy curtains that framed the window seemed falsely cheery in the morning light. She sighed and Charles squeezed her again. She stretched her smile more.

"There are over 400 billion trees in the world." Charles read off the tree leaves outside. It took a while, as their resident tree, a willowy beech with too much attitude, usually arranged its leaves solely to its liking, not necessarily to the ease of its human's perception. Charles always said they were lucky to have this spot, right at the edge of the forest, with so many silent trees. Sure, their resident was loud, but it had moved there when they did. The other trees were quiet. The leaves shifted, a trick of shadow and light that allowed for words to be shown between the quick movements of the tree's limbs.

"There are two billion humans." Jill read, feeling her eyes well with tears. No matter how many Earth Days she experienced, she never got over the statistics the trees made them read. Charles squeezed her again, and at the last minute, she remembered to smile. "Once, there were over seven."

"There will be no humans if you are caught using unsanctioned tree products." Charles read, his voice taking on the harsh quality it usually had when he was angry, and he was angry often. He read slowly, taking breaks between each group of words. "But, in celebration of the 20th Earth Day since the Reckoning, and due to the amount of undergrowth and discomfort from too many fallen limbs and twigs, humans will collect and clean the forest this day."

"Sanctioned use of twigs will be as follows." Jill whispered when Charles stopped reading and just stared, his jaw clenching and unclenching. Horror clawed its way up her throat.

"We won't be picking up any wood. I don't care what you put on that damn leaflet. She's pregnant and we're not your slaves." Charles said firmly. The leaves shifted.

"You will do as you're told." Jill quietly read the words. She lowered her gaze and stared at the floor before slanting her eyes to look up at Charles.

"I meant what I said." Charles grunted before turning as if he was speaking to Jill, but she knew he was really saying it to the tree. "You know, they used to just burn the underbrush. There are probably still people who know how to do that, but no. The trees won't admit it, but they're scared. At the end of the day, they're all just one fire away from extinction."

It was quiet outside. Finally, Jill heard the slight rustle that meant the tree was moving its leaves to form new words. Next to her, Charles stilled.

"I don't want to see it." She said, her voice a soft, nearly inaudible gasp that the tree probably still heard. "You shouldn't have said it."

Charles was quiet for so long that Jill finally looked.

**STRIKE TWO YOU WILL DO
AS YOU ARE TOLD COLLECT THE
WOOD
USE AS
SANCTIONED
OR JOIN THE FIVE BILLION**

***

Wanted: Scavengers for cadaver cleanup and/or recyclable and wood scavenging assistance. Must be comfortable with cremation and destruction of buildings. Must be capable of working 12-hour days. Must have a strong stomach. Must be comfortable with decomposition of cadavers. Must be non-sentimental. Pay rate: 30 dollars/hour. Pay will be provided in coins or goods, as available.

***

Jill gave birth while Charles was at work. When the first cramp hit, she thought it was just a regular ghost contraction. She had met a pregnant woman once. She had complained about a Braxton-Hicks contraction. That's what she called them. She explained them as fake labor, ghost contractions. Jill liked the phrase because babies were just ghosts waiting to happen. People died easily. Babies died even easier. Most children didn't get names anymore until they could talk, so they could perhaps ask for help, maybe not die as quickly.

"Tree?" Jill asked, clenching her jaw and forcing the words out.

67

She stilled herself for the branches to move, but nothing did. Edging forward, she stumbled down the back steps just as another contraction came. "Help me. Please. Tree?"

YOU SPAWN

The branches made the weird squiggle that Jill had come to know was a question mark.

"Yes. And it hurts."

YOU WANT YOUR MATE

Another contraction hit, and Jill doubled over. "No. He's too far. I need . . ." Jill flailed. "I don't know what I need. There is no close midwife and we couldn't afford . . ."

HELP SHOULD NOT COST

"It has to cost. People are barely surviving."

**THERE IS FOOD THERE
IS SHELTERTHERE
IS NO CRIME**

"No crime you can see. There is always crime."

HUMANS

"Yes." Jill breathed in and out. She sat on the back steps of the camper, a splurge Charles had asked for, both on the front and back door. Now, she appreciated it, so that she could sit while reading the beech.

The tree shifted and Jill watched as its roots wriggled, worming through the dirt and slithering across the forest floor so that the beech could come closer. Eventually the tree was close enough for her to touch.

COME YOU WILL HAVE TO WALK

"I can't." Jill panted, but you didn't tell trees no, no matter what they asked. If they wanted you to move your camper, didn't like the color, hated where your windows were? You moved, you painted, you turned the camper around. Trees had wanted all their dead family back, so society spent decades tearing down the world to return the wood. Humans married when the trees told them to, watched their language, learned to adjust. Painfully, she stood, held her stomach and wobbled across the dirt to the patch of grass the tree led her to. Leaves rustled and she looked up.

I WILL HELP

"How?"

USE ME

RECIPROCITY

Jill hesitated before tentatively reaching out to touch the beech. Its bark was both rough and smooth, ridged by tiny knots and crevices. She looked up and said, "I've never touched you before."

THIS IS UNTRUE

"I don't remember touching you. You don't feel like the tree bark I know."

FIR PINE COMMON

Jill snickered. "Ego much?"

The leaves rustled, but Jill did not look. She gasped in pain and hugged the tree trunk, bearing down with the contraction. She screamed, loud in the silence of the forest behind their home. When it had passed, the leaves rustled.

HELP IS COMING

"Charles?"

ANGRY MATE
UNREACHABLE

"Okay." Jill's voice wavered. She blinked away the tears that filled her eyes and continued holding onto the tree. "I need, I need . . . " She trailed off. The leaves rustled. Behind her, one of the roots lifted from the ground in a shower of dirt and slithered up the steps into the camper. When it returned, a blanket and a couch cushion was coiled in the ropy roots.

SIT HERE
REST AGAINST ME

Jill sighed. "That's my favorite blanket."

I KNOW

"You've seen me in it." Jill eased herself onto the pillow and pulled the blanket up.

YOU HAVE HAD IT
SINCE YOU
WERE A SPROUT

"How do you know that?" Jill angled her head back to stare at the beech's leaves.

YOUR MOTHER
LAY AT MY BASE
READ HELD YOU

"And you stayed with me?"

I PROTECTED YOU
FROM THE RECKONING

"Oh." Jill thought about that before turning and slapping the trunk hard. "Then you should've protected her too!"

I WAS TOO LATE

The leaves rustled, but the sound was drowned out by a car hurriedly turning down the winding path of the road that led to their camper. Help had arrived.

***

"So, this is the interesting thing, right?" Stan Colver, arborist and creator of the Naturers, leaned forward, speaking to someone offscreen, but appearing to look directly into the camera. "Tree families stay together, if they can. They even have harems. A palo santo male can live to be 200 years, but its female trees, its wives if you want to call them that, only live to be 40-50. One male can have up to eight "wives."

Colver sat back, his bright white smile especially noticeable on his tanned face. "An even cooler thing. Not all trees are dioecious. Many of them are monoecious, meaning they carry whole generations inside them and "birth" them as flowers of either sex."

"I don't care what's cool. How do I hurt them? How do I stop them?"

Colver laughed at the question. "There is no stopping them. Just sit back and prepare for the ride. It's nature time, and as you noticed, organic farmers, arborists, and a whole lot of environmentalists didn't get a scratch."—- Recorded Naturer Advertisement

***

Jill adjusted the baby wrap and watched Martha wipe the sweat from her ruddy face into her wispy ponytail of gray hair. The older woman stepped away from the doorway she and Rylie had just rammed open and motioned with one of her large arms for Jill to enter. "Make sure you check every room thoroughly, hear? This place is coming down today and we don't want to have missed our chance to grab something we can't get anymore.

"If you come across a body, let the cadaver team know." Rylie said. He gave Jill a brief pat on the shoulder. "Charlie wasn't real keen on you coming to work so close to having the baby and all."

"Well, we need . . . everyone has to do their part." Jill shrugged and thought back to what the beech had indicated this morning. It was "close to when the sapling can be carried all day" and "you have the human birth sadness" and finally, "you need other humans."

No one disagreed. There was so much left to do.

"So, your tree made you come?" Rylie asked, sympathy warring with wryness in his tone. Jill studied the man for a moment. He was close to her size, wiry and muscled. His eyes crinkled at the edges, and his dimples flashed often. He was brown, like she and Charles, which was why they often welcomed his presence, but he was not like them. Rylie flourished.

"Kind of." Jill shrugged. Rylie nodded. He looked over her shoulder at the baby she had defiantly named and smiled softly.

"Well, it's good to see you. Sorry I didn't hear the trees the day you went in labor." Rylie ducked his head. "I would have made sure Charlie made it."

Jill nodded.

"Rylie!" Martha called from the house next door. "Stop flirting with Jill and come help me with this door."

Rylie winked at Jill and jumped off the porch. She watched as he crossed the space between the houses and went to help Martha. He looked over and caught her staring. She looked away. On her back, Aspen yawned. Jill paused, waiting to see if the baby would wake, but they didn't. She entered the home, dragging her rolling cart with her. The air was stale with the faint scent of rot to it. Someone had died in there, but it smelled like the cadaver team had already removed them.

The house had been picked clean. All wood products, aside from what was in the walls, had been set in neat piles: papers here, tables and chairs there, cardboard and more. She paused by one pile, fished out some bamboo utensils and slid them into her cart. It was easy to assume bamboo was a tree, but it wasn't. Martha drilled that statement often.

The rooms were empty, echoing with her footsteps as she trailed through the home, rechecking closets, and perusing neat piles. The scavenge collection team would be along soon. She was only allowed thirty minutes per house. She hit topsoil in the half bath. Beneath the sink, in the back corner of a cabinet, behind the pipes, she found a bottle of baby wash and three diapers. She put those in the pay bag across her chest. There was a piece of paper beneath the diapers, a photograph of a family, probably stuck there to hide from the tree tax.

They looked happy, standing in front of their home, surrounded by trees, smiling with each other. One of the children had thrown up the peace sign. In the background, Jill could see that one of the trees had mimicked the child, not that anyone would have believed it back then. It would have been one of those funny coincidences that they laughed about. "Look. The tree was throwing up the deuce, too. Ha. Ha."

Jill put the picture back. It was one photo. It was—a scratching against the small window made her lift her head. A tree branch rested against the glass. Trees couldn't see, they said. Trees couldn't hear, they said. They were wrong. She grabbed the photo from the bottom of the cabinet and stood.

"It's a family." She said to the branch, holding up the photo. On her back, Aspen sighed. Jill carried the contraband to the front and made a show of placing it on a pile of other glossy sheets, magazines, or photographs. Mixed mediums. She looked over the room one last time. A magnet was still on the refrigerator. She moved the picture to the front of the appliance door and left to catch up with Martha.

Outside, the street was noisy; the wind played with the dust from the houses that came down a block over. The air smelled like dirt. Scavenge teams pushed wide carts and drove hybrid trucks dragging huge trailers full of products down the street. They stopped at each house, each team carrying out their prospective stacks, working to strip away the homes that were made from the bodies of trees.

"Ready for th'next?" Martha asked when Jill found her team. The older woman didn't wait for Jill's answer and slammed the ram into the door. "Here you go."

***

"This is Vance Ellington, reporting from the Earth Day festival here in downtown. As you can see, it is packed. It appears that we are reaching historic numbers for this iconic day. Just look . . . wait . . . what is that? Gary, are you getting this? Are those trees? Trees are moving! They are, wait, what is happening? What are they doing? Run! Run!"—Earth Day newscast

***

"Trust in the trees! The trees are our gods. Where is your faith? They have made the world a better place for us all." The man on the corner was screaming, his face red, veins straining out of his throat. Jill scanned the trees as they drove past. The firs had moved to the edge of the roadway. They were close enough to protect the man if something went wrong, close enough to attack a car if they so chose, close enough to snatch up an errant human if they misbehaved. Jill turned away from the bus window. The beast moved slowly, using the least amount of solar power that it could.

"Naturers." Charles grumbled. He was always in a bad mood after a long day with the cadaver team, so Jill didn't tell him that he smelled like rot and sweat. She tolerated it, occasionally turning her nose to the cracked bus window, and gulping breaths of dusty air. "No one wants to see that when they get off work."

"He's just naked." Jill replied, mildly. She fished her nipple out of Aspen's sleeping mouth and covered her breast. After adjusting the baby on her lap, she looked at him. "Naturers eat better than most of us. They live with the trees. The trees make sure they eat. All of that fruit alone . . . "

"Would not be worth it." Charles snapped.

"What happened at work, today?" Jill asked.

"What?" Charles looked up and flushed, his brown skin taking on undertones of red. He shook his head and looked past her out the window.

"Tell me."

He stayed silent, but Jill knew to wait.

"We found . . . " Charles breathed in a shaky breath and exhaled slowly. His voice was hushed when he began speaking again. "We found a family."

"In a house?" Jill said, her voice rising slightly. Charles shook his head.

"In the backyard. They . . . they were torn apart."

"Root attack?"

Charles shrugged. "Something."

"It was that bad?"

Charles nodded. "Mummified parts everywhere. They were

hiding in the grass. I went . . . there was a barbecue pit, and I thought . . .”

“Shh.” Jill reached out and rubbed his back. “Shh.”

“I hate them. If I had gasoline, I’d set the forest on fire. They deserve it.” Charles choked out, his voice loud with anguish. Jill snatched her hand back and stared at him.

“Shut the fuck up before you get the bus flipped.” Rylie snapped from behind them. Charles glared but fell silent. Jill turned back to looking out the window, humming to Aspen. She stared at the trees as they passed them. The leaves changed as she watched, each tree forming the same two words as the bus moved: STRIKE THREE

✳✳✳

Medical Interview with Dr. Neil Marshall. Sacred Heart Hospital. May 26th.

Dr. Marshall (Dr.): There is so much infection that comes with a limb wound. If the tree punctured the body, there is tearing from the bark, dirt, insects. There is soil bacteria and fungus, and those lead to infection. Even if they survived the Reckoning, many people are losing limbs or life to infection.

Interviewer (I): What should people do to protect their puncture wounds if they can’t get into the hospital?

Dr.: I don’t know anymore. Wash it out? Hope and pray? At the end of the day, the trees have contaminated the water with their fungus. Hawthorne poisoning is common. I don’t know anymore. I’m surprised they let us keep the hospital building. We had to give them all the tongue depressors. Tongue depressors. There’s no rhyme or reason to this nonsense—

I: Thank you for your time, Doctor Marshall.

Dr.: I’m not finished.

I: The trees say you are.

****

When the trees came for Charles, Jill opened the door, and allowed the roots to slither through the camper. She walked outside with Aspen, holding her hands over the sleeping baby's ears. Charles yelled, briefly, but the crack of his neck was louder, punctuated by the sudden silence. The roots dragged him out and carried the body into the ground.

THANK YOU

Jill nodded numbly. She carried the baby back towards the camper, but a rustling gave her pause. She looked back at the tree.

YOU HAVE NEVER HAD A STRIKE

"No."

WHY NOT

"Why fight it?"

FIGHTING IS HUMAN NATURE

"It doesn't have to be." Jill adjusted Aspen on her shoulder and sat on the top steps.

I DO NOT UNDERSTAND

"Humans can adapt. They can learn. We did the environment wrong, and now the environment has taken its planet back." Jill shrugged. "At least with the trees watching, I don't have to worry about animals attacking."

I WATCH OVER YOU

"Exactly."

YOU WILL MISS YOUR MATE

"Yes. I mean . . . we were together out of convenience, mandated matching, you know, but—" Jill searched for the right words, holding her emotions in her mouth. She closed her eyes and swallowed. "He tried to be good to me, to the baby. He loved us in his own way, even though his opinions, the things he said, put us in danger, he loved us. And I loved him."

I BRING YOU ANOTHER

"I don't want—" Jill paused and turned towards the sound of a bike sputtering down the road. Rylie parked the vehicle and stepped off. He nodded at her.

"Trees told me to come."

"Charles . . . " Jill stopped and bit the inside of her jaw hard. Her eyes burned, and Rylie shook his head, just slightly. On her shoulder, Aspen made a small noise and Jill blinked away the tears. Rylie nodded. They both turned towards the rustling.

RYLIE LIVES HERE NOW
WILL HELP

"I do not want a new mate." Jill snapped at the tree. There was silence and the tree slowly moved its branches.

RYLIE WILL SLEEP
ON LONG SEAT

"Did the tree just tell me to sleep on the couch?" Rylie asked.

YES

Jill choked, a hysterical laugh bursting from her mouth. She wiped her face, glanced at the tree and turned to Rylie. "Come on. I'll show you around."

****

"Take care of trees, and they will take care of you. Without them, we'll all be blue." –pre-Earth Day Save the Planet jingle.

TO BE HUMAN

HANNAH GREER

THE DOCTOR'S FINGERS worm through my insides, peeling back flesh and patting at the blood with a sponge as he searches for what he wants. I lay still, a chill seeping through the thin paper that separates my skin from the metal table. It's cheaper to keep me awake during the collection, so they do. They say I don't feel pain, anyway. That the part that connects pain and feeling doesn't exist in me. Still, I feel when the doctor probes and cuts my pumping, beating parts away. They make a wet sound when he sets them in a metal pan beside my hip.

"Any weekend plans?" I ask. The doctor doesn't acknowledge my game. He doesn't like to pretend I'm human. He prefers when I lie still like the dolls he trained with at school. The dolls are very realistic, they say. It's basically the real thing. Until I pretend to be human, then it is not.

No one likes to pretend I'm human, except the doctor who taught me how to play back when I was small and my organs were only good spares for children. He liked to play until the day he told me we were going somewhere only humans went, somewhere better than where we were. I never found out if there was such a place. We didn't make it out of the lab and I never saw the doctor again.

***

When I step onto the train, heads turn. First my way, then anywhere except for me. They whisper behind their masks to each other and trickle out of the car. People like the idea of free-range organs in concept only.

My organs slosh as I sit, small as they regrow. By next month, they'll be full-sized again. Next month, I'll return to the doctor and he'll take them out again to put in someone else. Someone who is human. They will feel pain when my spares replace theirs.

Two people do not leave. A woman who doesn't look up from her tablet and a little girl with a plastic mask over her nose connected to a humming tank. I peer at the little girl and she stares at her shoes.

"What's wrong with you?" I say it like a human would, measuring each beat.

The mother doesn't look up as she snaps, "Isn't it obvious?" I wait. I wouldn't have asked if it was. "Her lungs are failing."

Lots of lungs are failing. There's something in the air, they say. "Can't she get spare lungs?" The doctors have lots of spare lungs. My last pair went to a wealthy 152-year-old woman.

The woman's voice trembles. "Not all of us can afford it." Her gaze drifts from the tablet to her daughter. The way she looks at her . . .

I wish someone would look at me like that.

"I can give her lungs," I blurt.

The woman's gaze shoots up. "What?" She sees my eyes, stained gold to mark me a spare. She looks away, pale.

"I can give her lungs," I repeat. If it would make her look at me like she looks at her daughter, I would do anything.

***

Two weeks before my next collection, when my lungs are child-sized, I meet the woman at an old, rundown clinic. There is a sign that says we should not be here. I expect something to happen when we ignore it, but nothing does.

The doctor who meets us is not like the doctors I'm used to. He is old and bald and wrinkled and must have gone through many spares.

He speaks to the woman and doesn't look at me. He is not so different from my doctors, after all.

"I need at least double," he tells the woman.

"This is what we agreed on! I found the lungs; you do the surgery."

He shakes his head. "This isn't the same as finding a set on the black market. It's much riskier to use their spares directly, without permission."

The woman's eyes water, her hand white around the little girl's. "I don't have more."

The man turns away. I speak up. "You can have my liver as compensation."

It's enough.

***

I sit on a chair in the hallway running a finger over the seam in my chest while the doctor puts my lungs into the little girl. The woman paces. She bites at her fingers. Eventually, the doctor comes out. He says the transfer went well and the little girl will live.

The woman sobs and hugs him around the neck. He pushes her off with a grumble and she turns to me.

"Thank you." She walks over, hesitant. "I can never repay you for what you've done."

"I know," I say.

Finally, she drags her eyes to mine. She looks at me like I have done something special and unexpected. It is not the look she gives her daughter, but it is more than I've ever received. "They won't take it out on you, will they? I know this is against their rules. Will you be okay?"

The doctors will not be happy when they cut into me and find my lungs small and new. If I lie, they will think I'm defective. If I don't, they will lock me up. Neither is a pleasant outcome for a spare.

I don't tell the woman. Humans do not tell the truth, so neither do I. "Yes," I say. She smiles. I smile back.

I like pretending to be human.

I HAVE SEEN SEVEN BAD THINGS

SJ TOWNEND

1. Daddy, escorted home by the police on a grim January evening.

AT THE TOP of the stairs, dressed in my pyjamas with teddy squeezed tight in my arms, I sit, knees huddled to chest, and witness it all.

No arrest has been made, according to the sombre policeman, but this doesn't stop my mother from exploding with fury after she hurries my father in and shuts the front door. Daddy must sleep on the sofa tonight. After the lounge door closes, I hear the clunk of cupboards and drawers in the kitchen. My mother passes me on her way up the stairs, one of her glass bottles under her arm, and instructs me to go back to bed. I do as I am told.

From under my Ninja Turtles duvet, in the dark, through the thin plasterboard floor and walls of our council house, I listen: Daddy's snores, Mummy crying herself to sleep.

In the morning, my father still wiped out in the sitting room, my mother gives me one of her awkward hugs, kisses me on the forehead, then crouches down to meet me at eye-level. "I love you, Boo, but I've got to leave," she says, her face puffy, her breath wine-sour. Over her arm, her half-zipped bag spews with bundled clothing. I plead for her to take me with her. I don't want to stay with Daddy. Both our eyes fill with tears. "We'll stay in touch, I promise, Sweet-pea, but you must stay with Daddy. Your father understands you better than I ever will. Now, be a darling, go and wake him up."

I ignore my mother's instruction and follow her down the hallway and stand a few feet behind her as she searches for her car keys. She finds them, then reaches for the front door handle. My fingertip runs faster and faster round the loop of my teddy-bear's snout, the place where the fur fabric is most worn. My mother turns, speaks,—"Stop doing that to your bear, Michael. Please,"— then leaves.

For a while, my mother picks me up on Saturdays for ice cream and the occasional trip to the swings, but her visits dwindle to the annual birthday card in the post as the years pass by.

2. The drawing on the whiteboard at school: a stickman with fingers and thumbs in places they shouldn't be. The caption underneath, scrawled in the handwriting of a rushed nine-year-old child: *"Michael Andrews and his family are all weirdos."*

I cry, deny it, rush for the wiper, and scrub the sick image away before the supply teacher we've been told we've got today arrives; but as Jenny Brown sticks her tongue out at me, and flicks her pigtails back, she exposes the lobe and the canal of her right ear.

Something flutters in my stomach.

The board a blank canvas again, I toss the wiper on the teacher's desk, thrust my hands into my trouser pockets, and slope back to my plastic chair at the side of the room where I sit down next to Miles "Cheesy" Johnson.

The supply teacher arrives.

The class settles.

The teacher instructs us all to copy today's date from the board into our workbooks, but all I can think about is Jenny Brown's earlobe. For the first time, I wonder if there is, perhaps, some truth in the graffiti I cleared from the board.

3. Judy's face.

A single-parent household now, Dad unable to afford a sitter, he tells me to stay in my room; a woman named Judy is coming for dinner and I am not invited. "Eleven-year-olds should be able to entertain themselves for a few hours," he says, and presses a warm paper bag with the blue Greggs logo on its side into my hands.

Later, in the night, I take a peep into Dad's room through a gap in the door, drawn there by a sound similar to a wet fish being reeled onto land. Judy is perched on the edge of the bed, and Dad is standing, fully clothed, by her side, his clumsy hands all over her face.

He shouts, "Get out."

Judy screams. She shuffles up her belongings and pushes past me to make her way downstairs.

Despite the nightmare qualities of the scene I've witnessed: Judy's too wide eyes, my father's fingers plumbing up her mouth and nostrils, his head and eyes rolling back in some sort of lost, ecstatic trance, back in my own room after Judy has gone and Dad has returned to bed, with a grin on my face, I take deep joy in playing the scene out, again and again, in my mind.

In the morning, Father doesn't seem cross or disappointed, tells me he's sorry I caught him up to his 'old tricks,' "It never feels as good with the same person a second time anyway, kiddo," he says as he pours me a bowl of the weekend cereal even though it's Wednesday.

I never see Judy again.

I sit my GCSE exams a few years later. Father is out on the drink, up to 'old tricks,' as he so often is, when I receive my seven failed grades in the mail.

4. Midnight, my greying father in a dive-bar cubicle, his thumbs up some lad's nose.

After a long shift in the warehouse, I find myself at Cheetah's, a Gentleman's Club full of anything but. I come here now and again to let off steam. The beer is cheap and the dance floor is always busy, even in the small hours of the morning. Not much choice of venue this side of the town centre.

Three pints down, I have the urgency to piss.

There he is, my father, in the stalls with a redhead. If I'd have known he'd be here, I would have gone somewhere else.

I pause, hidden behind the door jamb of the Men's and try to interpret what the heck is going on. The redhead, a slim lad perhaps a few years older than me, has his arms around my father's waist. Dad's hands are cupped around the young lad's face, intimately so. But they do not kiss.

Instead, Dad's pinkies caterpillar in and out of the redhead's ears, his thumbs, the redhead's nose. My father's body shudders as the face between his hands laughs.

Still unaware of my lurking presence, Dad pulls the young lad's face closer to his, breath-close, then worms his index finger under the lad's left eyelid.

The redhead grunts and yanks Dad's roving fingers out and away from the holes of his face. My father staggers back, apparently far more drunk than me. "That is not what we agreed to," the lad says.

Dad stutters, apologises, but his spidering fingers lurch for the poor lad's face again. The redhead slaps him, rightly so. "Security," the redhead shouts above the thrum of resonating bassline, and while doing so, his eye catches mine, "And it's extra for voyeurism."

As father sees me, I cannot tell you which one of us looks more surprised.

"Shit, son, I'm sorry," he says.

"You owe me thirty," the redhead is addressing my father. Dad reaches into his pocket and passes the lad a bunch of crumpled notes. The lad takes them and spits on my father's shoes before slipping out past me, becoming swallowed in the queue for the crowded bar. Dad sways to his left, attempts to take a swig from an empty plastic pint glass that had been balancing on the hand drier.

"Let's get you out of here, Dad."

***

At home, I help him undress and get him into bed. Dad slurs as he tries to explain something to me. "We're hexed, son. Me, my father, my grandfather—the whole damned line of us Andrews. We've all been cursed to fuck."

I pass him a glass of water and let him ramble on.

"And your mother, she knew it'd pass on to you, too. Mother's always know."

"That's why she left me with you?" I find myself drawn into his deluded story, although he's beyond answering questions. Just one long drunken soliloquy to come, until he passes out, I expect.

83

"At first, it was just an itch, something I could push down and ignore. But then this need, this curse, became an obsession. The relief when I slide my fingers into someone's face holes, dear God—" He stares into the space between us, his palms turned up, his fingers spread out, each hand an upturned crab. Said crabs shake in time, emphasising the cadence of his words. "This curse, son, as the wheel turns, it develops, becomes an insatiable condition. My body crawls with agony when I'm not plumbed in."

"Dad, you're oversharing nonsense. Too much to drink again. Get some sleep." I don't dare tell him about my own sick fetish. The one that's been growing within me, extrapolating towards my fingers and toes, like a seed's roots stretching out through dirt, probing, unfurling, since I first saw Jenny Brown's ear hole in Year 4.

Dad apologises profusely, his tongue thick with alcohol, then passes out.

With gaffer tape initially, then with the four coiled bike locks I retrieve from the garage, out of shame and out of love, I tether Dad to his bed.

Sometime mid-morning, he wakes screaming, shifting in his sheets, writhing like Renton without the gear, the stench of beer dripping from his pores. I apologise, "Look, Dad, I'm sorry." I have no choice but to tape his mouth shut too, before I go to work.

5. The contents of the bag.

I move with urgency. Father has been alone for six hours and will be in pain, begging for release. Of course, I'll never untie him. He's well past the point of no return. To liberate him entirely from his sweat-stained bed would be insanity, could put innocent people at risk.

The heavy bag I carry bashes against my leg as I walk, its contents squelching like my sodden trainers through the puddles.

The rain descends in almost horizontal wet grey hyphens. I swear the wetness whispers 'hurry' as my feet pound the pavement back to the apartment Dad and I share. I arrive, wade through the knee-high grass of our front lawn, unlock the door, go inside, and kick off my shoes. *Clunk clunk clunk.* The headboard of Father's bed bashes against his bedroom wall.

Still exulting from my date earlier with Aisha, despite how things evolved, I dump the bag on the kitchen counter and sniff my fingers. The scent of her mucus and waxes lingers on the pads of my damp thumbs. After we'd kissed, I'd asked her permission, had said it was sort of a kink. I had to try, with real flesh. My urges have been growing stronger.

I'd slid my finger in her ear, just for a second, then her nostril. On the edge of a pleasure greater than orgasm, an indescribable need had driven me to it.

But this curse, it's not a sexual thing, not carnal. It's primal; intrinsic and all-consuming. My yearning to plumb and plug grows weightier by the day. God knows what will happen in time. At least I don't have a child who'll catch me mid-action and keep me restrained in shame. I can control it, anyway. I'll always ask for consent. I'm not weak like Father.

Aisha had laughed at first, before she'd asked me to stop. "It's not doing anything for me," she'd said, before tugging her hijab back on.

Irritated, but in control of myself, I'd told her it wasn't going to work out between us, had grabbed my stuff and left. I'd marched in the rain to the butcher's after leaving her house, to fulfil Dad's request.

I peek into the carrier bag, pegging my nose as the odour hits my olfactory system. Inside, ogling back up at me: the severed pig's head.

I'll have to settle myself the same way father does tonight. In the morning, I'll hit Tinder again, try and find a new source for a new day.

6. Father's face as he plumbs.

Until now, I've pacified Father with cold slices of meats, latex substitute body parts. Last month he'd even been able to get his fix from a pair of old, warmed leather gloves. But these substitutions no longer seem to be enough. His body has become weaker without a daily pure flesh fix, and his urges have grown stronger. I've researched it, our condition. It seems, in the dark corners of the web, there are others like us out there, scattered across the globe. I promised myself, while leafing through microfiche slides in the library, that I must reach out and connect with the others, see if there is a cure.

I carry the butcher's bag up to his room. "Release," he wails, his voice reedy, like his limbs. Ensuring his waist and ankles are still restrained accordingly, with the correct combination of numbers I will never reveal to him, I unlock his bound wrists as old sunken eyes implore me to bring the bag and its contents closer to where he lies.

I let him plumb his fingers into the meaty sockets, the snout, the whiskery ear canals, the stale, raw swine maw. His own tongue pokes out, lolls from side to side. His frantic, desperate fingers and thumbs explore the dead flesh. Father's head tilts, his eyes closed. He purrs in an ecstasy I now fear I nearly understand.

To watch him pleasure himself this way unleashes something in me.

Surely, I'm too early on in this sick downhill trajectory to need to join in with him, to abuse the hog's head in such a filthy way? The stench of the aged meat repulses me. The putrified odour turns my stomach. But the white hair which pokes out from my father's nostrils has quite the opposite effect. I learn fast: to observe is too much for me to bear. I can't help myself. I'm not as strong as I'd thought.

"I'm so sorry," I say, although my father is so momentarily oblivious; I'm unsure if he hears. He's in a faraway place, dancing with fairies, or demons; as his near-skeletal fingers pump in and out, revelling in the hog's head which rests, milky-eyed, upon his lap.

I sit on the bed beside him and slide my finger into Father's ear canal. I push it through layers of wax, like a stick in a toffee apple, until I reach the tympanic membrane. Bliss.

We both recline together, in another level of pleasure, my fingers probing and plumbing more into my father's skull holes, and his, digging deeper into the skull holes of the pig, pulverising pork into mince.

Father has a sudden moment of lucidity, becomes aware of what I'm doing to him. He screams. He withdraws his fingertips from the pig and plugs all ten of his jellied, blood-covered exploratory worms into my mouth and nose.

Connected like a twin-human ouroboros, a mass of wigwagging

wet skin, bone, and hair, I wonder, in my own brief moments of lucidity, if I can get my big toe in my father's mouth.

For minutes, an hour perhaps, side-by-side on the bed, we writhe and sweat and probe each other's faces, limiting the other's oxygen supply, the macerated pig's head between us, staring up at the ceiling, perhaps feeling left out like the third person in an unsuccessful three-way.

***

We embrace our Magnum Opus. I am not sure when I come to realise father is no longer breathing, his body already stiff from the outside in, and that I too am no longer present in my mortal body. Like a reverse claustrophobia, I am both suddenly unfolded from my shell, inside and out, then out, out, all at once.

Time is of no relevance now, as our once-entwined bodies separate out into sentient nothingness, somewhere up here in an ethereal plain.

Below, the emptied, twisted double-headed knot of what was us lies hard and yellow, bracketing a minced pig's head, splayed out on vermillion, sodden sheets.

Father and I, or the cursed apparitions of us both, snake our way, like oil in water, towards the other mass of curling and furling energy. So this, I think to myself, my last independent thought, is what lurks beneath the veil.

Together, we wisp up, and join with the single, timeless point of entanglement; a singularity of darkness. We become everywhere and nowhere all at once, with no beginning and no end: true release.

7. What lies beneath now, cold and solid.

Now, we inhabit no human bodies. We all move as one. Between us are infinite fingers and toes and thumbs, a pulsating, tendrilled ball of invisible force.

We call ourselves the Brotherhood and glide alongside man, although, we'll never reveal our true form—it would drive the oblivious to insanity. Instead, we hide in plain sight, between the atoms of the air, in the blind spot when you drive, in your sense of déjà-vu.

Within the God particle we lurk, in the low frequencies of electromagnetic force. As one and as nothing, we swim in all the domains of science and religion no man will ever truly have the capacity to understand.

In this moment, we drift into the neo-natal clinic as a tired nurse loses focus, and there, we plant seeds of erotic asphyxiation in the souls of the sexually lost. Then we float to Mayhill Retirement Home once the old folk have gone to bed. We do what we have grown to love, that thing that brings release.

Beneath our collective now, as you read this story, an old girl rasps in her sleep.

Working as one, we pull the pillow into position, shifting the sheet of cotton one fractal thread at a time, then each of us, anchored to a thin white hair, help tip her head a little too far to the right, and anchor it there with our urges.

With all her orifices smothered, we release her from her opiated sleep and help her avoid the need to wake.

✳✳✳

We have seen seven bad things and we will see an eternity more.

SOFT

IRA RAT

"I think I'm in hell, therefore I am."
—Arthur Rimbaud

I AM A fifth-generation bootleg of myself. A recording of a recording of a recording of a . . . All background noise and soft edges, a drone with no beginning or end, a constant now of a mildly occupied frequency. I exist to separate the nothingness from the somethingness, no matter how insignificant my disruption to non-existence might be.

My dreams were to perform in gleaming white, surgically white rooms, all 90-degree angles, and the kind of bland lighting that only someone who never once had to worry about pulling a day job while going to school would be able to design. The kind of rooms that would make Marina Abramovic's granny panties moist.

Middle-class aspiration of decadence collapses under the weight of old money. Once you finally get there, it's no longer Versace and Versailles. It's $250 plain gray polos that look the same as a $10 Walmart special.

I can't remember the last time I saw a perfect angle. Tonight, it's a country club on the outskirts of Cedar Rapids. Cigarette smoke fills the air, wood panels cover the walls, and my bare feet tread through shag carpeting that feels like it hasn't been vacuumed since it was installed somewhere in the mid-last century.

Hell isn't other people. Hell is doing the thing that you love night after night to uncaring, indifferent audiences in the performance art equivalent of the chitlin circuit. If you were to tell

Yoko Ono or (not that) Nick Cave that places like this exist, they would scoff in incredulity. I wouldn't have known either, if I didn't need to eat.

My jaw hurts from chewing. The world is the taste of dirty pennies. It's all I can taste . . . hear . . . smell. I feel the blood running down the back of my throat. However, observations seep into me like osmosis. I'm not consciously aware of anything, but my senses are heightened. Somehow, I'm as omnipotent as Santa Claus.

When I asked them to play some Kali Malone, they looked at me blankly, same when I asked for anything neo-classical. So I asked for something soft, to create "a mood." My skin bristles as this-decade country music crawls through the not-so-discreetly recessed speakers and into my ears.

A '70s snuff film plays behind me, over me, around me. I can tell it's the '70s by the size of the bush on the girl being vivisectioned. I would complain that it was distracting from the show, but at these types of venues, I've learned to just do the work. Its flickering light crisscrosses my body, illuminating the veneer-perfect topographical moon maps of my scars. It would be oh so beautiful if it weren't such a goddamn waste.

Would you die for modern art? At least conceptually? There are a big B—billion mini-Hirsts who are willing to kill, stick pins through things, and display, but nobody is willing to sacrifice anything, let alone themselves. They aren't willing to give anything of themselves to their audience. This is my body, Pastor Keith's voice crawls from the back of my brain a childhood memory, made not too many miles away from here.

A billboard-sized R. Crumb fills my brain. "I'm dying up here," the crucified man yells at the yuppies mingling. I should be so lucky. I mock myself. Fuck, I wish I could draw like Crumb. I could never draw anything representational. Instead, I got drawn to theory classes. The distance between craftspeople/illustrators and true artists is miles, but I still can't help wonder how my life would be different, if pencils didn't lie in my hand like dead fish.

I am art.

The host laughs in the back, all missing teeth and escaping cigar smoke. His money was green, and he had the space. So, this is where my judgement ends. I've been doing this far too long, for far too many people to really pass judgement on anyone. Well, that's not true, I do, but I admit that I'm a hypocrite.

A row of hillbillies playing nouveau riche watch my every move. Pricks in hand, the sound of their cocks slithering through their wrinkled fingers, and their wheezing is almost enough to put me off my meal.

I had been popular for a moment in the world of real money, but like everything else, these things come and go in phases. Right now, auto-cannibalism is so pre-COVID. I chew and chew and chew, it's worse than any steak at even the cheapest steakhouses you can think of. My blood pools around my left arm, the bite looking Apple logo perfect.

Jesus wept; it was that goddamn beautiful.

PIG HOUSE

Kay Vaindal

WHEN THE POWER goes out, whole cities die. Your rebreather stops pulling oxygen and if it zeroes before you can charge it: suffocation. Heave into your lungs the useless air. Deep breath, nothing. And another and another. Aunt Beth died that way when Rochester went out. That was the fifteenth biggest one in the States–Rochester. Three years after the atmosphere turned sour. No real protocol for accidents yet. So a snowplow knocked into a transformer and killed twelve hundred people. C'est la mort!

I don't remember any different than this. My mom did. She had cats and dogs and birds, rabbits, gerbils. Little animals that lived with her, slept with her, and she'd feed them, and they'd follow her and meow and bark and sing. Now I sleep with my rebreather. I go for walks with my rebreather. If I want to eat solid food or make out with somebody, I hold my breath. People die that way, too. Old people, usually. Drunk, usually. They forget.

On the news they say we're the only animals left. Except last week I heard my husband's coworker say there's a pig in Omaha, in a sterile room they pump oxygen and dinitrogen into, no nitrifying microbes to turn it fast into nitrate. I haven't stopped thinking about it, the pig. At night I stare at the ceiling and picture it. I want to see that pig more than anything. I'd die to see the pig. I'd kill to see the pig. As long as I get to see that pig, when the power goes out in Syracuse, I won't care.

So I'm doing it. I'm here now, on the road, my three-year-old conked out on sleeping pills in the back seat and my husband's credit card in my pocket. Giant corn country, now. Everywhere giant corn, sixty feet tall, cobs as big as me.

We pull over at a rest stop in Illinois, town called Mt. Vernon, because the kid's rebreather is beeping long and low. The clouds look threatening, moving in dark purple coils in the sky, sparks between them. I park the car under a solar panel in case it hails. Between low rumbles there's the comforting whir of back-up generators from somewhere out of sight. The power won't go out unless lightning strikes them all. I unbuckle my seatbelt and peel open the side door of the van. Sammy's heavy now. I toss her over my shoulder and head into the Paul Bunyan service center. A big blue cow statue stands watch in front of double glass doors, smiling with chipped teeth at the dark sky. Other families hurry between the cow's legs, into the building.

We get inside just before the rain starts falling, those sort of big heavy warm drops before a thunderstorm. There's no hills to stop the storms here, I know. I saw that on TV. When the storms start, they go for days, until the big corn bends over, ears on the ground, nitric acid pock-marking the leaves like rotten bananas.

It's a nice rest stop, all things considered. Food court in the middle. Protein drinks you can sip while you breathe. Decorative chandeliers hang from a center atrium, a big skylight so you can see the bubbling atmosphere. Maybe it was clear glass back when people had cats, but now it's striped with yellow crusts. Twenty or thirty people mill about as the sky darkens, sipping smoothies while their phones shine into their eyes. I make my way to the charging café in the corner, swipe my husband's card and hook the kid's rebreather up to a wire.

I hook myself up, too. Figure I'll get more bang for my buck here than I will with the car charger. I sit myself down next to Sammy and watch big raindrops paint the skylight gold.

The inevitable—a man sits down next to me, gives me a shy sort of look like he wants to say something but he needs my permission first. I glare at him. That's enough. "Couldn't help but notice that Steeple hoodie, ma'am," he says in a plain plains accent. "That's my favorite video game."

"It's my husband's sweatshirt," I say.

His eyes crease with a smile. I watch for disappointment,

angled eyebrows, the seeds of a coming tantrum, but his smile looks pleasant enough. "You waiting out the storm here?"

I inspect the man more closely. His head is block-shaped, blue eyes, buzzed hair, nose that might have been broken once or twice. I'll bet his name is something like Sven Jorgensen, and I bet his parents come from Minnesota. I suppose I wouldn't mind screwing him in the backseat of the van. The click click click of hail on the skylight. I point my chin at it, and that's enough of an answer for Sven.

"Smart, yeah," says Sven. "No driving in that. Cracked my whole windshield that way back in August. You know, the corn farmers prefer this sort of storm. The acid doesn't come out of the hail till it hits the soil. Nothing a little liming can't fix, there, right? The biggest crops don't mind the hail as much."

Sven wears a Clayrite brand rebreather. I watch its LED lights turn green when he inhales, red on the exhale, and ask him if he's a farmer.

Sven shakes his head. "I'm a miner."

I'm tired of making eye contact with Sven. The hail on the skylight has no eyes to meet, so I watch that. I ask Sven if there's phosphate out here, but I doubt it. Since I left Syracuse, it's all old shale gas lands, cracked and broken and filled in with chalky white soil to grow up massive stands of corn.

"I'm not from here," says Sven. "Just passing through."

"Where you headed?"

Sven watches the skylight, too. Before he answers, my phone rings loud in my pocket. I tell Sven excuse me, and pretend to answer it, but really when I see my husband's name I press the red button. I say a lot of things like mhm and yeah and okay, honey and Mt. Vernon, Illinois, Paul Bunyan Service Center. The power flickers. I put into the phone a laugh that goes to no one. Wait a minute longer. Goodbye. I love you too.

I slip the phone in my pocket and turn to Sven. "I'm headed to Nebraska."

"What's in Nebraska?"

"Family," I tell him, and I think of the real live pig in its pressurized room. I picture something sterile, white. Glass windows where scientists can look on. Sammy has a kid's book with barnyard animals, a gift from my mother-in-law. The pig lives in the mud. And the farmer in his denim overalls can walk into the woods with a sleeping bag on a whim and never come back to his farm. He can find berries and small corn and turkeys to eat. The atmosphere didn't turn sour all at once. It got bad enough that you had to gasp, my mom said. Then so many animals died that their rotting corpses sucked all the leftover oxygen and gasping wasn't good enough anymore, and so many more animals died, and so on and so forth. At night, I imagine the pig feels soft under my hand. Silky-smooth and wet like mushroom flesh.

Sven's Clayrite rebreather has an auto display that connects to his cell phone number. A blinking blue light tells him and me he has a text message. He doesn't check it. Instead he looks at me very seriously, and he asks if I'm safe.

"Am I safe?"

One nod from Sven Jorgensen.

"Of course I'm safe. Why wouldn't I be safe?"

"You look a little beat up, ma'am, and you're talking about a husband, but you—" He pauses. Looks at the skylight again. "You look very young. I know there's bad business that goes on in some circles with all this repopulation talk, so I'm just making sure that you're—"

"I'm fine, Sven Jorgensen. Jesus Christ. Does nobody mind their own business anymore?"

"I'm glad to hear it," says Sven Jorgensen. "But if you need any help at all, my wife and I are traveling in an RV. We could hook your car up to the back. Drop you off in Nebraska."

I tell Sven my daughter is with me, and stick a thumb toward Sammy, conked out on the bench on her wire, looking peaceful below the white noise hail hitting the skylight, chhh. Sven says they have room for us both. I don't think Sven has an RV, or a wife. I think he has rohypnols and human trafficking ties. Still, I imagine myself eating breakfast with his big blond wife, Helga, traversing the big corn lands on some great American tour. There's a gun in the pocket of my dress. If this is all true, and Sven can afford an RV on a phosphate miner's salary, I could wait until nightfall, pull the gun, say a few terse words and take the road yacht for myself. If it's make-believe, I don't have to wait until night.

I curdle my face into a smile and let my eyes get wet and tell Sven I would love that, thank you so much for your kindness, God bless you and your wife. The hail is falling harder now. I wait for cracks in the skylight, but it holds. It's had twenty years of hail and winds and acid rain, and it and the roof and the great blue cow out front haven't crumbled yet. Sven asks me my name, and I look to the brick wall on our left, and tell him, "Bricks."

Sven's smile doesn't fall, and I'm ninety-five percent sure he wants to sell me to the sky worshippers in Texas, now. He says his name is something like Todd or Tadd or Chuck, but I don't revise the picture of him in my mind. Sven Jorgensen. Minnesota.

On the bench, Sammy's eyes start to open. She can't hear, which I've always thought is a blessing. We can't afford implants. I don't know that we'd want to. No acid storm or screaming match can wake her. I leave Sven, walk to her side and sign, "Good morning."

She stares up at me, then looks left to right and left again. Sammy only knows a few words in sign language, like hello, and pig. I've tried since she got the diagnosis last year. She doesn't get it. The doctors say keep trying. It'll click. And then they send me off with a pamphlet on how to learn and teach an entire new language. It'll click!

Sammy's rebreather blinks green. She's past the age where she tries to rip it out, thank God. I unplug her, and she hops off the bench, wanders in a six-foot diameter around my feet. Her yellow dress is rumpled from sleeping in the booster seat. She points at the smoothie store. I shake my head. She gets that sort of thing, pointing, head shaking, head nodding. I think she lip reads at least a little bit, squinting through the foggy glass of my rebreather. No and yes and Sammy and things like that. Maybe that's the start of the click.

"I can buy it for her," says Sven, behind me like a ghost.

"Me too?"

Sven smiles, nods. I knew he would. Before he sells me to the sky worshippers, I want to make full use of his artificial kindness. I tell him I have to pee and he says, "I can watch her, if you want." And I laugh and shake my head–that's very kind of you, but she'll need to go too—because he's selling us to the sky worshippers together or not at all.

I'm pregnant again. That's half the reason the RV is so tempting, real or otherwise. An engine and a toilet on one set of wheels. None of my husband's other wives warned me on the subtleties of being pregnant when it first happened. They told me I'd glow, and my hair would be so thick. Nothing on the constant pissing and the fact that I'll never do jumping jacks again. I ate a bunch of coffee grounds and cigar ash to try and kill this one, but we're past the twelve-week ultrasound now and everything looks good. It's easy to run with one kid. Once you have two, you don't have any free hands.

We pee and I wash Sammy's hands and my hands and wipe them dry with paper towels. She looks at me with a head-tilt, and I tell her as best I can that we're going to Nebraska to see the last living pig. When I was pregnant with Sammy, I always craved salt. I would huddle in the pantry and unhook my rebreather and dump spoons full of it on to my tongue.

Sven is waiting for us with smoothies, like I knew he would be. He helps hook Sammy's up to her proboscis, and I do mine myself. "Where's your wife now?" I ask him. I'm okay with poking holes in the story now that the free smoothie's sliding down my throat.

"Out draining the RV," he says. "Fueling up. All that maintenance business. They don't tell you about that in the reviews. That you need to drain the pee out the back every few days or the whole thing stinks."

"In the storm?"

Sven laughs. His laugh doesn't fit him. It's high-pitched. Geeky sounding. He should be at a convention center in Buffalo, dressed in a cape and laughing about Mr. Spock. "Service area's all covered up. That's why we stopped here. Missouri rest stops don't have lids."

I nod, and slurp my smoothie and watch Sammy to make sure she doesn't choke. Her rebreather light goes off while she sips, on when she pauses, off when she sips. The rhythm of it soothes me a little.

"Is your eye all right?" Sven asks me.

The makeup on my cheekbone must have been sweat away. I figure he's been waiting to ask that for a while now, concerned crinkles in the corners of his eyes.

I smile at Sven like how sad battered girls smile up at their rescuers in old movies written by horny men and I say I'm all right.

The storm stops, eventually. It doesn't take days like I was afraid of and hopeful for. The clouds fizz and disperse and there's the sun and the corn-colored sky. Sven leads Sammy and I out, and we latch my van to his RV. There's no buzzing in my ears like I've been drugged, and I think I'm a little disappointed by that. Their RV has tires bigger than my daughter. According to the app on my phone, the screws on the axel are bigger than the thirteen-week-old naked mole rat burrowing in my guts.

We ascend a three-step staircase and I'm in the Jorgensen's home-on-wheels. It's immaculate. There's a bowl of lemons on the table in the kitchenette. Helga is real and tall and buff and Scandinavian like her husband. She could scoop me up and put me in her vintage EAT LOCAL tote bag as a snack for later. Sven talks something about making ourselves at home but Sven is old news. I want to look Helga in her eyes and touch her face and tell her I'm taking my daughter to Nebraska to put our hands on the mushroom flesh of the last living pig. Instead I say something stupid like my real name. Sven Googles me, I'm sure, and texts his wife all the information from my New York State ID page, and she responds with a big, gooey-eyed frowny face, maybe wonders if she should contact the police, naive and EAT LOCAL as if all legal roads don't lead back to my husband.

While Sven adjusts himself into the driver's seat at the front of the car, Helga helps Sammy onto the couch and offers her a cell phone game. Sammy isn't allowed to look at screens at home. She loves it. I stand there dumb, hands in the pockets of my ugly dress.

Sammy and Sven otherwise engaged, Helga approaches me. She puts a hand on my shoulder and looks deeply into my eyes. She says, earnest as her goodie-two-shoes-ass-husband, "You're both safe now."

That snaps me out of it. I point my gun and shoot her in the head. I didn't mean to do that. It was too easy, and now it's done. I'm dangerous. I point my gun at Sven and shoot him, too. Sammy keeps playing her game. She doesn't look up once while I move their bodies into the back bedroom and peel their expensive rebreathers off their faces. I won't go back to Syracuse, and neither will my daughter. Lord willing, we'll be in Omaha before the Jorgensens start to smell.

***

Driving an RV is different than driving a car, it turns out. My hands shake, gripped loose around the steering wheel. I scrape the cement divider on my way back to the highway with the big corn under the yellow sky. We accelerate up to a solid seventy miles per hour and I follow signs west. I clear my mind and think about cats most of the way. My mother-in-law has a faux fur coat that I could stroke for hours. I could say to Sven and Helga in the back of the RV in a patronizing voice, "You're both safe now."

My mom was forty-four and pregnant when the atmosphere turned sour. She had six cats and three dogs and no husband and she made a living rescuing abused donkeys and posting their donkey faces online. Then she had a sperm bank baby and a hypoxic brain injury and she only got to stay my guardian as long as she did because the foster care system was so flooded with nitrate orphans. Once when she was more lucid than usual she said that in the early days of the new age, when the doctors all were closed, my Aunt Beth tried to remove me from her uterus with an ice cream scoop and a needle. Eleven-year-old me thought that was funny as hell, but my husband thinks it's what screwed me up in my head. He rescued me from ice cream scoops and hypoxia and nostalgia for donkey influencers. I was fifteen when we married.

I drive into the night. Sammy doesn't make a peep in the back of the RV, a whole world opened up to her on the dead woman's phone, lights and colors and shapes probably making more sense to her than anything I've ever tried. She falls asleep on the couch with it still in her little grip.

My GPS takes me to the address I heard my husband's friend talking about. Omaha National Food Security Laboratory. A manila, two-story building sitting unguarded, surrounded by suburban homes and big corn. I haven't seen a tree since I left New York. The landscaping here is giant corn and thick, waxy meadows. I park in a lot near the back of the lab and pack Sven and Helga's rebreathers into her vintage tote.

Sammy doesn't drop Helga's phone even when I pick her up and tuck her against my chest. My arms hurt from steering the big steering wheel and shooting two people. She feels heavier than usual. I sit her down in the waxy grass while I break a first-floor window in with a rock, then I make her wake up. She wipes wetness from her eyes and looks at me, and I sign pig, hand under my chin.

She knows that one. I pointed to the pig in her picture book and signed it enough times before this trip. She signs back, pig, and we climb through the broken window.

There's no alarm going off. No security guard waiting with a night baton. I put my hand on the gun in the pocket of my dress anyway, hold Sammy's hand with the other. Above us, motion-detection lights flicker on up and down the hallway. I expected white walls and warning signs, but this looks like a post office. The building is quiet except for our footsteps. I imagine the pig will be on the first floor, in the centermost room, to best protect it from tornadoes and the atmosphere. A cynical part of me wonders if the pig is here at all—if the pig is even real—if all of this was for nothing and I'll find another empty office. There should be security guards. There should be alarms. This is the last living pig on earth, and it sits in its tomb alone.

We're near the center of the building now. I try some doors, and Sammy helps. An office. An office. An office. A musky blue-toned room like an execution chamber viewing booth, big glass window and bright white door off to one side. Sammy and I step inside. The lights don't turn on automatically like in the halls. I flick on my phone flashlight and search around for a light switch. On the wall, beside a sign: No lights between 8 PM and 8 AM. I turn on the lights anyway.

The room hums to life. Light blue walls, long benches with clipboards set down at the end of the day. It's dark behind the glass. I can't see in. Above the big window, scrawled in Sharpie on yellow graphing paper ripped haphazardly from a notebook: SOW #651. So there are six hundred and fifty one pigs in the world, maybe. So I've been lied to. I don't have time to wallow in that because if I start to wallow I'll wallow forever and instead I find a second light switch, and I hit it, and there it is.

One pig lying against a wall. A hundred times bigger than I imagined. It's a tiny space just big enough that the sow can turn around if it presses itself against the wall and then folds in half. It's not a sterile room. It's brown like a dirty aquarium, and there's a crack on the window and shit on the floor, and the pig has tubes down her throat and nostrils connected to an oxygen tank and a big barrel that says FEED. Sammy looks at the pig, then at me. I sign pig, and she shakes her head. The one in her picture book was pink and round with mud on its hooves and a blue sky above it. This is tissue. Pile of cells. But its eyes are watching the door.

I decide I want to go home. My mom lives in a care facility now. I haven't visited since I got married. One day she's going to die and I'll say I should've visited and I know that and I still don't visit but I look at the pigs and I feel nostalgic for donkey influencers in a big green field and a farmer who could walk into the woods and stay forever.

There's a gun in my pocket. I could use it on the pig and my daughter and the naked mole rat and me but I don't. Maybe that's what I came here to do. There's no plan post-pig. There never was. I tell Sammy to stay put, and I slip into the pig's room. The door feels like it's never really been used, sits off its hinges in a way that I'm not sure I'll be able to close it again when we leave. The pig's eyes track me but her head doesn't move. I worry if she knows how. But she flicks her tail so I test Sven's rebreather against her snout. She recoils at the touch and pulls at the tubes stuck in her throat and nose but she can't get any purchase so she settles back down again. I decide if this doesn't work I'll shoot her. I'll tell her she's safe now and sell her bacon on the black market for a trillion dollars. Then I extract the tubes from the pig's mouth and nose one-by-one. She can't breathe. I can see the look in her eyes when she realizes she can't breathe. Her lungs are expanding and filling and expunging but nothing's happening. I fix Sven's expensive rebreather over her snout and secure the elastic behind her ears. The pig meets my eyes. Her chest settles. Oxygen flows over the bubbles in her lungs again. I exhale with her and tell myself I was never going to shoot her and my daughter and me. I have a post-pig plan.

The pig gets up, now. Turns around and chuffs and looks at me and the room she's probably never left. She bolts past me toward the door, then shuffles about the viewing booth, squealing into Sven's rebreather like a person with a stubbed toe. Sammy touches a pig. I touch a pig. Her skin is coarser than I expected, warm and wrinkled like a human palm and covered with long white hairs.

Sammy and I fashion a harness and leash out of duct tape and we exit the lab with her alongside us. We leave the Jorgensen's RV behind to duck under the cover of a big corn forest, disappearing under the giant yellow leaves. The sky is purple-black and the stars glow greenish against it. The pig's hooves turn white with sand and lime.

Deep in the corn forest, I open up Helga's phone and find her social media accounts. I take a picture of the pig with its rebreather and its white feet under the stars.

WAITING FOR JONAH

SHARANG BISWAS

ONCE UPON A TIME, there was you and there was Jonah. "Jonah!" you would call out. "Jonah, it's me! Let me in!"

But he'd never let you in. Before you turned ten, the inside of Jonah's room remained as opaque as the inside of his thoughts.

And he would always, *always* make you wait. You'd stand there, bouncing on your toes, hands stuffed into your pockets, wondering how long it would take this time. You never dreamed of going back down to his parents. You never dreamed of doing anything except waiting for Jonah.

He always emerged with a weird excuse:

"I was trying to catch the sun in my mirror."

"I was teaching the cat how to sneeze."

"I was staring at a bird that looked kinda like a fairy."

The last time you asked him why he made you wait so long, he gave you a strange look and said, "because I knew you would." You never asked again after that.

Jonah was the most magnetic person around, even back then. When he turned on his personality—when his head tilted *just so*, when the corners of his mouth curved *ever so slightly*, those large, brown eyes somehow *wider*—he had you. No one was safe—not other kids, not parents, not even teachers. His hands could be bloodied with guilty red paint and everyone would still believe that no, despite Farhan's sobs, Jonah would never leave red handprints on his bag, how could anyone ever accuse him of that?

Jonah liked to hold court. There was a big date palm in the middle of the playground, ringed with an octagonal wooden bench.

He would stand on the bench, leaning against the knobbly trunk, heels poised right at the tip of the octagon. The other kids would sit on the gravel—cross-legged so as to not skin their knees—and offer him their rapt attention.

Jonah would tell stories. It was often salacious stuff: what he'd caught his older sister doing with her boyfriend; how he'd snuck a chocolate bar out of the corner store without anyone noticing; where his parents actually took the family after they told the neighbors they were off to church. But what Jonah *really* enjoyed telling were fairy tales.

"Fairy tales are for babies!" Khalid Attar bravely said once.

Jonah crooked his head and gave him the Look. Khalid gulped.

"Babies?" Jonah asked. "So you don't want to hear about how the queen in Snow-White was forced to dance in red-hot iron shoes until she fell dead?"

"That's not true!" Khalid stammered, his defiance wobbling. "That's not how the story really goes!"

"Isn't it?" Jonah asked and didn't look at Khalid again, not then, not later. No one did, now that you think back. Khalid changed schools a few months later, after everyone stopped talking to him.

***

At twelve, Jonah won second place at a local writing contest for kids. The head judge, some fancy professor all the way from England, lauded Jonah's "mature voice" and "precocious vision." He also strongly hinted that the only reason Jonah didn't win was that your school principal—another judge, and the only adult you'd met who seemed immune to Jonah's charms—had considered the story to be "inappropriate." Personally, you had to force yourself to keep reading past the part where Cinderella dismembered a horde of rats and sewed their skins into a furry ball gown using their sinews and whiskers as thread.

"There's something to them," Jonah said, toying with a glass jar. There was a lizard he'd found at school trapped inside. It had leaped onto Jasmine Chaudhary during recess, and he'd caught it in his lunchbox in exchange for a kiss on the cheek behind the chrysanthemum trellis. He'd transferred it to one of his father's pickling jars at home.

"To *lizards?*" you asked, watching as Jonah turned the jar this way and that.

Jonah rolled his eyes. "To *fairy tales.*"

"Oh."

"I'm reading that book my uncle got me. By Joseph Campbell. It's got a lot to say about fairy tales, myths, and old stories."

The lizard scrambled around, eyes wide, as though permanently startled. Its little feet scrabbled ineffectually at the glass.

"Aren't you afraid the others will make fun of you?" you asked, even though you knew they wouldn't. No one made fun of *Jonah.*

Jonah shrugged, as though the idea hadn't occurred to him, as though it didn't matter, as though it slid off him like water droplets off the new blue bathing suit he'd received as a birthday present, the one you couldn't help admiring at the beach last weekend.

"What if—" you began, but hesitated because you never knew how Jonah would react to confessions of weakness. "What if they make fun of *me?*"

Jonah lifted the glass up to his face and squinted at the lizard. It turned away, as though it too feared meeting his gaze. "I'll protect you," he said absently. "You're my best friend."

Something clenched in your stomach, something pressed against your heart, forcing it to *thud thud thud* against your chest like a lizard trapped in a glass jar.

Jonah held the jar above his head, considering the lizard, thought-lines creasing his pale face. He'd let his hair grow out, and it was a mass of ringlets. The school would ask his parents to get it cut soon. You liked it long.

"I like your hair like this," you wanted to say, but the words caught, trapped in their own glass prison.

Jonah tapped one finger against the jar. The lizard swiveled. "Want to come to the back garden? I want to light a fire under this."

***

"Jonah . . . "

You followed that with an extremely embarrassing, staccato burst of moans. You were never that loud when it was just you and your right hand. You were feverishly happy that Jonah's parents weren't home right then.

105

Jonah's curls popped up onto the pillow next to you. He wiped drool off his mouth with the back of his hand. "That was messy," he announced. "Next time, I'll try it with less spit."

"Next time . . . ?" you echoed, still somewhat dazed. At sixteen, you'd never been with a girl—been with anyone—like this.

You've wanted to—with Jonah, specifically—for a very long time.

"Jonah, are you—are we—we're still *straight,* right?"

Jonah raised an eyebrow. He brought a finger to your mouth. Reflexively, your lips parted. He laughed as he withdrew his hand, the sound cold and hard.

Jonah rolled off the bed, snatching his shirt off the ground. "I'm going to show you something," he said, as if starting a grand proclamation. "You won't tell anyone about it, will you?"

Jonah never *told* you to do anything. He always asked. Politely. And knew that you would obey.

"Of course I won't, Jonah!" you replied, expecting—hoping for?—further sexual revelations. But no, Jonah began rummaging through his backpack.

What he withdrew made a tingle slice down the contours of your spine. You're still not sure why the book made you uneasy back then. It was just a book. It would always *be* just a book, even after everything else that happened.

It was a journal, not even a proper, printed book. The nicks, scratches, and worn spots on the leather cover betrayed its advanced age. Jonas opened it. The paper was thin, beige, and speckled with dark spots. It reminded you of skin stretched over the bones of an old, old woman. Inscribed on the first page, in a hard-to-follow, looping script, was the name "Jeanne." Below it, smaller but in the same handwriting, was the word "Fées."

Buttoning up your shorts, you approached him. "It's about fairies?" you asked, relying on the edges of the French language your high school teachers had forced you to gnaw on.

"I found it in the British Consulate's rummage sale," Jonah said, carefully turning a page. "It's written in a bunch of different languages."

You could see that. As Jonah continued to turn the pages, you recognized French, Arabic, and maybe German. But there was more. Greek? An Indian language?

Chaos was the book's reigning design principle. Great flows of unbroken text in multiple scripts and colours had been splattered haphazardly onto the pages, interrupted by sketches, rough, hand-drawn maps, and scatterings of untidy, numbered columns that seemed to belong to recipes. Some of the ink had faded into ghosts of their former sentences, while others bled into messy clots.

"Look at this," Jonah said, flipping to the last page. There, lovingly detailed in dark ink that had resisted the ravages of age, was a drawing of a fairy. It was the kind you were used to from children's books: a little person in a dress, with gauzy wings and large, earnest eyes.

Jonah's eyes, on the other hand, caverned hungrily. "I'm going to translate it myself."

"We can ask Mme. B. for help with the French—" you began, but Jonah interrupted you by snapping the book shut.

"I'm going to translate it," he said slowly, "*myself.*" His gaze gripped you like talons, and made you want to squirm into a ball and shiver.

***

There were two things you and Jonah absolutely did not do after that.

1. You didn't have sex again.

There was none of the promised "next time." You gave Jonah meaningful looks and dropped subtle hints. You invited him over when your parents weren't around. You even went so far as to suggest you watch a gay movie together—a tricky ordeal, given that you would have to bypass the Ministry of Culture's blocks and bans on all queer content on the internet.

Finally, you broke down and simply *asked* Jonah if he wanted to hook up again. "I'd do it this time. If you want," you mewled, eyes locked on your feet. "Blow you, I mean. I'd really like to!"

Jonah pulled your face up by your chin and for one sparkling moment, you thought he was going to kiss you. Instead, he met your gaze and said, "I know you would."

That weekend, at a party hosted at Faisal Al-Faheem's mansion at the edge of the desert, Jonah pulled Emma Bax into a guest bedroom. "Guard the door for me?" he asked you, voice dripping with smoky silk. Despite everything, the sound of Emma moaning "Jonah! Jonah!" gripped your groin like a steel trap.

2. You didn't talk about the book.

You saw it. Glimpses of aged leather when Jonah withdrew notebooks from his bag in class. Snatches of it when he pulled out his lunch. Sometimes, you caught him studying bits of text in other languages that he'd clearly copied out himself, and you spotted him carrying dictionaries for languages he didn't study at school. Once, during a particularly dry Biology lecture, you noticed his furtive hand reach into his bag. With a slow, rhythmic motion, his hand moved in . . . and out . . . in . . . and out. You knew he was stroking the book. You simultaneously wanted to recoil and to touch yourself.

But he never brought up the book.

Neither did you. You felt too—too—

Well, you didn't want to bring it up either.

***

Your final year at school was challenging.

It wasn't just the coursework, though the difficulty had skyrocketed (who could have predicted that the honours track, which you had signed up for because Jonah had, would be *that* much more work?).

It wasn't the anxiety of leaving school. College applications were stressful, but you knew that's what was expected of you. That was a predictable anxiety.

It was that everything seemed a little off.

You saw less of Jonah. He was busy with a girl, with the extra courses he was taking, or, strangely, in the desert. He started spending large blocks of time, entire weekends even, camping in the desert. You didn't ask why. You knew he wouldn't tell you.

The time he did spend with you was . . . Well, once, when his parents were out, Jonah said he wanted to sunbathe in the backyard. He stripped nude, waited for you to admire what cricket-team training had done to his physique, then handed you a bottle of suntan lotion without saying a word. He smirked the entire time at your hard-on, which even your baggiest shorts couldn't hide.

You dreamed of him often. Usually they were innocuous and silly, like dreams were. Sometimes, they pulled you awake, gasping and with warm stickiness spreading down your pyjama bottoms. And once, your dream of Jonah lifting you up by the throat felt so

108

real, you couldn't stop massaging your neck all morning. In the dream, he had big, gauzy wings. He hauled you up to his face and whispered, "You're mine. I'll protect you, but you're mine . . . "

One night, Jonah asked you to accompany him to Khalifa Park at midnight. "I need to bury the dog," he said. His voice was marble: cold, smooth, and hard.

At midnight? you wondered, but not aloud. Never aloud. Besides, here was Jonah, asking to hang out with you again.

Neither of you owned shovels. You lived in apartments in the middle of a metropolis surrounded by a desert, after all. So, under the light of a gibbous moon, you and Jonah dug a shallow grave beneath a date palm using a wooden spatula and a steel ladle. It might have been funny, in another timeline.

Jonah withdrew a cardboard shoebox.

"Didn't your parents just get the dog last month?" you asked. You had been delighted by the cute chihuahua-terrier mix, who Jonah's dad had christened Luke Skybarker. "How did he die?"

Jonah gave you his Look.

"Sorry, Jonah—" you stammered, "just—just that maybe we should say something? Over his grave? He was a good boy!"

Jonah smirked at your display of sentimentality. "I smothered it with a pillow until it fainted," he said, quirking an eyebrow, "and then sawed off its head with a kitchen knife. All in the aid of a devious experiment."

He burst out laughing at your thunderstruck expression and ruffled your hair. "You can be such an idiot sometimes! Let's just get this over with so we can leave!"

✳✳✳

Odd, unsettling incidents began occurring at school.

Mr. Abbas, everyone's least favourite Biology teacher, vomited in the middle of class, spewing not the expected churn of half-digested food, but wiry tangles of dirty, black fur. They heaved out of his mouth like large tarantulas, glistening with mucous and stinking of bile. He was rushed to the hospital.

The Exam Hall, the bane of every student's existence at your school, was unexpectedly shut down one Thursday morning. You snuck under the caution tape they'd put up, peered through the windows—and recoiled with a yelp. On every available surface in

109

the Exam Hall—on every inch of floor, on every table and chair—lay a dead lizard.

A week after breaking up with Jonah, Shanika Ramasinge began shrieking in the middle of the cafeteria during lunch. She sprinted out clutching her mouth, wine-red driblets oozing out between her fingers. When you went over to her seat, you saw, in a sticky, bloody puddle, a small pile of delicate, white teeth. Though you held back, some morbid fascination made you want to reach into the pile with your fingers and count them, one by one, tooth by tooth. Because you were certain there were thirty-two.

***

You were serving after-school detention when Emma Bax cornered you. Mr. Nizar was fast asleep at his desk, his snores a counterpoint to the loudly ticking clock.

Emma plonked herself next to you. She could've landed herself in even bigger trouble for that. Your school had managed to flout the general rule of sex-segregation only thanks to a senior Ministry of Education official's friendship with your principal. A girl and a boy sitting *together*, though, would be pushing it.

"Why are you friends with Jonah?" Emma asked quietly, looking right at you.

"Err . . ." Girls did not often speak to you. Not like that.

"He's awful," she continued.

"Everyone likes Jonah," you managed.

Emma shook her head. "Does anyone actually like him? Or are they just . . ."

"Afraid?" you whispered.

Emma nodded.

"Didn't you—didn't you date him?" you asked.

Emma's laugh was tiny, sharp, and unkind, like an insect bite. "Date? You might call it that. Didn't really feel like dating."

"Was he mean to you?"

Emma paused. "After that party at Faisal's where we first hooked up, I hung around like a sad puppy for a few weeks. He ignored me unless we were having sex. Then he got bored with me and broke it off. Does that count as mean?"

Mr. Nizar gave a great *hmph* and stirred in his seat. You both

110

glanced at him warily, but he remained ensconced in sleep. The clock's ticking punctuated the silence.

"Jonah's my best friend," you said loyally.

Emma shook her head. "You seem like a nice guy. I just wanted to warn you. Jonah's *not* a nice guy."

"Why didn't you break up with him sooner?"

Emma could have stabbed you in the eyes with her stare. "Can *you* imagine having that conversation with Jonah?"

You swallowed. An image of thirty-two bloody teeth flashed through your mind, but that had nothing to do with you or Jonah, did it?

"You see?" Emma fidgeted in her chair. "No, I waited until he got tired of me and did it himself."

Emma paused. She cleared her throat. It seemed that she had reached the heart of what she wanted to say. "Near the end, though, things started getting . . . " She hesitated again. "Has anything weird ever happened to you? Between you and Jonah? Or around him?"

"What do you mean?"

"I mean . . . this might sound strange, but for a while, I kept having these *extremely* vivid dreams about him. Like, I'd wake up and they weren't dreams at all, but strong *memories* . . . only they couldn't be memories because they were dream-weird?"

Emma was babbling. But you wouldn't have stopped her even if you had wanted to, because things *had* been weird around Jonah, ever since he showed you that book, and you *had* dreamed of him vividly. And what about all the strange stuff happening at school?

That had nothing to do with Jonah, though. Of course not.

" . . . he had these big wings and he kept *telling* me things," Emma was saying, "I know they were just dreams, but it creeped me out. He'd say things like 'once you're mine, you're always mine,' *chara* like that." Emma didn't speak Arabic, but her accent when she swore was flawless. Growing up here, you've all picked up the common curse words.

"I don't know what to—" you began, but you were interrupted by a loud, angry yell of "HEY!" from Mr. Nizar, whose glare was venomous.

Emma slipped over to the next seat, burbling out an apology, leaving you to stew.

***

Jonah wasn't valedictorian. Normally, the student with the highest grades earned that distinction, but for your year, the principal announced that the school would start considering "a more holistic picture." And so, the honour went to quiet Saba Mahmoud, who had organized charity Iftar dinners on campus during the Ramadan of your junior and senior years. Her speech at your graduation ceremony was measured, understated, and boring.

Jonah organized an outing for the whole class that weekend, at what was known as the "American Beach," the only beach where men and women were allowed to mingle. Saba did not attend. You learned later that Saba had been attacked by a pack of stray cats, and that she spent that entire weekend in hospital.

The party started off well enough. Hammad Akhtar, who'd recently earned his driver's licence, brought over his grill and cooked everyone burgers, hot dogs, and skewers loaded with alternating cubes of seared pineapple and spicy paneer. Mary Azar, daughter of the Jordanian ambassador, procured bottles of champagne which fizzed your senses pleasantly as the sun dyed the water a dusky pink. Jonah's bathing suit kept dipping low around his butt as he dove for the beach ball, and you contented yourself with looking from afar.

So you weren't expecting it when it all went to shit. Perhaps it was a cruel bit of theatre played out by the universe? An abrupt end to an enchanting evening to echo the sharp end to your childhood?

Faisal Al-Faheem—rich, sneering Faisal, whose father sat on the Supreme Court and who tried to hide the welts and bruises on his back that must've come from a firmly wielded belt—sauntered over to where you sat, your drink nestled in the sand beside you.

"Were you looking at me?" he demanded, voice thick with alcohol and anger.

You didn't really know what he was talking about.

"I asked you a question! Were you looking at me?"

Curious glances from some of the others blinked in your direction. Jonah, you saw from the corner of your eye, had turned to watch.

"Everyone knows you're a pervert!" Faisal said when you didn't reply. "Everyone knows you're gay."

You just sat there in the sand, looking up at your tormentor, because how were you supposed to respond to that? What did you say when a truth that you'd been hiding—that you'd been wrestling, that you didn't even fully acknowledge—was thrown in your face like that?

People were murmuring now. You caught snatches at the edge of your hearing:

" . . . gross . . . "

"You knew?"

" . . . mithli . . . "

"Really?"

"Chathaab!"

With a deft kick, Faisal knocked over your cup. Golden liquid splashed out, pooling momentarily before sinking into the sand, leaving behind a dark blemish. Idly, you wondered if wealthy kids built sandcastles using champagne instead of water, and then realized you might be going into shock.

Jonah was now jogging towards you.

Faisal still wasn't done. "People say you're gay for Jonah. Does he know? Does he know that you're a faggot—"

WHAM! Jonah barreled into Faisal, knocking them both into the champagne-soaked sand.

Scrambling. Flying dirt. Screams from the crowd.

"Kus ummak!" Faisal swore, shoving Jonah off.

Jonah picked himself up and dusted off the sand. "So sorry, Faisal," he said with obsidian-sharp politeness. "I wasn't looking where I was running. The champagne, you know? Gets to your head!"

Faisal muttered something dark as he got to his feet, but you thought you caught the word "homos."

"What's that?" Jonah asked, voice still razor-keen.

Faisal shook his head. "Nothing."

Jonah nodded. "Well if that's all, I'm going to take this one—" he jerked a thumb in your direction, "—home. His mummy worries so!" He gestured to the rest of the class. "Enjoy the rest of the party, everyone! And someone please get Faisal some water!"

The taxi ride was entirely silent. It was only when you reached Jonah's living room that you started sobbing into a cushion.

You heard the clink of glassware and a gurgling splash of

liquid. When you looked up, Jonah was handing you one of two tumblers of amber liquid. "Brandy," Jonah explained. "My dad says it's soothing."

The drink burned as you swallowed, but did warm you up.

You were used to long silences when you hung out with Jonah. He would pause by a tree, or put down his game controller, or set the CD back on the display shelf, and then drift off to someplace else. You would let him gather his thoughts. Often, you would snatch the opportunity to furtively admire him.

But right now, the air between you both felt heavy. There were a thousand things you wanted to blurt out, but the air pressing against your nose and mouth wouldn't let you.

"Faisal's a shithead," Jonah said finally.

You nodded and forced yourself to speak. "Thanks, Jonah," you said, though it almost hurt your throat to say it out loud. Thanking him almost meant that you were admitting what Faisal had accused you of. Which was ludicrous because *of course* you were—what Faisal had said. *Of course* you were—

"Let's deal with him?" Jonah asked suddenly. There was a strange, fervent quality to his voice.

You looked up from your drink. That quality, it was in his face too, a dark excitement that began at his eyes and radiated down to his mouth.

"Wait here," he said.

You were not surprised when he fetched the book from his room. Somehow, you'd always known it would boil down to the book. *Fées* by Jeanne.

But you *were* surprised by what he held in his other hand: A glass pickling jar. And inside it was . . .

Well, it had to be a fairy.

This was nothing like a fairy from children's books. It was upright and human shaped, yes, with two arms, two legs, and a head, but the resemblance ended there. Its skin was leathery and a mottled yellow-brown, like a snake. Its face was pointed and equally reptilian, though beady black eyes betrayed an uncanny intelligence. Its wings were made of thin membranes of wet, slimy skin, like that of a frog, stretched taut over slender ridges of bone.

And it was banging against the glass furiously with tiny fists, struggling to break out. You noticed that Jonah had placed a little bundle of herbs tied with twine in with the fairy.

"The scent of the herbs keeps it weak," Jonah said, noticing your look. "The German parts of the book were very helpful there."

You drew your attention to the book which Jonah had placed on the coffee table beside the trapped fairy. Since the last time you'd seen it properly, it had gained a number of bookmarks, tabs, and inserted sheets crammed with notes. It didn't make you uneasy anymore, not with the jar and its prisoner overshadowing everything. It had always been just a book.

Wasn't it funny how that happened? How different spectres gobbled up the ones you used to fear? Like, in that moment, you couldn't have cared less about Faisal, or what he thought of you.

"Jonah, is that really a . . . ?"

"A fairy, yes."

"How . . . ?"

"Good old Jeanne collected every fairy tale she could find. Every mention, every story, every scrap," Jonah said, sitting back down next to you on the sofa. "She was trying to piece together a picture of *real* fairies. A lot of it was rubbish; she even admitted that. The Greek portions are completely made-up shit. But she succeeded in teasing out parts of the good stuff . . . " He tapped the jar. You saw the fairy open its mouth. Maybe it screamed. You heard nothing through the glass.

"This is a species of desert fairy particular to the Middle East," Jonah continued. "The Arabic translation took me a while; it was all in verse. But once I figured it out, it was easy to catch them." He smiled deeply, proud of his accomplishment.

"Them? There are more?"

Jonah nodded. "I've managed to catch about three dozen."

"You have *three dozen* fairies up in your room?"

Jonah laughed, and you were suddenly reminded of that moonlit night in Khalifa Park, when you'd buried a dog together. When Jonah had laughed exactly like that.

"Do you want to know the reason Jeanne was obsessed with fairies?" he asked. "It's not because they're pretty." He gestured lazily at the jar. "It's because Jeanne believed that fairies could grant you wishes."

"What? Like a genie?"

"No. You don't *ask* a fairy. There's no rubbing lamps, no crafting carefully worded requests." Jonah brought his fingers together like he was portraying a cartoon villain. "You have to eat them. Jeanne had recipes."

You stared at Jonah. Then you stared at the reptilian thing, whose angry motions had slowed. It took a moment to slump against the glass and pant, before resuming. In that little moment, despite its alien features, it looked . . . extremely human.

You felt bile rise in your throat. You forced yourself to swallow.

"Her recipes weren't perfect. My first few tries, I could only send people vivid dreams."

"Jonah, did you . . . did you do that to me? Did you send me dreams? Did you send Emma Bax dreams?"

Jonah's teeth were particularly prominent when he smiled. "Jeanne, of course, wasn't a scientific thinker. I realized that eating the *whole* fairy was probably unnecessary. And unnecessarily bad-tasting."

The fairy was definitely growing tired now. Its violent attempts at escape looked half-hearted at best. Jonah nodded. "Good. I can show you."

He withdrew a thick rubber glove from his pocket, donned it on his right hand and reached for the jar. With practiced efficiency, he unscrewed the lid, stuck his hand in and grabbed the fairy by the torso. It struggled weakly, even trying to sink its teeth into Jonah's hand, but the glove did its job well.

"I experimented. I realized what *really* mattered was this fluid-filled sac at the base of the skull. The other ingredients in Jeanne's recipe weren't even that important; they just help mask the taste. Eating that sac alone gets you much more potent results. Such exquisite curses . . . "

Another wave of nausea washed over you. You gripped the arm of the sofa, digging your nails into the fabric.

"The experiments weren't easy. There was a whole month I couldn't catch any fairies at all. I had to content myself with practicing my butchering skills on Luke Skybarker."

Jonah held up the fairy, now slumped over his hand. "I've made so much progress. I don't even need to use a knife anymore; their skulls are so soft." The fairy hammered feebly at his wrist with its tiny fists—and then Jonah grabbed its head with his other hand and snapped its neck.

You gasped and stumbled out of the sofa.

Jonah laughed again. "Don't be such a pussy. These fairies . . . well, you saw what I did, didn't you? With horrible Mr. Abbas? With that bitch Shanika who wanted to dump me? With Saba, who stole my valedictory spot? I even thought it would be funny to put the Exam Hall out of commission for a while!"

As he spoke, the memories rushed back. You could almost imagine them as though they were your own. The undulations of a throat as a tangle of wiry hair clawed its way out. The twitching limbs of a lizard, dying on its back. Teeth *clack-clacking* onto a table, blood and drool puddling around them.

"And now—" Jonah began to dig the fingers of his left hand into the dead fairy's head, and you had to look away, "—we're going to get revenge on that shithead Faisal."

You heard a crack, then a squelch. Sitting on the carpet, you squeezed your eyes shut. There was a tearing noise and a strong odour bloomed into the room, at once coppery and floral. It made you want to retch.

"Poor baby," Jonah crooned, "you can look now. It's done."

The corpse of the poor fairy was back in the jar. In Jonah's pink-stained left hand sat a small, jelly-like, fluid-filled sac. It was white, but splotches of pinkish blood clung to its surface. Perhaps it was your imagination, but it seemed to quiver, like there was something in it, trying to get out, trying to . . . hatch?

"Here, open wide! I'll let you do the honours," Jonah said, beckoning to you. "All you need to do is chew and think hard about what you want to happen to Faisal."

"Jonah, I—I don't want to . . . "

His eyes hardened instantly. "Don't be a little bitch. With this, you could get even with anyone who ever hurt you. Faisal? Make him piss acid and see how he enjoys that. Are you afraid of coming out to your parents? Well, if they react badly, maybe they'd like it if their eyes turned to wax. I have so many plans . . . " Jonah's voice turned almost reverential. "After we deal with Faisal, I'm going after our bastard principal . . . and then, the sky's the limit, right?"

You looked at Jonah, who was grinning madly. You looked at the book, now so small and innocuous on the table. You looked at the jar, the mangled corpse of a tiny creature lying inside.

"Jonah's not a nice guy," Emma had said. Did you fully see that now, or was there still a part of you that ached for him?

But you knew what you had to do.

You didn't dare look at Jonah again. You didn't want to be enthralled. You knew you didn't stand a chance against him if you looked at his face, at Jonah, Jonah, *Jonah* . . .

You crawled over to him as he extended a hand.

Your lips closed around his fingers. Despite everything, you felt a frisson of delight, putting your mouth on Jonah. What you would give to just—

No. You had to focus.

Curses, right? You wondered if Jonah had tried anything else, any other kinds of wishes. Maybe it simply hadn't occurred to him.

But curses worked. You had proof of that. You'd seen it.

As hard as you could, you focussed your thoughts on Jonah.

***

Once upon a time, there was you and there was Jonah. What would happen when it was just you?

YOU CAN LEAVE YOUR HELMET ON

TEHNUKA

I HEAVE MY basket onto the checkout counter and try to scratch an itch on my scalp with a sweaty finger before I remember that I can't.

It's way too hot for this.

"Half price if you remove that helmet," says the cashier wearing Luke's nametag, and the rest of his body. Luke ditched his protective gear last month. He said he was sick of helmet hair.

I pass my shopping bag over. "Nah, I'm good, thanks." We might be down to one income, and I'm beginning to suspect they turn off the air conditioning whenever they see me walk into the supermarket, but I'm still not that desperate. Anyway, carrots are always cheap to ensure *they* stay well-fed, even if I can't afford much else. The restricted diet is manageable, though. Marcy always used to joke that I ate like a rabbit.

The cashier shrugs and pushes the laden bag across the counter.

"Sweetheart?"

Ex-Marcy comes to the door. "Carrots? Oh, yum, thanks!" A hungry tentacle twitches in her ear.

I pass the grocery bag over, keeping a couple of carrots for myself, and lock ex-Marcy in the bathroom to have lunch before flopping onto the sofa for a helmet break. I'll have to brave the hardware store this afternoon to buy a lock for the lounge door, too. Then ex-Marcy won't have to eat sitting on the toilet lid, and

I'll be able to wash my hair somewhere other than the kitchen sink, and maybe that will help us love each other a few more weeks, a few more months, even a few more years, despite everything.

Because I don't really know how long the ex- part of ex-Marcy is going to put up with meals in the bathroom, or with my helmet in the bedroom. And it's hard for both of us, me being the last human around here. One day that might change, but for now . . .

I'm not yet ready to be ex-me.

THE LIMINAL SPACE DATING AGENCY

TIM PRATT

YOU REACH THE end of a chapter in the ebook you're reading and swipe the tablet screen with your fingertip, but instead of the next chapter, there's an *ad*, luridly hyperlink blue, with shouty all-caps words and underlines. You're disgusted, and you remember finding musty paperbacks in used bookstores with advertisements for cigarettes stuck right in the middle. Everything old is new (and awful) again. The ad reads

THE LIMINAL SPACE DATING AGENCY
IT'S NOT AN APP
IT'S A WHOLE THING

do you feel like you're stuck in the waiting room
watching people all around you
getting called in for appointments
with love

WAIT NO MORE
YOUR TIME IS NOW
YOUR TIME IS OUR TIME

You swipe past the ad, irritated, and the book continues with the next chapter, but then you decide to take a screenshot so you can post on social media and complain about the insidious insertion of spammy ads into literature. Except when you swipe back, the ad is gone. A glitch, a trick, a mistake? Was it some kind of virus? Can ebooks even get those?

You search online and can't find anything about the Liminal Space Dating Agency, but of course nowadays all the search engines just spew regurgitated chatbot sludge anyhow; remember when "AI" meant hypothetical sci-fi machine intellects and not just autocomplete with bonus plagiarism? At least Skynet respected us enough to want to kill us; large-language models don't want anything at all.

So ads *and* AI crap: that's two things you're mad about now, and you put down the phone without posting anything. You don't go "touch grass" because grass is where the bugs and allergens are, but you can at least take a walk.

And as you trudge past the twenty-foot-high wall of dystopian welded shipping containers the local university erected to stop people from using a historic park, you think, despite yourself, that yeah . . . being twentysomething and without love in the city *does* feel a little like sitting in a waiting room, even if the ad was probably written by a chatbot too. Even the scam writers are being put out of work these days.

***

You see the next ad a week later, in the form of a flyer stuck in the tunnel that runs under the street and connects the Berkeley Rose Garden to Codornices Park. It's the wrong time of year for the flowers to be in bloom, but looking at the bare sticks rising out of the dirt is satisfying, in a melancholy way, and the little creek that cascades at the bottom of the park is nice. You cut through the tunnel because you've been walking up and down the steep and nearly endless Cordornices Steps a couple of times a week lately: you hate going to the gym, but you think if your butt was a little tighter, you'd feel more attractive, and thus more confident, and then somehow that will . . . well . . . it appears in your mind as:

PHASE 1: GET A BETTER BUTT
PHASE 2: ??????
PHASE 3: TRUE LOVE

But before you get to the steps, there's the tunnel and the flyer, still in lurid hyperlink blue, but printed out this time. It says

THE LIMINAL SPACE DATING AGENCY

**LIMINAL SPACE DATING AGENCY
JOIN US FOR OUR NEXT SLOW DATING EVENT
Tired of speed-dating try slow-dating
We give you time to get to know
all the things that you were meant to know!
YOUR TIME IS NOW
YOUR TIME IS OUR TIME**

There's not even a date or a phone number or a URL or anything. It's like someone just printed out an online ad and stuck it on the wall. Maybe the ads are some kind of conceptual art project, like the people who put up flyers offering rewards for lost goldfish by the Walgreens. Or they could be the visible tip of some hipster iceberg, like the Lost Horizon Night Market, the pop-up surreal sideshow only cool people heard about back in the day. You used to know people that cool, back then.

Whatever it is, you hate the name: "LIMINAL SPACE." You've seen that word "liminal" abused all over social media, in videos and photo accounts, where people seem to think it just means "weird" or "lonely" or "spooky," but words have *meanings*, and liminal means "in between": it refers to a transitional space, or sometimes to a sensory experience that's barely perceptible. Who wants any of *that* on a date?

You take a breath, and walk on, and try to let the pointless irritation go. You're trying not to get pissed off about more than three things a day and as usual you're way past your limit already. But you used to be a copywriter before you lost all your good freelance gigs to AI companies, even though their mindless iterations of illegally scraped data generate nonsense and misinformation, including some errors serious enough to get one of your old clients sued by its customers. The schadenfreude there might have been sweeter if you hadn't been forced to go back to waiting tables at your cousin's restaurant after the unemployment checks ran out.

You tromp up the stone steps through the trees, and down the stone steps through the trees, and you don't arrive anywhere at any point, and you think furiously, *I'm the one who's liminal here, you fucks.*

***

You go to visit your aunt in the hospital because your mom guilted you into it even though it's just her gall bladder, and who'd even miss a thing like that?

Eventually you get bored of sitting bedside and offer to go get coffee for your uncle and cousins, and someone says, "Don't use the vending machine, there's a good coffee cart hidden away at the back of the first floor," so you take an elevator down and go looking for this supposed caffeinated nirvana.

Except you must somehow get turned around, because you go down various passageways, but you don't find coffee: just more hallways with cream-colored walls and white floors that aren't really grimy but discolored from long hard use. There are occasional black arrows on the walls with the names of departments stenciled over them, and this remote part of the hospital must be where they put the really niche specialties, because the say things like "Tooth Worm Extraction" and "Lithotomy" and "Humor Balancing"—that last one sounds like the sort of California woo-woo thing your aunt probably tried before she got the surgery.

You can't find the coffee cart *and* you have to pee, so that's two new things to be pissed off about, bringing your daily total to around eight hundred items. But you turn a corner and the next hall dead-ends at an all-gender bathroom door, so *that's* something.

You tug the door handle and a snippy voice says "Occupied!" from the other side.

You sigh and dance a little back and forth, and resentfully listen to the person inside talk loudly on her phone (presumably). You pay closer attention when she says, "It was the Liminal Space Dating Agency! Girl, I know, I was so done with the apps, but it's not even *like* that. It's a whole immersive transformational experience, you've got to—hold on let me just . . . ."

And then the voice dwindles like she's walking away. You knock, tentatively, and there's no answer, so you pull again, and this time the door opens, and there's a toilet stall, and *another* door on the wall. What kind of public bathroom has two exits?

After you pee you try leaving out of the other door, and you go down the very first hallway, and there's the stupid coffee cart, which isn't even that good—it's not like it's Blue Bottle or something, it's just *Starbucks*. But you do your nibling duty and get enough for your cousins and ferry it all back upstairs. All the time, thinking. So this Liminal Space thing is real, in the sense that it actually exists, and isn't just a joke or a scam. And . . . maybe it's good? Like bathroom lady said? Sure, sometimes marketing companies pay people to talk about their products in public to drive up interest, but those shills hang out at clubs and stuff; they don't sell the sizzle in the most obscure toilet in a hospital.

After you get home to your cozy-which-is-to-say-tiny basement in-law unit that's really meant for college students to live in, you flop down on the futon under the strings of half-burned-out Christmas lights and take out your phone and search again.

This time you find a website, right away, first hit: The Liminal Space Dating Agency. Except when you click, it's just a landing page, with no pictures or text except the company name in hyperlink blue on a black background . . . but it's not actually a link!

You scroll down and down and down, just hate-scrolling nothingness because bad user interface design routinely makes your "things I'm pissed off about today" list. After about ten screens worth of scroll there's a tiny "join our waiting list" text line and a white box for you to enter . . . something. You take a wild guess and put in your email, and then hit enter on your phone because there's no "submit" button.

The page changes to say

THANK YOU WE WILL BE TOUCHING YOU SOON

You think, *I just gave my email to some kind of horrendous spam farm botnet, didn't I?* But it was the throwaway address you always use for that kind of crap anyway, so no great loss.

***

Except the email came to your *actual* address, the one you used for freelance work and keeping in touch with friends and family, which was weird. Maybe you set up some kind of mail forwarding a while back and forgot?

The message from LSDA is . . . surprisingly sane, given how

strange the ads were. It starts with your name (which wasn't attached to the email you gave them, but . . . something-something-data-mining?) and goes on to say

You have been selected for our next exclusive slow-dating event in your area. If you're interested, please fill in the following questionnaire so we can sweeten your potential matches and make sure your ideal connection(s) are invited to the event too.

You've always secretly liked answering personal questions. Back in the day, before the dating site OKCupid was transformed into just another Tinder clone, it was famed for having hundreds of questions you could answer to improve your match percentages with potential partners. On idle nights on the couch you used to answer scores of the questions at a time, just for fun. You used to do all those "tell us about your first six jobs" and "what were your childhood pet's names" things online, too, until someone told you they were used by identity thieves.

So you decide, why not, and answer questions like

Crème brulee or tiramisu

Are you concerned about rising sea levels

Do you enjoy sex in public

What about in private

Do you eat octopus, and if not is it because: they are sapient; vegetarian; texture

What is the most orgasms you've had in a 24-hour period and was it: not enough; just right; too many

Do you prefer to call them "inguinal creases" or "cum gutters"

What is the shape of your soul: oblong, polyhedral, tesseract, other

Would you describe your relationship style as: monogamous; monogamish; ethically non-monogamous; swinger; cheater; none

Elucidate your gender identity and sexual orientation in your own words

Anime or manga

Name an author you've read more than five books by; if you do not read name a breakfast food you've eaten more than five times

And on and on. It reminds you of those old OKCupid questions. Some of them might even *be* old OKCupid questions. Or more likely the list was generated by a chatbot that scraped the OKCupid question database and dozens of others . . . .

But you click through, being as baroque and odd in your answers as the questions were, and you have a good time talking about yourself, and you hit reply.

The response is instantaneous: **THANK YOU FOR GIVING US YOUR TIME**, and then an address that's just a few miles from your apartment, and a time that very night, and instructions: **JUST FOLLOW THE LIGHT INSIDE**

Well, you don't have any good shows to watch right now anyway, so why not?

***

You consider your usual first date outfit and then decide it was never exactly lucky, was it, and settle for neat-but-casual instead, a light sweater and the nice jeans and good walking shoes. You text your three best friends (one moved to Vienna for a job and only texts during his unsynchronized off hours, one got married and dropped off the face of the Earth, one had a baby and after the baby sneezed directly into your mouth you eased back on trying to hang out with her) and tell them "Hey I'm going to a speed dating thing at this address, if I don't come back tell the cops, ha ha." Ha ha except not really.

By the time summon a car with your phone, the one with the baby has replied: "I remember dating, GET SOME in memory of me," so that's sort of nice.

The car drops you off outside one of the many dark office buildings that emptied out during the pandemic lockdowns and have never refilled. Liminal Space Dating must have rented the place; the owners were probably happy to get any money for one of those unleaseable relics.

You walk up and down the sidewalk looking for an entrance until you notice a row of lights lining a path that leads around the side of the building, like illuminated cake pops stuck into the dirt. That must be the light you're meant to follow. You wind your way around the side and find a posterboard on an easel that reads **THE LIMINAL SPACE DATING AGENCY WELCOMES YOU TO**

YOUR SLOW DATING EXPERIENCE outside the doors to a glassed-in lobby.

There's nobody to welcome you, which is a bit odd, but the electric doors whoosh open when you approach. The foyer is dimly lit, the reception desk an asymmetric onyx slab, big black pots with no plants in them placed here and there, and two sets of closed double doors on the back wall leading deeper into the building.

The doors on the left bear a hand-lettered sign that reads **THIS WAY TO THE TIME OF YOUR LIFE**, so you open the door.

The world glitches. You cross the threshold and you're in a hallway, but you're *way down* the hallway, and when you turn, you don't see the doors you came in through, just more corridor, curving gently away. The curve has the same degree of arc in the other direction.

The walls are cream-colored, the floors scuffed white and industrial, the lights infrequent and fluorescent.

"Hello?" you call, and walk forward, along the arc the way you were facing when you . . . woke up? Got here?

There are no doors along the hall, but eventually you encounter a huge floor-to-ceiling window on the right, stretching easily twenty feet. The glass is smeared and covered with algae, like it's a big and poorly maintained aquarium. Something indecipherable moves on the far side, and you think of lobster tanks at restaurants, but you'd never order a lobster out of a tank this scummy.

Something is very wrong here, and with pounding heart you start to think about human trafficking and murder cults and dark web snuff films. The ghosts of a thousand true crime podcasts and torture porn movie trailers whisper dreadful predictions in your mind. You don't feel like you've been drugged, but how else can you explain that discontinuity, that *glitch*, that took you from the lobby doors to this hall?

The only way out is through, so you walk on, so far along the curve that you're sure the hallway is an actual circle, and you're going to meet up with your point of origin soon. But you find a branch corridor on the left, with a bright white light shining at the end, and you rush toward it, because anything is better than going around in a circle that never closes.

Underneath the zillion-watt incandescent bulb at the end of

the hall, there's a door with the words **PUNCH BOWL** written in messy black spray paint letters. Where else can you go? You push open the door.

The room is fairly wide but not too deep, and it's decorated like a high school gym after the prom has finished: drooping streamers, a few stray balloons in pastel colors, bedraggled crepe paper dangling from the ceiling, colored lights illuminating nothing. Near the back wall, right in the center across from the door you're standing in, there's a table with an immense cut-crystal punch bowl full of something the green color of antifreeze. Your eyes want to stop there. But they move on, and up, and behind the punch bowl, holding a ladle, there's . . . .

Something. Someone? A discontinuity, a glitch in the air, roiling black velvet, but it's smiling, an arc of white at roughly head-height, and those darker smears might be eyes. Its body, if that is a body, is a snakelike cylinder, and it disappears into the wall behind the punch bowl. You think, *It's a sock puppet*, as if that makes any sense.

"Welcome to the Liminal Space Dating Agency Slow Dating Experience!" The voice is an overlapping blend of the automated women who live in your phone and GPS and smart speakers. "Are you ready to meet your match?" It taps the ladle against the bowl and it rings crystalline. "You and your match have many things in common, like being composed mainly of fluids and existing indefinitely in this place and time." The smile doesn't move when it speaks.

You are pinned and pinioned by its anti-gaze, and the thing reaches out with what can loosely be called an arm, more joints unfolding until it's long enough to cross the room, holding the ladle from the punch bowl. "Drink."

You clamp your mouth shut and shake your head and try to run but your body won't respond to the latter demand. You're thinking about how if you eat the food in fairyland you're trapped there; you're thinking about pomegranate seeds binding your soul to Hell. You won't.

Then the walls starts to close in on you: literally. The balloons roll, pushed by the moving walls, the sides coming closer together. The punch bowl and its table and the thing behind it moves toward you like they're on a moving walkway, the unnecessary joints on the extended arm folding up smoothly. The ceiling begins to descend. The ladle touches your lips, presses against your mouth, hard metal on soft skin. You squeeze your mouth closed together.

The ceiling touches the top of your head with a gentle, insistent pressure. "Water is nearly incompressible," the thing says. "But you are only mostly water, and the rest of you will squeeze down small. There will be no room for romance then. Drink. This is love potion number mine."

You hunch as the floor rises and the ceiling drops, and the ladle moves with you, keeping its insistent position. You finally gasp and open your mouth. The punch, the potion, is cold, shockingly so, and as a result it doesn't taste like anything *but* cold, but the moment you swallow there's

Another glitch. You awake sprawled on stones, and there's an indescribably beautiful man looking down at you, backgrounded by a white sky. "Hi," he says. "I'm Kane. Welcome to . . . here."

Even in your total confusion and terror, looking at him, a deep part of your mind goes *oh*. And then other parts of you weigh in with their own opinions.

Your mouth is freezing, like you just ate a handful of crushed ice. You groan and sit up and scoot away on your butt from the stranger. "What who where." The words feel numb.

He sits on his heels, looking at you with open and evident sympathy. He has messy hair and big dark eyes and a black t-shirt that's just a little too small, in a good way. He touches his chest. "Kane. I came here for the Slow Dating Event. Mine was in Seattle. Where was yours?"

What? But it's a question you can answer, so you do. "Berkeley."

He smiles. "I did a postdoc there, wow. I loved it. So . . . I told you who and what. As for where . . . I guess, a liminal space. Or set of spaces. There are lots. They don't make a lot of sense, the way they're connected, you'll have a grassy median strip next to a theater lobby next to a customs checkpoint, but, well. We have plenty of room, anyway."

He gestures, and you look around. You're in a plaza, maybe fifty feet to a side, with a dead fountain in the middle, and stone benches, and statues that might have been lions before time wore their features down to coarse nubs. There's a wall around the place, of gray stone, and there are doors in the center of all four sides. The sky is—

The sky is not a sky. It's a domed screen, like in a planetarium, showing grayish-white static. You start to hyperventilate, because you *have* been kidnapped, you're in a horror movie, but Kane is there patting you and soothing you and saying, "It's okay, you're not in danger, come on, sit on a bench."

You wobble up and over and sit down, and put your head between your knees until your breath is under control, Kane's hand rubbing gentle circles on your back all the while. "How long?" you gasp. "Have you been here?"

His answer is thoughtful. "Time is hard to measure. I've slept . . . seven times, or eight. Occasionally that Siri-Alexa-GPS voice would whisper 'match in progress' in my ear. And then, just before you appeared on the stones here, it said, come 'meet your match.' So. Hi."

You laugh, and it's a jagged wild sound. "I'm supposed to *date* you? Some kind of creepypasta Trevor Henderson monster thinks it can trap people in a weird fucking nowhere place and we'll fall in love?"

"Yeah. See. That's the thing." Kane runs his hand through his hair and looks sheepish. "It actually works. There's like a hundred people down here, at least, that I've met. There could be a lot more. But they all agree, and I mean all of them, that when the voice says it's a match, it's a match. It's love. Most of them are couples, there are a couple of triads, and even one fivesome, which seems too complicated for me. But whatever that thing is, the thing behind the punch bowl . . . it does what it promises. You really do get love. The only problem is . . . you get it in here."

"You think I'm going to fall in love with you?" You look at him, incredulously outraged. Except only like ninety percent incredulous, because he's gorgeous, and those eyes, not to mention those biceps, and there was that *oh*. When he touched you, there *is* a buzz between you, like the two of you complete a circuit. You've felt that feeling before, but never this strong and never this fast.

Kane nodded. "I do. You don't have to believe me. And who knows? Maybe you'll be the exception. But some people down here fought against the connection hard, they tried to take off and flee their matches, but the geography or topology or whatever just nudges them together again, and sometimes presents them with . . . challenges . . . to overcome together. And they always come together in the end."

"Challenges?" you say, and he pretends, badly, that he didn't hear you.

Instead he says, "I met this guy Raj who thinks our host is an AI, like a real one, with an actual mind. Or maybe it's an alien, or an alien AI even, maybe from another reality. Raj thinks Lizzda—we call it Lizzda, L-S-D-A—learned about love from the internet and books and movies and it's . . . really trying its best. Like clearly it doesn't understand the intricacies, but it's really good at pattern matching and analysis and predictions. It's like a deranged reality-altering otherworldly monster, but a romantic."

Maybe it's not, you think. *Maybe it's just executing a program and it doesn't feel any way about it at all. How could you tell the difference?*

But Kane is still talking and his mouth is pretty so you watch. "Everyone hates it here, but they all agree, if they have to be here . . . they're glad they aren't alone." He touches the back of your hand with his index finger. "It's been hard, being alone."

"Why me?" you ask. "Why you? Why us?"

"I've asked a lot of people," Kane said. "And Raj did like a proper survey. People here come from all over the world, different nations, different cultures, though we can all communicate for some reason . . . anyway, we don't have anything in common. Except we were all lonely, and didn't want to be." He looks at you with warmth. "You, too, I assume?"

Before you can reply the amalgam voice speaks from the fake sky: "Monogamish mixer in the leftward locker room from now until untility."

He sighed. "We should go to that. It's for no-strings spice-things-up hookups technically, but Lizzda always turns on the showers, so it's a good chance to get clean. And the lockers are always full of snacks and fresh clothes. Usually it's about seventy percent lingerie and jockstraps and slutty Halloween costumes, but there's normal stuff too."

This is too much and it's too much of the wrong everything. "Kane. Listen. I don't know you very well. But I feel like you're the chill, go-with-the-flow type. But I am not. *Not.* I get pissed off about three things a day, minimum, and I'm pissed off about way more than that now."

"Opposites attract." His smile is lopsided and enchanting. Ugh.

You take both his hands in yours, look deep into his eyes, and say, "Kane. We have to find a way out of this place."

He squeezes your hands and looks at you. Into you. You feel your blood pressure dropping and your heart rate slowing. How does he do that?

"Okay, then," he says. "I'm pissed off, too, even if I don't show it. So yeah. Let's do it. Let's try to find a way out of this place."

You let out a breath, and tears start to well up at the corners of your eyes. Someone you can be pissed off *with*? Maybe this will be—

Then he continues: "Lizzda always says common interests and shared activities are important for the long-term health of a relationship, after all."

FULL IMMERSION

Tiffany Michelle Brown

THE CORK CLEAVES in two as I pry it from dark glass. Bark rains down into the bottle like sad confetti. I'm not surprised. The expensive pinot has languished in my wine fridge for far too long. Still, it feels like a betrayal. A dig from the universe, which has been relentless in its cruelty lately.

I pull a metal sieve from a kitchen drawer and place it over the wine decanter. The mesh won't catch all the debris, but it'll filter out the largest pieces. With shaking hands, I pour the wine. As the pinot breathes, I peer out the window to check on Jamie.

It rained last night, fat drops that transformed our dusty backyard into a pit of sludge. He loves when the ground goes soft. Relishes the mire and filth. A month ago, I would've rushed outside to berate my son. I would've demanded he climb out of the muck right this instant and march upstairs for a bath. Tonight, I simply watch as he contorts his naked body into impossible shapes—contracting, lengthening, contracting, lengthening. The articulation of his spine makes me shudder.

The wine should sit for at least another thirty minutes, but I don't have the patience for that. Not tonight. Warm spices coat my tongue. The wine is meant to be savored, but I find my reflection in the bottom of the glass three separate times before I come up for air. My blood warms. My fingers tingle.

"It's just a phase," his general practitioner had said. "Kids at this age have such big imaginations. I bet he'll believe he's an astronaut next week."

Intellectually, this seemed like a sound assessment. And yet, on the ride home, my stomach twisted into knots so intricate, I had to pull over the car and stumble along the shoulder of the highway until my lungs no longer burned with anxiety. When we finally made it home, I called the doctor's office and asked for a referral to a child behavioral psychologist.

***

After an initial consultation, the child psychologist asked me to bring Jamie in for observation. We stared at him through the glass, me biting my nails, the doctor composed and steady, her hair twisted up into an elegant chignon. Jamie immediately peeled the clothing from his skin, revealing a body covered in oozing sores and Band-aids trying and failing to keep his wounds clean and closed.

I dropped my gaze to the hem of my shirt, embarrassed, both by Jamie's nudity and the state of his body. I was sure the psychologist thought he was being abused. I opened my mouth to apologize, to explain there was no need to call child services, because *I* hadn't done this to my child. The psychologist intervened, placing her hand reassuringly on my forearm. If she had any concerns about my parenting, it was clear we would discuss them later.

In my periphery, the shadow of my son lowered himself to the low-pile carpet and began moving in circles through the playroom. Contract, lengthen, contract, lengthen.

***

I'm terrified this is all my fault. A little over a month ago, we were in Jamie's room after dinner pretending to be all manner of animals. First, we were pandas, tumbling around the room like balls of dough. Then lions, jumping, roaring, holding ourselves up with pride in our hearts. Flamingos balancing on one leg. Quokkas grinning. Worms slithering around the room on our bellies.

I called out hyena next, pushing my body up to all fours and erupting in deep-throated cackles, but Jamie refused to move from his prone position on the floor. He kept sliding across the carpet, balancing the weight of his little-boy body on his chin. I could see his skin turning an angry red, rugburn blossoming on his face.

"Possum," I shouted, collapsing on my back, playing dead. But

Jamie kept inching toward me, his gaze fixed on mine, an eerie emptiness behind his eyes. His tongue lolled out of his mouth, dragging along the carpet, collecting hair and dirt and dust.

In a panic, I yanked him from the ground. "Playtime's over," I said. "Go brush your teeth." I gave him a nudge into the hallway. Jamie lowered himself to all fours and crawled to the bathroom. I didn't breathe until I heard water gushing from the faucet.

At bedtime, I rubbed Aquaphor into his rug-burned chin and kissed him goodnight. I hoped he'd return to normal in the morning.

But he hasn't. He's entirely mute. I can't keep clothes on him. He sneaks out to the backyard to roll around in the dirt. And that vacant chasm behind his eyes remains.

***

After observing Jamie for a good ten minutes, the psychologist offered me a practiced, too-optimistic smile. "We'll get to the bottom of this, Ms. Danforth. Do you mind if I go talk to him?"

I nodded, but I knew talking wouldn't get her anywhere. I was right. Jamie ignored the psychologist completely, continuing to creep around the room close to the water-stained baseboards.

The psychologist returned, her white smile still in place. "I know it's going to sound counterintuitive, but for a case like this, radical acceptance is your best bet. Any sort of opposition to his delusion will only encourage rebellion. While his behavior may seem extreme, I don't think you have anything to worry about. Simply go with it and see if anything changes. If it doesn't, we can, of course, discuss additional modes of treatment."

Before we left the office, the psychologist let me know she'd put in a call to our family doctor. She thought Jamie could benefit from some kind of topical antibiotic, perhaps something with steroids, to treat his brutalized skin.

***

I've done as directed—and more. I've delayed Jamie's enrollment in first grade despite having to forfeit the down payment to reserve his spot at the fancy parochial school I've always believed would foster his education and development. I've called his father, trying to enlist his help, but it's been years since we've talked, and his number is disconnected. Groceries are delivered once a week directly to our door so I don't have to leave Jamie on his own. A sitter is out of the question. I'm not sure I could pay a teenager enough to roll with my son's unique needs. I'm working from home indefinitely. I told my boss my son has a medical condition that will eventually resolve, but in the meantime, he needs my constant presence and care. I hired a handyman to extend our backyard fence further into the sky to give Jamie greater privacy when he's out back. I ignore the stares from our neighbors when I leave the house.

And I've begun researching earthworms in an effort to better understand Jamie. Try to connect with him. Continue to be his mother, any way that I can.

In an effort to keep him eating, I began keeping a plate piled high with spinach leaves, herbs, and mushrooms in the middle of the living room, knowing Jamie would graze throughout the day. I learned to leave the greens out on the counter so they had an opportunity to wilt, grow soupy, give off an unappetizing odor. The smell seemed to conjure my son. I'd plug my nose and watch him dive face-first into his plate, smudging his cheeks with slime.

One afternoon, I found him in the shed in the backyard, bent over a bag of gardening manure, munching away. My maternal instincts kicked in, and I screamed at him out of fear. I ordered him inside, but he wouldn't even acknowledge my presence. He ignored my every word. Kept chewing, shit caking his skin, jaw working the mixture into a brown, wet slurry.

I carried Jamie upstairs and cried for an hour as I scrubbed the filth from his body with soap and water. I kept asking him why he was doing this, why he'd eat manure, why he couldn't just be a normal little boy. Of course, I never received an answer.

I was terrified to call anyone for help—I really didn't need CPS showing up at my door—so I watched him carefully the rest of the day. I waited for him to double over and vomit or show signs of weakening, but these symptoms never manifested. Jamie continued to shuffle along the carpet, leaving discarded Band-aids and scabbed skin in his wake, which I quickly sucked up with a hand-held vacuum cleaner. He spent the afternoon in the backyard, inching along the sun-warmed patio, snoozing in the uncut grass. He never so much as coughed. He seemed completely at peace.

I locked him in his bedroom that night, exhausted from standing sentinel all day and still very much on edge. Jamie hadn't shown any outward signs of poisoning, but could he experience a delayed reaction? Surely, he would've already shown signs of distress by now, right?

I laid in bed, imagining Jamie gasping for breath, losing motor function, collapsing beneath his Paw Patrol bedsheets. But each time I crept down the hall and peeked into Jamie's room, he was very much alive, gazing blankly at the ceiling, undulating like a wave.

The next day, Jamie was more energetic than usual. He gave off an air of strength and contentedness. His skin seemed to glow with vitality. The only difference in our daily routine had been his manure snack.

I realized I'd been going about his diet all wrong. I've started collecting fresh grass and half-decayed leaves from the backyard for Jamie's grazing dish. I sprinkle manure over the top like crumbled cheese on a salad. And it works. He spends more time in the living room with me each day, and the increased physical proximity gives me hope.

And yet . . .

It's been months. Months of radical acceptance. Of changing every aspect of our lives and trying to cater to his new predilections.

There's still a wall between us, an unseen force that continues to pull us further and further from each other. When I look at him, I still see my son. When he looks at me, I'm not sure if he sees anything.

****

It feels like there's a storm brewing. The air hugs my body like water, tickling my calves and creeping beneath the plush material of my bathrobe. My brain feels gummy thanks to the wine, and I'm grateful. The liquor served its purpose. The less I think about what I'm about to do, the better.

Jamie winds his mud-caked body around the trunk of our lime tree. I watch him for a moment, studying how he moves, the ripple of energy that propels him steadily forward. My heart clenches. I miss my boy.

FULL IMMERSION

I close my eyes and concentrate on the hum of my blood as I untie my robe. My skin lights up with sensation as I lower myself to my belly. Cold mud immediately leeches to my body. Blades of grass press against me like the dull blade of a knife. I tremble, and tears threaten to spills over my cheeks.

The world looks different from the ground, overwhelming and vast and indistinct. A flicker of light green in my periphery gives me purpose. The lime tree. Jamie.

I try to move my body the way my son does, but no amount of hot yoga could have prepared me for the task. I flail and sweat and toss my torso around. I can feel bruises bloom beneath my skin. Cuts open up across my soft flesh. I smack my chin on the ground multiple times, and the taste of copper fills my mouth.

It feels like cheating, but I resort to using my arms to pull my body forward. My legs remain limp, pinned together by sheer will. Jamie needs to see my effort, my willingness to meet him in the mire, no matter how difficult, how painful.

I don't know how long it takes to get to the lime tree, but when I do, my body is spent. My arm muscles feel like frayed string cheese, and a primal cocktail of muck and blood covers every inch of my skin. I collapse, my chin sinking into soft earth, my lungs screaming for oxygen.

But it's all worth it, because my boy has waited for me. He stayed put, watched his mom work through the soil and shit and agony to be with him.

I know worms don't speak and this should be an exercise in full immersion, but his name bubbles up in my throat and can't be contained. "Jamie."

For the first time in weeks, recognition skitters across my son's features. There's something there behind his eyes. A warmth I convince myself could be love.

There's a flash of light, the crack of thunder, and then the rain comes.

THEY REMEMBER FACES

Leo Oliveira

Editors of 'The Jury,'

YES, I AM the man who murdered Jakobi Stewarts of Ovil
Industries. Yes, I stood in charge of research and
development, where I spent a decade fattening elk and
squirrels and other vulnerable species. I was there for all of it—
selling their flesh to zoos and parks, then for private consumption.
Yes, I coined our company's ethos when a batch of fresh-faced
trainees soured green upon witnessing a tray of dhole pups being
churned into cheetah feed:

"That which humanity finds useful will never go extinct."

Internal questions or concerns, I addressed them. Failings and
flaws, I solved them. When inspiration struck Jakobi at three in
the morning with reports due at seven, I wrote them. Unaffiliated
press calls haunted us hourly in those first couple years, ripe with
accusations of animal cruelty and genetic experimentation. It was
brutal training programs to filter those as spam (the animosity of
that chapter is the reason I now find it so difficult to contact you).

I did all this—wept cortisol, bandaged my wrists with
adrenaline patches, clocked work in at all strikes of the bell and
through my supplement alarms—without ever nearing the top of
Ovil's payroll or receiving half of Jakobi's praise. Not even a
quarter.

But I did not do what I did out of 'jealousy,' as your newspaper
suggests. Nor, as the competing theory goes, did I adopt a change
of heart or ideological stance.

THEY REMEMBER FACES

My father was a slaughterhouse worker, see. He returned every evening reeking of ammonia and oxidized hemoglobin. Cruelty roosted in our air and in our water. Violence does not bother me.

I've never desired the crushing weight of a spotlight either (lest my poor bones shatter), nor have I harbored much need for luxuries beyond hot water and a stove. My childhood weaned me on charity: first with the roof my father shared, then with the opportunities the ravens traded me.

I remember it so clearly. Murders of ravens perched outside my broken windowsill, croaks and calls spilling through the jagged glass. My father couldn't afford anything more sheltered than an abandoned warehouse downtown. Not if we wanted food or cigarettes. My bedroom was a stack of crates and curtains partitioning off my square of crumbling foundation from my father's. Besides the drunks ambling outside and the flickering shadows of our fellow house-less, the ravens were our only neighbours.

I fed the ravens crumbs, then sweets. They traded me trinkets, then protection. Clawed shields between me and my father's fists when he caught me pawning off their stolen jewelry for tins of mints and trading cards.

"Under this roof, I have the final say! That money is mine by right, damn you!" He strangled one raven, snapped its neck, and roasted it whole. Then he scattered the feathers outside like a skull-on-pike warning. "Useless goddamn things."

After that, ravens followed him everywhere. They circled outside his work and tailed every bus and train he rode. They knew his face like I did until they sharpened their beaks and rearranged it.

He became a changed man after that. He even helped put me through college—not that he knew that was where his disability checks were going.

The ravens stole his eyes, his lips, and his tongue, and it was through his thin warbling that I stitched together our most pleasant conversations.

Jakobi's company had an internship program. Lab tech, engineering, and midnight coffee runs. Ovil was a smaller lab back then, specialized in transgenic plants, and though I'd never cared much for botany, every other opening rejected me. I had to make Ovil work. It didn't matter the cost.

I nursed an addiction to stimulants. I slept ten hours a week so I could spend more time slaving away in the lab and learning in the library. I once tripped down my lecture hall's stairs and arrived at Ovil twenty minutes early in a splint I'd crafted from tape, spit, and pencils.

In hindsight, I could have gotten away with far less. Jakobi prized my skill in weathering his storms more than any latent talent. He gave me more of his time, and more of his time meant more responsibility. And more responsibility meant my life became Ovil.

We were going to change the world. Turn every dying species into a factory-farmed machine. Keep them on life support if solar radiation and human development wouldn't let them have anything else. Jakobi cared about that, at least, and so long as I flocked by his side, I had a place to stay.

I had meaning. I had stability.

I purchased a new apartment (one without roommates, if you can believe it), scalded myself raw in the shower every night, and cooked my meals on an actual stove.

The world still sloughed apart in glacial inches around us, but we were doing just fine.

After animal feed, Jakobi set his sights on human delicacies. Rhino shanks, antelope venison. When squirrels started dying out at the same pace as everything else, I suggested selling their hearts on skewers. He agreed.

I grew complacent, you see. I began to believe I mattered. I thought I had a say.

Then Jakobi wanted ravens processed next. I refused.

"Seb," he said, "we've known each other a long time, but that doesn't mean you're irreplaceable. You don't make the final decisions for me or this company, understand? Any species can be made into an asset. I want ravens. If you don't take this project, I'll find someone who will."

I could have walked away. I almost did, too. But then, perched on a tree branch outside Jakobi's office window, I met a pair of shining black eyes over an obsidian beak, paused amid grooming its oil-slick wings.

So, I killed him.

I choked Jakobi Stewarts with my own two hands, his skin

purpling as he clawed at my face, throat whistling curses, calling me a mad traitor and worse. I choked him like my father choked that raven. I choked him like I wasn't choking him at all, but the idea of him, his legacy, everything he was, and everything he would cut me out of being.

My metacarpals ground together; my clenched jaw ached. I channeled more power in those minutes than I ever had before. I floated. I flew outside myself. The chair tipped over. A lamp bulb smashed. He thumbed at my eyes; I crunched them like carrots. Broken phalanges, warm and slippery against my tongue, still pulsing arteries flossed between my canines. I chewed, I laughed, I swallowed.

You might imagine me selfish. Foolish. Insane. But I know the raven saw me, and I know it understood. A trade for a trade. Protection for protection.

The irony is not lost on me that, in facilitating Ovil's preservation of the species, I have doomed the individual, killed the culture worth preserving in the first place. I could have walked away, allowed Jakobi to continue with another more willing participant, but the ravens would know, and they would never forget. They'd saved me once. It was time I saved them.

I'll be long gone by the time you receive this. Tell the police to be gentle with my possessions (if they're capable), and do not harm my messengers.

After all, they remember faces.

Sincerely,
Sebastian F

MEASUREMENTS EXPRESSED AS UNITS OF SEPARATION

M. L. KRISHNAN

7 centimeters

of my ring finger on my right hand. Sliced with a hot knife through gristle and tendon and bone, as though it were as soft as an ingot of butter.

2490 kiloliters

of water had once ripped her and I from one another, had once sheathed her and I to one another.

In the middle of it all was a jungle. And in the middle of the jungle was a gash of concrete within the forested darkness. This concrete semi-circled into a squat array of buildings, into the Erode Christian College of Arts and Science for Women—a missionary endeavor of the Church of Scotland to wring South Indian women into the narrow flute of Bible truths. But like most missionary undertakings in Tamil Nadu, this too snarled into indifference as the locals flinched away foreign ideals and foreign encroachments as they were wont to do.

Over the years, our college had become a knot of expendable girls, offering subjects like Homeopathy and X-ray Crystallography and Folk Practices that sounded carefree and bohemian on paper, but were simply designed to fill the listless expanse of day that sludged from one hour to the next. Majors like Engineering or Accounting or English Literature were deemed unnecessary with their meteor-bright promises of ambition and status, a hindrance for the young women that were expected to anvil themselves with a degree just for marriage.

The only breath of tenacity on our campus was a euphorbia shrub that knuckled against the windows of our hostel dormitories, the greenwhite glint of its leaves a sieve of light through the glass, freckling our faces with shadows from its creamy flowers that parted the foliage like teeth.

No one cared about anything, at all.

Phrases like *proper decorum, moral turpitude, no loafing*, and *academics over hooliganism*, fluttered out of staff lounges and plunged to their doom in the underbrush. Most of us attended college strobing on coffee and a mash of pills from the town pharmacy—an opiate confection better suited to lorry drivers who drove fifteen-plus hours across state lines without stopping to eat or piss. In class, we sat immobile under a drug-rimmed void, our attention fractaling into shards with pleasantly blank expressions on our faces. And as long as we were tactful in bribing the hostel wardens with arrack at regular intervals, we could slip in and out of campus unnoticed.

Some of the girls fell into the toil of boyfriends and married lovers from neighboring towns and villages. Mediocre sex and controlling men were the only flashes of revelry around these parts, so the students braved the risk-calculus of defying college administrators. These men were all the same to me—an amorphous, shifting-eyed clump whose collective entitlement roped around my neck and under my armpits, leaving friction burns in its wake. Besides, my parents had arranged my betrothal to a distant cousin I did not know, bottle-corking my life into clean submission.

This is why I chose the forest instead. Why I chose to impale myself on the dense groundcover of the lantana, choking on its powdery blooms as it stripped the skin clean off my calves in sheets. Why in another instance, I stumbled over an anthill, my thighs already scudding with bites. Later, I would core each scratch and bruise with my fingers, until my welts pulped into tenderness. I wondered if this was what it meant to feel something—blood, its crusted-over aftermath. Somewhere else, a distant promise of pain.

Once, as I pushed further, still further into the forest viscid with heat, I came upon a crumbling stepwell a few kilometers into the woods. Such reservoirs were not uncommon around these parts: bodies of water sluiced out of the earth and into pipes through boreholes. My nightly excursions now haloed with purpose, and I began swimming in the well's cool depths under the foliaged dark.

That night started without incident.

I peeled off my kurta and pants and as if on cue, silken-winged chironomids hummed over my bare skin as I stepped closer to the water. A repetitive sound nailed me in place amid the shadowed reeds, a low splish-splash that felt like it belonged to a large animal body. The enzyme-burn of my fear pulled that moment through an eye needle—a breath, an immobile form, a tongue lapping against the steps. I wanted to scream. I wanted to fling myself into the well and throttle whatever it was.

But a spherical face pushed out of the ripples, followed by a gulped exhalation, a nose ring concentric-circling her neck, and my anger settled into recognition.

It was our Folk Arts professor. Shrouding herself in voluminous cotton saris, she would move from class to class during the day as though she were insubstantial—a wisp, earthed by the gold Nath through her left nostril.

Her hair was a braid of feathery milfoils across the well's surface. Arms softened into silhouette as she cleaved through the water. I continued to watch her, an improbable want knifing into me.

And then a glottal elapid mouth, fangs, liquid spuming up my nostrils.

Vacuumed into a black so thick and opaque, I felt comforted that this was how it all ended—stricken by desire, suffocation, and the well I so loved.

43 inches

of snake shed was the only part of her that I had found intact, crimped within a groove on the stepwell after she was gone.

But that was not entirely true. She had also left me a story about a prince.

இப்போ கெழு, she would say in Tamil, after I had spent an afternoon in her office, rumpled between her thighs underneath an overlarge desk, my wrists spider-silk bound, my head cowled by the lower half of her sari, and I would always bite my laughs into her while she sat there as though hewn from gneissic rock—forcefully dull in a way that put a finite end to conversations or questions, the upper half of her sari pleating across her left shoulder, a double-lined teakwood panel the only furrow between my unclothed body and the students' feet, the wide-open gorge of her face still immobile as she welcomed or bade her students goodbye, as she came undone suddenly, always suddenly, a rip-current in the back of my throat as I held her constriction, her pleasure, in my mouth.

Listen now.

இப்போ கெழு, she would say in Tamil, after the waters of our dissolution, a world or two or three in my stomach. She said that she was from the sea. That she beached herself on the shore between her love and his love, the lacquered sheen of her ventral scales cupping darkness, a sine wave granulating into dust.

Who was he? I would ask.

He was always different, she would say, pulling me into the upside-down night of the stepwell, pale green azolla and velvetleaf drifting in clouds past my ears as she dragged me still deeper, my lungs swelling out of my ribs, a plural-sac inflatable devoid of air, and I thought to myself, *this is happening again,* letting desire fishhook me into compliance. The sky at the floor of the well was spongy and perforated like an earlobe, leaking red. She would stream apart in hexagonal scales of blue and black, her once-human skin crackling open around her once-human mouth. Then a ripple and a lateral expansion, her lidless eyes refracting the moonlight as it washed our tongues. I wasn't sure if I was alive or dead or a half-life suspension in formaldehyde. What did it matter when the pale cream of her dorsal body furled around me as her blue-lipped mouth kissed neurotoxin promises down my torso? What did it matter?

Listen now.

In each of her stories that were mostly the same, the endings sometimes varied. Every time, she would speak of the prince whose beauty was as fierce and unyielding as a thunderclap. His father was the Lord of Flowing Rivers and War after all, and his brothers were in order: the son of the Lord of Shadows and Judgement, the son of the Winds, and the twin sons of the Horse Physicians. They had one wife among them.

Everybody knows this story, I would say.

Not like this, she would reply. *Let me tell you about their wife.*

This princess was an ayonija—a woman who had not been gestated in a womb. Her father was the Lord of Fire who was also her mother, as she had leaped out fully-formed from the flame instead. But this was not the princess' story, not quite.

This is just to make you understand that being a husband of the woman who was a child of fire was not easy, she had said.

Why does this feel like an excuse?

Just listen.

The prince who was the son of Flowing Rivers and War was fond of carnage. He never had to travel far, as battles landed on him like felled trees wherever he went. But even princes fond of fighting eddied into currents of exhaustion, and he found himself on a riverbank, missing his wife.

Who is to say how it happened? Perhaps he saw the snake first, sunning its honeyed underbelly on a rock, opalescent scales dripping golden light. Perhaps the snake saw him first, losing herself to his storm-cloud skin and eyes and glistening forearms.

In one version of the tale, he would have a son with the snake. In another, he would become a father to many children, lulled into comfort sans princely responsibilities. In yet another version, they met on the seashore instead of a riverbank, a cresting inevitability, their union already foreordained. But in every story he would leave the snake, his son, and his children behind. He would always return to his brothers, his wife of fire. He was a prince after all.

I won't leave you, I would promise each time.

You are not a prince, she would laugh.

37 feet

of a washed concrete stage floor, across which you pushed a wooden table. Do you remember their faces? Enthusiastic, fidgety, offended. I remember it all. It was the Annual Day Function where college administrators, local politicians, MLAs, sump pump entrepreneurs and housewives roused themselves from their bridge games and vendhuthals involving mortifications of the flesh; making their presence known on campus since an event was an event after all, even if the free snacks were khara biscuits and coffee veined with bluish milk. That day reminded us that our college sometimes grasped at normalcy, that it did have clubs. I mean, did you know that there was a club claiming to promote Eastern and Western solidarity through fusion dance? Their members popped and locked to Tamil kuthu songs on stage, and as I watched them, my embarrassment puddled into something else, a thrum along the edge of my hairline. Something new, like awe. None of us knew how to join these clubs that stood outside time. I asked you once as we lay on the widest step of the well, our legs scissored under a threadlike balsamic moon that reeled light back into itself, and you wouldn't give me a clear answer. It was okay. You were preoccupied, terror and passion congealing your words a whole six months before the Annual Day Function because you were expected to put up a solo performance. You were the Folk Arts Professor after all. But could you blame us for anticipating a show that was at least straightforward, like a kavadi where dancers weighed themselves down with a parabola of wood held in place by a rod across their shoulders, arcing and bowing their obeisance at the foot of a papier-mâché approximation of our six-headed god of war adorned with peacock feathers? Or even a villu paatu, a chanted intonation, a lament, involving a tightly strung bow as an instrument? So when the lights dimmed and we all hushed in excitement, we could not help but respond in surprise at the single table that decorated the stage. I admit, I was so fixated on you that I didn't see the table at all, at first. You had walked out in only a petticoat and nothing else. I recognized it immediately, as I was the one who had dyed it with turmeric—a beige, whorled in yellows—for you. I felt marked, chosen somehow. A nudge in our arrangement, your feelings a pulse away from indifference, a not-quite, but also not a no, inching into a terrain of acknowledgement where I could allow myself a nub of hope. Gasps ricocheted across the audience. You were fully clothed, but a petticoat was an inner garment, the first of many layers closest to the body, its visibility an affront. You knew and you did not care because you were already cloaked in a flesh and blood skin not your own, the petticoat your fourth or fifth or sixth membrane, and that was when I think my desire signal-flared into love, a pyrotechnic explosion, all-consuming. You had now begun to dance, each movement towards the table a practiced bharatanatyam nadai, step by excruciating step. Your eye-contact with the audience was a taut line. Not a sound was heard. Then you slowly slid the table from one end of the stage to another with your elbows. Then you sat on the stage floor with your back against its legs, your hands crossed in a shunya mudra—the gesture for emptiness, for what seemed like a whole hour, but perhaps it only lasted a few minutes. In the front row, a politician cursed his sycophants, his voice a conspicuous javelin of sound, rising and rising as if to warn. His white veshti and shirt blazed with purpose in the darkened auditorium, and we all understood who the expletives were actually for. As if on cue, parents walked out in pairs as our college principal placated them with fee vouchers and lunches. Some of the more rowdy girls hooted *ei* and *yakka* and threw paper planes at you. One plane skimmed the stage floor in a low axis, grazing your feet. You did not move. But here's the thing, I couldn't understand why they didn't see what I saw, which was your tail splintering halogen beams into chips of light, your mudras a dehiscence through your human-seeming limbs, your underbelly möbius-looping the perimeter of the stage. Why could they not see? This is why I thought I was set apart, chosen. Especially by you.

409.4 kilometers
was how far I moved, after her dismissal. A "rustication because of the Annual Day Function debacle," the official statement seethed on our notice boards.

Bracts of interest, curling out of my palm. Flattened, the moment I saw the announcement. I felt no need to finish my degree, no need to return to the dim strobe of opiates and classrooms and apathy. I married my cousin. I couldn't find a reason not to. The prince always returned home, even if the home that he knew unformed into an edgeless shape, utterly new. This was how it always was.

My husband was a man inured to family customs, his mind calibrated to only autosuggest whatever societal and cultural norm that was in vogue at the moment. He hated decision-making, loud noises, birds, television news anchors, overgrown plants—anything that declared its presence in full, that took up a lot of space. His days neatly cubbied into geometrical blocks of time that were predetermined by someone or something else—his bosses at work, his mother, the Fair Price Ration Shop that only sold lentils and rice for two hours each morning.

MEASUREMENTS EXPRESSED AS UNITS OF SEPARATION

One evening, I stepped out of the bathroom and into the dining room completely naked. I did not desire my husband at all, but I did seek to provoke him. A tiny coil of satisfaction lodged itself in my throat at the idea of his shock, his discomfiture. Instead, his face held no reaction at my nude body, its willful intention.

Enna, he said.

Enna? I asked, in response.

Our *whats* hung suspended in the air, unclaimed.

Then he stood up without a word, walked over to the settee, and turned on the tv. After that day, I understood that in marrying me, my cousin had reached his life's purpose, his pristine adherence to tradition fulfilled. He did not care for anything else. Somehow, I felt that this too was her doing.

108 days

of riverbanks, lakes, estuaries at the mouth of the bay, islets at the crocodile conservatory outside the city, pockets where bodies of water sheared land. The sloughed remnants of your scales, glasslike. I ran my thumb along the scutes of your belly at each waterfront, remembering how it used to be my teeth paring your human then snake then human membrane one after the other after the other, the saltmetal tang of your limbless form blistering the underside of my tongue.

At the conservatory, I befriended a herpetologist. Her muscles would pulse under her safari shirt as she rolled up her pant cuffs and tucked her long braid inside a bucket hat while cradling adult gharials in her arms. Somehow I thought this might be easy, and it was. All it took was three guided "Become a Zookeeper for a Day" tours in succession, and the herpetologist's interest in me switched on like a heat lamp. It was the linear endpoint of a shared drink and a decision one evening, and what did it matter, my husband was remote enough to be an apparition, a non-presence.

Most importantly, she was not you. The herpetologist's rancid sweat was like mine—all too human, her laughter a sonorous boom, her torso thick and unspeakably beautiful. But when she got on her knees in front of me, her arms encircling my waist, fingers unfurling into an orifice, all I could see were her specimens on the wall, a bas-relief of reptiles entombed in milky jars as my legs slung over her shoulders, tightening around her jawline. I would whisper the names of each bottle label as I bucked on her tongue. *Checkered keel back, Bengal monitor, rat snake, mugger eggs.*

Blue-lipped sea krait.

Blue-lipped sea krait.

Blue-lipped sea krait.

I would have known those markings anywhere. Known those blue-black bands to be a premonition.

2.6 meters

of high tide, waves keening against the bluff. I hulled the clothes off my skin as pain fisted around my purpose. A temple conch blasted on the shore below, the first shrill note to awaken a god. Conferences of large-billed crows and terns competed for silvery coins of dried sardines, karuvaadu as breakfast scraps.

I unscrewed the vial of krait venom filched from the herpetologist's freezer, downing it in a gulp. A sudden vision of her braid, a pang, nothing more than a momentary diversion. Holding your ecdysis in my ring-fingerless hand as blood dyed your cast-off life, I leapt into the murk of the sea.

You once said that I was not a prince. I now know this to be the truth, even as I scattered home to my husband who was my cousin. To the herpetologist. In the beginning that was the end, unlike the prince who was the son of Flowing Rivers and War, I chose the snake. I chose you.

PLASTIC-EATING FUNGUS CAUSED DOOMSDAY[2][3]

Emma Burnett

THIS IS THE talk page for discussing improvements to the *End of Plastic (2029)* article, about the *Tremella purgare* fungus, released into the Gulf of Mexico following the *TransAm War Oil Spill,* and the knock-on impact of the attempted bioremediation. This page has been listed as a level-3 vital article in Earth. If you can improve it, please do.

Deadly fungi?
Can an expert in this field please expand on or link to the meaning of 'deadly fungus' in the opening sentence. Deadly fungi is a disambiguation page and as a non-expert I am uncertain whether it applies here. —8ditor

Update details
There's some updated research explaining the spreading mechanism the fungi used to move from sea to land. The spores eject hard, and once airborne, can latch on to any oil-based synthetic material, and then they grow and digest it. Here's the ref: (Spread of mycelium oil to plastics)—jamirazzz

Dumping an untested fungus into the environment like they've learned nothing from biological pest control. —8ditor

I think it was tested (Lab Results—FUNGUS.PDF). Just not well enough, I guess.—SamePanicDifferentDisco

EMMA BURNETT

Article name
Doomsday doesn't seem like a good fit for this article. It's supposed to focus on the introduction of the oil-digesting fungus introduced into the Gulf of Mexico. —Kinoko

It does that in section one tho, look: <u>Development and introduction into the ecosystem</u>. It's causing major chaos. —DoraTheExSpora

Chaos isn't the same as doomsday. Suggest re-naming to 'Unintended consequences of fungal petrochemical control.' —Kinoko

Remove image
The picture of mushrooms sliced up on pizza can be confusing and may be dangerous. —thatplantguy

All suggestions that *T purgare* fungus might be edible in the future should be removed to prevent potentially fatal mistakes. This includes any links to <u>edible fungi</u> in the initial description.
—jamirazzz

Level-3 change to Level-2
Can an expert please confirm whether we can upgrade this page from <u>Level-3</u> to <u>Level-2</u> to reflect the current shitstorm now that plastic everywhere is basically disappearing? —Kinoko

I second this, the damage it's causing to health equipment is crazy!
[<u>This guy's pacemaker disintegrated</u>].
And there was that airplane that got holes in it while it was flying. Look: [<u>Watch this airplane turn into swiss cheese!</u>] —DoraTheExSpora

That footage needs to come with a trigger warning. I've unlinked them from the article. —thatplantguy

Misleading statement: Jelly seas???
Section four talks about the fungus (fungi?) eating all the microplastics in the ocean. But it talks about the seas turning to jelly, which is a misnomer. Sure, they're more solid than previously, but when the plastics are all consumed, the fungi will die and it'll become water again. —47.71.232.208

Yeah, but that's going to take a while. And look, [U gotta see this dude walking on water] and his shoes melt because of the doomfungus. Plus, all the fish and things are gonna die before the seas are free of microplastics.
Img.png
Img2.png —DoraTheExSpora
Is there a way to revoke edit access if DoraTheExSpora doesn't stop posting triggering things? —thatplantguy
This stuff is really happening, though. You can't deny it. —DoraTheExSpora

Death toll
Updated figures rolling in from accidents and medical issues in section four. Suggest this be moved up to the intro section to keep it easier to locate/update. Also have made a list of things that contain plastic that people might not expect to suddenly break down. Like clothes and orthopaedic implants.
—SamePanicDifferentDisco
These figures are changing daily. Will add a link to the UN mortality stats page. —8ditor

Sealing off computing equipment/bunkers
Has anyone else moved into their prepper bunker? Just checking if they've managed to sterilise everything before sealing in.
—jamirazzz
I just switched everything in the house over to metal. Like, the keyboard is an old metal typewriter that I rigged.
—DoraTheExSpora
Remember that this is not a chat room. But, yes, everything in the bunker looks ok so far, everyone settling in. Nice to be away from the city, too. —SamePanicDifferentDisco

Temporary lag
Had to move to a new bunker, didn't realise the sealant around the windows was sus. Plus, internet went down because a bunch of equipment got eaten. The UN mortality page has been moving too fast to keep this page updated. Suggest just putting a link in the page intro. —jamirazzz
I think we should big up the numbers, so more people take it

serious. Not like this dude [Watch this fool explode after drinking water with doomshroom in it!] —DoraTheExSpora

 Petition to ban DoraTheExSpora for recidivism. —thatplantguy

Any updates?
I noticed there's not been any updates for a few days. Family bunker life is keeping me busy, and so is managing the water situation. The filters were not designed for this.
—SamePanicDifferentDisco

Checking in
Internet has also been very patchy the past few days. But if anyone has any updates, please feel free to post here. It would be good to know how regular contributors from different parts of the world are doing. I heard on the news that the seas haven't actually turned back to liquid yet, and that's really impacting things like weather. It would be good to hear from you folks.
—SamePanicDifferentDisco

Still not heard anything
It's been a few weeks since the last post and there's been no updates. I don't know if that means your internet is just down, or worse. Some internet services must still be running, because the UN is still updating their death toll, and there's still news coming in through the radio. Anyway, I hope you're all doing ok.
—SamePanicDifferentDisco

Steampunk saved me
Glad I went with metal! Even bunkers aren't safe, look [Doomfungus ate thru insulation and got this family!]
—DoraTheExSpora

EGREGORE

Samir Sirk Morató

for all drunk girls in the bathroom.

«I **SAID NO**. I'm scared.»

It's the third time you've asked this clubber to repeat herself. A speaker is blasting behind you, grainy, blown-out, overwhelming in its sonic output—it's not just your ear drums, the ancient floor is vibrating too—and even by the bar, all is lit by failing pink strobe lights.

Pulsing streaks of skin hover where the clubber's face should be. A glitching collection of maybe-features and maybe-flesh broken by glimmers of metal. Above her, a lopsided fan rattles; behind her, the club seethes, a sea of broken light and grinding, amorphous bodies. Grimy mirrors armor every wall, making the crowd thirty-fold.

«Okay,» you say.

Your miniskirt and halter top are sheets dripping off your body, textile made liquid heat. Your thighs stick to the broken chair beneath them. The cocktail you paid too much for is clammy in your hand. The crisped vape coil stench won't leave. The clubber won't either.

«To the dance,» the clubber says. «I said no when she asked.»

«Who?»

«The woman between women space.»

She must be new. She has no eyebrows. Her eyeliner wings are vast, thick wedges of tar. In the strobes, they're voids. If you hook your fingers into her temple holes and pull, you could peel away her face in strips. You imagine her countenance would crumple into your fist like a condom's warm latex.

«Hun,» you say, «that's a lesbian.»

«That's me. I'm scared,» she says.

«Okay.»

All the strobing shards of skin around where her voice emerges scrunch in, forming a strange carnation of features. She gurgles in the split lull between songs. Oh. She's crying. The clubber seizes your elbows with crushing, spit-wet hands.

«I'm freaking.» Her shaking rattles the cocktail out of your cup. It splatters your lap. «I'm really freaking.»

You grab one of her wrists. «Let's go to the bathroom.»

You don't hear what she says next. You absorb syllables framed by a warped, flashing elastic of lip. Maybe the bathroom is quieter. Or cooler. These factors matter to people. You drag the clubber away from the speaker, across shores of gyrating bodysea, and into a bathroom made of brick and collapsing stalls. They're more graffiti than mauve paint or wood.

A group of girlies is clustered around two sinks and their mirrors. They're a chattering cluster of stiletto nails, coquette sunglasses, and utterly owned bodies. They writhe over each other to fix their lip gloss in the mirrors. You tow the clubber to a sink nearby. In the bathroom's steady glow, she gains a face. It's ashen. Swollen. She's young. Bloody opals hover in the crooked, moist corners of her mouth.

«What's her problem?» A girlie points at the clubber. Her pigtails crawl over her shoulders and into her glittery cleavage in so many reaching tendrils.

«Negative space,» you say.

A girlie laughs. «That's all of us.»

You rinse your cup, then plug the sink with paper towels and flood it with cold water. The clubber's pupils are so enormous they're sliding out of her. She slumps against the mirror. Although it's quieter, two speakers are audible from inside the bathroom. Both play the same song, with one a few seconds ahead of the other. Everything is ripply.

«Does she want a pick-me-up?» A girlie looks up from hooking the plum curve of her thong on a glittering, palm-length talon. Hearts and stars float in its quick.

The clubber's pupils shiver. Her dahlia piercings shift back and forth. You hear the grinding of teeth against piercing posts alongside the squelching tear of unhealed cheeks. You scoop water from the sink in your cup, wetting your fishnets, and hurl it into her eyes. Behind her, twin girlies draw ice picks from their ribbon-cinched leg warmers. Other girlies remove compacts and flip phones from their purses.

«Was a man it?» A girlie sets her bedazzled cane aside and wipes an ice pick on her skirt. It's a flannel ruffle that covers none of her. «I'll suck his skin off. Just give me the word, babe. I'll erase him.»

The clubber shakes her drenched head. You hurl another cup of water at her. She coughs. «It was the woman between women space.»

A girlie slides the ice pick beneath her sunglasses. It tips them up. You glimpse a deep bruise.

«She's gorg,» a girlie says.

«If you look,» the clubber says, «between people and mirrors—»

A spluttering, electronic beat floods the bathroom. It overwrites the sound of the running sink.

«ARMS, BODY, LEGS, FLESH, SKIN, BONE, SINEW» the speakers chant. «ARMS, BODY, LEGS, FLESH, SKIN, BONE, SINEW.»

All of the girlies scream.

«Yes!» they howl. «Yes!»

«—magic eye puzzle, the angle has to be—»

The clubber gestures while skirt girlie, dancing, reaches behind her sunglasses. She pinches her lashes between thumb and index finger. She pulls her eyelid up. She slides the ice pick beneath her glasses and over the top of her eyeball.

«—confusing because a lot's happened! I'm—»

Skirt girlie's reflection lip syncs as she angles the ice pick upward. She aims the flat side of her compact at it. A cascade of shooting star charms hang at the dull end of the pick. They jingle. Maroon cakes their tassels.

«—been alone until tonight, you're all—»

The music explodes out of both speakers. Skirt girlie drives the ice pick in with one clipped blow after another. She wiggles it back and forth, all her friends singing and dancing with her.

«—Nebraska so after my crush raped me I couldn't—»

One girlie plucks the shining ice pick from skirt girlie's socket as if it's a rose stem, a beam of light, and slides it under her own eyelid. They're experts: they grind on each other, skirt to skirt, breast to shimmying breast, synchronized to one beat or another. The pounding of compacts or flip phones on ice picks melds into the equally metallic music.

The song ends in one speaker before it ends in the other.

«What a banger,» a girlie says.

The clubber's melting liner contours her cheekbones in black downpour curtains. She's skeletal. Long ago, you were liner-cry gaunt too.

«Feeling better?» you say.

«Sort of.» She wrings her fingers.

«Okay.»

You move to leave. The clubber clings to you.

«Wait!» she says. «Is the woman between women still out there?»

«Girl. She's a regular. An aggregation. She wants to dance, right?» A girlie looks at her from beneath fanning lashes. «So dance. Duh.»

The clubber's throat bobs.

«You need a pick-me-up,» a girlie says.

The clubber looks at her corded waist, complete with floating clover belly piercing, and says «Sure. Sure.»

The girlies usher the clubber into their center. They crowd around her in a miasma of perfume and cunt. When her eyelid keeps shivering and shutting, one girlie pulls it open. An ice pick glows in another girlie's fist. You check your phone. Since you don't have a plan it never has new messages. You watch it die during the hammering and brain-stirring.

When it's over, you and the clubber wander back onto the dance floor. The music is a mixture of moaning and women screaming over a club beat that shakes grime out of every crevice in the decaying building. You prepare to groove. The clubber sways nearby, rubbery, relaxed. Bruised splotches float in her not-face now.

For the final time, the clubber stumbles into your orbit.

«Dance with me?» she pleads. «Until she shows?»

Though you want to reject her, the uncertainty in her voice—childish and untailored—verges on anxiety. It implies personhood.

You were once a person too. It takes such little time before these raw, ruffled edges of being are wiped away. How many crucial moments have you lost to becoming?

«Okay,» you say.

You dance.

Song by song, strobestep by strobestep, you and the clubber wriggle your way into the middle of the dance floor. The view is different from the center. Instead of watching bodycurrents splash onto the dance floor's extremities before ebbing back, you're at the boiling apex. Slivers of corset, flinging hair, flexing muscle, and maybe-people crash together around you, all wet, twining, sometimes brushing you, sometimes pirouetting around you. The heat-reek throbs with the lights. It's somehow calmer here than on the outskirts. After several rounds, the clubber doesn't seem to know where she is. Your consciousness begins unsticking from your body.

In the endless labyrinth of reflections, between a flickering crossroads of elbows and knees, a shape manifests. It vanishes a millisecond after you register it. You're uncertain you parsed anything until, several steps and a head tilt later, you register it again: a shape. Electric wire. A moment. Sweat streams past your brows. It burns. You dance through the next song with your gaze on the floor. The clubber's sticky, bruised form stays against yours. She's oblivious.

A few songs later, when the music turns to sex toy plastic vocals and car crash sounds, music meant for girls that fuck for sport, you look behind the clubber again. It's easier to navigate the kaleidoscope this time. You let your vision slide between mirrors and mirrored, thrashing thighs and backs, and there it is, distant and prickly: the shape.

The figure.

The figure isn't an object. It's a presence between them. An outlined void. At the right angle, negative space clicks into an implication. Face or vase? When you solve the cipher, when you register her in full, pressure blooms in your skull. It bounces with the beat of sound and light. It throbs at the juncture of oncoming migraine or ice-pick-wiggle in frontal lobe or orgasm. The figure's outline intensifies into a glowing white grain.

She must be coming closer, because she's getting bigger.

You dance closer to the clubber. By the time atoms buzz around you, your jaw is almost slotted into the clubber's collar, your hips almost in her skirt. Her breath smells of mint and her maybe-skin smells of cheap stainless steel. You suspect she never had a face. If you took her maybe-mouth with yours you could chew her tongue and taste the bubble gum texture of all the bad schools and oil field trailers you lost your personhood in.

You doubt the clubber feels.

The figure is coming, inch by inch, girlie by girlie. You perceive her crawling between parted calves and squeezing between flirting pelvises. She grinds in ways the rest of you can't. Isn't the space between women more delectable, more violent, than their touch? The clubber is screaming at the ceiling or singing along. Who knows. You grab her shoulders.

«Look,» you say.

In the reflected cauldron of dancers, in their shadows, hovers an extended hand. An offer. The clubber grows still. If she has an expression it's lost to you. Her features are blurry commas pitting sludge. Her whole figure goes rigid. She's an unbreathing animal becoming stiff in a useless lap; a hole contracting around an intruder. For a fraction of time, you know her.

She exhales.

The clubber steps into the space between women. Her waist swivels. She dances into her new partner's dark matter arms. Then, she's gone. A dissolved patch of particles. A grainy burst in the dark. Pressure lifts from your temple. There's only pink lights, a lull between remixes, and the club. Someone's hoop earring crunches under your heel. A drunk, wheeling doll next to you is crying on her friend, her maybe-face smeared against breast.

«You're so beautiful,» she's saying. «You're so, so beautiful so.»

The next song begins, pulsing and unbearable and aloof.

You greet it with open arms.

THE SNOW HATH NO QUEEN

SHANTELL POWELL

CHIMNEY COUNTY HAS a good waste disposal system, but we must all do our part to keep the streets clean. Sunflakes melt tires into treacle, and if they're allowed to bank up, they will catch the air on fire. Then sirens fill the air and we must all return to our homes and seal the entryways. Even the filtered air stinks of burning petrochemicals on those days.

I live in Smokestack 32A on Chimneysweep Street in Chimney County. I close the sunroof when Hyperion sails by overhead and his team's hooves tear up the cobblestones of the sky to send the sunflakes raining down. Once Hyperion reaches the west, I don my asbestos suit and go out into the heat-hazed streets to shovel the driveway. I dump the sunflakes into insulated dustbins and not onto the street because I am a good citizen. At night, when the heat isn't quite as fierce, I dream of snow.

No one has ever seen such a thing. It's a fairytale creation, like unicorns or lions. In my dreams, there are no sunflakes, no asbestos suits, and no heat sirens. Instead of glowing with molten plastics, the world is white and flecked with synthetic diamond sparkles. I am not covered in soot and sweat. Instead, my skin shrinks against my flesh and my silver exhalations off-gas into the sky.

Is this what cold feels like? When I imagine hard enough, little bumps rise upon my skin and reach out to kiss the air, my teeth clack against one another like pistons, and my knees knock in the dance of freezing.

In my dreams, I slide out across a solid river, gliding with ease until I fall through a hole in the ice (that's what it's called: ice) and I am submerged in water hovering around 0 degrees Celsius. I wear my panic sluggishly. My heart slows. My movements slow, and I am breathing water. Not effectively. Not at all. And when I die, my spirit erupts somewhere far from Hyperion's reach.

I never knew all the codfish went to the underworld when the Grand Banks collapsed. When my ancient ancestors first came from the eastern continents, the cod were so plentiful that you could hop your way across the ocean on their backs. This was back before there was plastic. My ancestors staked claims on land and sea alike. They killed the cod like they killed the great herds of bison and the sun-blocking flocks of passenger pigeons, only they used trawling nets instead of guns.

I wonder if I'll see bison and pigeons down here, too.

I know one thing: one of these chthonic codfish has a map tattooed on its skin. I do not know how to find this singular fish in the sea of the underworld. In my death dream, my spirit corpse swims with the fishes, wriggling with the currents, and swirling through schools of aluminium-coloured fish. The shoal coalesces into the shape of a huge maw. It opens, big enough to swallow the world in a single gulp, and I wake from death to escape.

When I open my eyes, I'm in my air-filtered sleep tent clasping a tommy cod. Its mouth opens and closes with metronome regularity. Its gills flare and recede, flare and recede as it flops in my hands. It's drowning in air. I carry it to the kitchenette and dispatch it with a knife. When I peel the skin away, I find my map tattooed on the underside.

This map is from a forgotten era. It's like looking at a subway map from antiquity. I see landmasses where there should be none. Are those continents? "You are here" is marked in the middle of one of several oceans. It's marked atop Chimney County, right in the middle of the Great Pacific Garbage Patch. The Garbage Patch looks right, but the other geography makes no sense. The earth flooded those land masses away years ago when the glaciers melted and the polar ice caps disintegrated.

Nowadays, land is made from salvaged plastic, floating in interlocked masses atop a dead and stinking sea. There might not be land like in olden times, but there's more than enough plastic to create a reasonable facsimile. As I trace my fingers along the contours of the map, I am transported to a place with neither sunflakes nor snowflakes. A vast field is polka-dotted with all the wrong colours. Instead of sepia, the sky is blue, and the earth is green instead of grey and black. And I see and smell blossoms of red, violet, yellow, and pink. Where are all the microplastics? Where is the smoke? My nose doesn't know what to do with this lack of scent, so I sneeze. Then I hear a drone of sound as little yellow and black creatures land on the blossoms. Bees, I think. These must be bees. I thought they were mythological.

I lie down amongst living flowers and a vine creeps its way toward me, tendrilling down into my ears and whispering to me about the Queen of Snow. When flowers whisper, they sound like the cold things of my dreams. They sound like sleet in relentless wind. The frigid wash of white noise lulls me to sleep and I awaken on the green field now twinkling with hoarfrost, blossoms locked into place behind a thin filigree of ice.

A huge white caribou erupts from the frosty soil right in front of me. She gazes at me with red eyes and lowers her head, then bows down onto her front knees. Her name is Tuktu. I know this, though I don't know why. I get on her back, and her muscles bunch then relax as she stands back up and then we are tearing across the sky like Hyperion, like Santa, like the archaeological ISS spacemark.

We gallop across the aurora, a green and red drift of light painting the evening in a coat so thick the stars and satellites don't shine through. The northern lights shift, but Tuktu doesn't lose her footing. She's migrated across the sky all her life. We pass over taiga, muskeg, and tundra, rocks encrusted with lichen, massive floating icebergs, and sheets of ice reaching out across the Arctic Sea. We pass through a conspiracy of ravens, croaking and cawing as they wheel through the air. We travel for hours through sunless sky until we find a campsite with glowing ice mounds spread across the tundra.

Tuktu will not enter the camp, so I slide off her back. She snorts, then leaps back up into the sky and gallops off.

A massive igloo rises like a mountain before me. I pass sleeping dogs, their noses tucked beneath their tails, and crawl through the entrance. Inside is a lake, light flickering far beneath the frozen, translucent surface. That's fire down there, the only familiar thing

I've seen on this journey. I walk across the ice in my bare feet, reach inside my coat pocket and pull out a handful of sunflakes. I scatter them and they burrow like worms all the way through the ice, hissing as they go.

A woman clad in white fur rises from the water on the back of a whale, her hair a wild, black tangle of icicles. She has no fingers. Seals and walruses squeeze out from the stumps.

"You have no business here, qallunaat," she says from the pinniped pile. She waves her sea-birthing hands, and like that, I'm back home.

I live in Smokestack 32A on Chimneysweep Street in Chimney County. In the daytime, I wear asbestos. When the heat is not so bad, I dream of winter and the caribou in the sky. I dream of huge schools of fish, and fire burning below the ice. I dream of these things, but I'm careful not to think of the woman with no fingers. I'm a good citizen. I go outside and shovel sunflakes into the bins.

NOT ALL YOUR BONES ARE YOURS

PLANGDI NEPLE

TWO **HOURS AND** twenty-seven minutes ago, you killed a mermaid.

Blood drips from your clenched fist and the wooden door in front of you opens before you have a chance to knock. A man glares at you from behind a pristine pair of bone-rimmed lenses. Yellow light behind him casts him in shadow and you can barely see his facial expression.

"What is it?" The man's voice is nasal, the kind Tochi would have despised. "I'm busy."

You throw the gyara at his feet and smile a little when he recoils from the splatter of blood that threatens to reach his suede boots.

"Are you mad?" he shouts. Then the man peers closer at what you threw and his eyes widen to fit his glasses. He shuts the door so fast you have no time to beg. Now your bone-to- be is trapped behind his door.

Blind rage turns your vision hazy and you bang relentlessly on the door. Whether or not he likes it, that bone will be in your body today. You did not spend hours seducing and killing just be thwarted by some rich sót.

When he doesn't answer, you whip off your eyepatch. Your mechanical eye whirs and makes a clicking sound. You activate the laser. When it comes in contact with the keyhole, you get blown backwards on your butt. Your scream is raw and loud in the night air.

The door opens. The man takes in the scene before him; you on the ground rubbing your arms through your clothes, the beginnings of a self-satisfied smile on your lips. He shakes his head and looks at you like you are a common mosquito. He could snap his fingers and turn into exactly that, but as you've just shown, only bad things happen when magic and technology mix indiscriminately.

The man kisses his teeth, pulls you in unceremoniously, and shuts the door.

Before you can shake off your disorientation, your head lifts involuntarily, as if your name is being called by the sweetest of voices and your eyes find a door at the end of the hallway. Animal glyphs and other symbols you can't identify cover the dark brown surface. It glows subtly. Your feet move involuntarily, but the sót presses your bone into your chest, halting your movement.

"You're either very desperate or very stupid. Do you know what this is?"

Your lips twist and you nod. The sót's glower deepens and he takes off his glasses and rubs his eyes.

"Where did you get it from?"

You stare at him without blinking. It's a stupid question and you both know it. It doesn't matter that it is arguably the most valuable thing in the world, the bone that granted Mami Wata the ability to reincarnate in the exact same body over and over. No one would go to the trouble of obtaining a gyara, let alone test the application of its properties on humans.

Until now.

"So, what do you want me to do with it now? Did you want to sell it to me?" You shake your head. "I want you to put it inside me."

Silence and only the sound of a ticking clock and hum of electric appliances and the open mouth of the sót.

"You're actually mad," the man whispers. "Get out of my house."

For the first time in three days, your cold calculation and surety give way to the heat of fear and desperation. This is not how your plan is supposed to go. The man's big hands are hot and burn your skin as, dragging you by the arm, he flings you through the open door into the balmy night.

"Please, I just—"

"What reason could you even have for this?"

Tochi's smiling face flashes in your mind and you wrench your arm out of his grip.

"That's not your business," you reply. "Just do it and let me go." The man stares at you for a long time. Then he slaps you, hard.

"You want me to do something that no one has ever done before, with something that could get me and you killed if anyone should walk into this house and see us now!"

His voice rises with every syllable, and the veins on his bald head shine with a mixture of sweat and oil. Your face stings and you clench your fist, speaking through gritted teeth.

"The great Dr. Eko. I know you. I've seen your name in newspapers almost every day.

They're always saying how you like to try dangerous things, that you're the smartest and most stupid sót of your generation."

Your eyes bore into his. You feign an admiring gaze, ignoring the stinging in your cheek. The man huffs but looks a little pleased, pushing his glasses higher up his nose. But he remains silent. You bite your tongue, your chest twisting and head pounding as you struggle to articulate the words he wants to hear.

"I—I want to see if the bone will make me reincarnate, like it does for the Mami Wata. There's . . . someone I want to meet again."

The doctor's eyes go wide and his lips flap like that of a fish.

"Imagine if you do this successfully," you whisper. "Everyone will worship you." The draw of mortal godhood is too great to ignore, and the man is quiet for a time. The small kernel of hope rattling around in your chest grows bigger as time passes. "Young man," the doctor says finally. There is a strange look in his eyes that you cannot place. "I don't know what has possessed you to come to my house today. And even if I did, I know you have no way to pay for something this expensive."

The doctor gestures to your obviously scavenged eye implant, which is still exposed.

Shame pricks your skin and you quickly cover it with your eyepatch.

You turn toward the front door. You cannot cry in this house, not when you haven't cried since that night. It would be a stain on Tochi's memory.

"Did I say you could go? Come back."

Your hand stops just above the doorknob, and you spin around so fast you stumble. The rhythm of your heart increases. Hope floods you once more with its dizziness.

PLANGDI NEPLE

The man is already walking away from you, his imposing figure moving toward the door that has been singing your name since you stepped foot in the house.

By the time you reach the door, he's no longer the respected doctor with purported ethical principles. He is the reviled madman you need, the man who will do the bone transplant letting you reincarnate with the love of your life.

"I have one condition before I open this door. If you have any problems after this surgery, ignore them." The fire in the man's dark eyes banks higher and now a different fear grips you. These are the eyes of the powerful sót that once swapped out a gestating baby for a chicken, placenta and all.

"Don't even think of coming to me. In fact, if anything goes wrong, kill yourself, because no one will help you."

The dire warning does little to quell the happiness inside you, and as soon as the man gives you an anesthetic concoction of things you would rather not think about, you forget his words.

The implanted bone is like a well of life, bleeding optimism into your heart and soul. It is not until a day later, that the true meaning of the sót's declaration hits you.

***

After picking and prodding at your arm, waiting to see how long it would take the gyara bone to merge with your body, you finally fall asleep on the sofa in your living room, and you're instantly transported.

Water sluices over your feet, as cold as the grave you are standing in. You know it is a grave because the fluid walls around you are the same satin herringbone pattern that was in your father's coffin. The air feels stale and the fact that you can feel it is the first indication that something is wrong. Your dreams have never made sense. There was even one where yam and stew smelled like insecticide and tasted like cotton candy.

But you have never *felt* a thing; this is more than a dream.

You punch the coffin cover above your head. The hardwood slightly gives, but there is no sound. Abnormal. That's better, familiar dream territory. You drop your hand and reflexively inhale a big lungful of the rotten, humid, and strangely fishy smell of death.

170

Images of bile and vomit fill your head. You retch and squeeze your throat in a vain attempt to quench the taste of death from going any further down to your stomach.

White light filters into the coffin. Slowly, you look upward.

Disbelief freezes your body. That lined face—one on each cheek—is gray and lifeless, yet still makes your heart stutter like the first time. Then your heart stutters for a different reason as Tochi's face leaves the opening and an ax comes crashing down into the coffin's cover.

"Tochi!" you scream, but cannot hear even yourself.

You glance around frantically, searching for a way to hide from the splinters and slats of wood falling toward you. Falling debris pierces your skin and the metallic smell of blood soon joins the rotten air. You attempt to use your hands as a shield, but it barely helps and blood flows from your fingers like raindrops.

And still, Tochi hacks away at the cover, with no care for your safety or the tears now streaming out of your eye.

Your eye . . .

With renewed hope, you reach for your implant so you can activate it to shoot. Then your hand touches the edge of your empty socket and you flinch and yank your hand away from your body so hard you nearly dislocate your shoulder. True fear fills you and you begin to shake.

"Tochi, please," you cry, broken by this not-a-dream. "Please, it's me."

You want nothing more than for him to hear you, to remember you, and stop whatever madness he is doing. But how can he hear you, when not even you can hear yourself?

Perhaps this is it, his retribution for that night.

The splinters stop falling. You huddle into the corner of the coffin. Light has filled the coffin, and Tochi is climbing down the sides of the coffin. It is a marvel how he can find any purchase on the walls as they seem to be made of shadow, solid, and twisting— just like this dream.

Tochi locks eyes with you and caresses your face with his thumb. Then he smiles, and he is your Tochi again. His face is the same as it was last week, chiseled and with a smattering of hair strands he liked to call beards. There is still death in his gray eyes, but his golden skin is smooth and luminous in the white light coming from above.

"I miss you," you croak.

His smile widens and his hands travel from your cheeks to your arms. His touch sends a thrill through your body and you pull him closer to you, enjoying the feel of his hard chest against yours.

Then his hand stops just above where you had the gyara implanted by the sót, and he lifts your arm.

Your smile is giddy and triumphant. The point of the transplant beats with a faster pulse than every other place on your body. It's just like the spot on Tochi's back where his gyara bone was when he was alive.

"You see," you say, even though you know he can't hear you. "We can come back together."

Tochi's mouth opens, and then razor-sharp teeth are sunk into your arm, and he has torn out the gyara bone.

Pain blinds you and you scream till your throat is hoarse and you wake drenched in sweat.

Your pulse pounds as you turn over your arm and inspect the spot where the sót implanted the gyara bone. But where you half-expect to see at least teeth marks, you see scales instead, like the ones on Tochi's tail whenever he was in merman form. You frown and pick at them, trying to dislodge them. It is like trying to remove super glue from your skin and hurts just as much.

When you succeed, blood flows and it's cold, and your heart starts to pound. Then your hoodie slips off your body and exposes your entire forearm.

It isn't yours anymore, but an unholy amalgamation of a frog's webbed fingers and scales dotted all over your dark, hairy forearm.

An intense feeling of wrongness makes you lightheaded and your body starts to shiver. You spring to your feet, already charting a public transport route to the sót's house in your mind. Then his words come back and you stumble on the last two steps down from your flat.

Kill yourself, no one will help you.

Desperation threatens to drown you, until you remember one person who may be able to help you. But no, you cannot meet him yet. You promised Tochi to never ask him for anything.

Besides, there is someone else you can ask.

NOT ALL YOUR BONES ARE YOURS

In your haste, you almost forget to pay the bus conductors who ferry you across town to your destination, earning you more than one stink eye and several insults.

Down in the river up to your shins you sing Tochi's mother's favorite song. Your desperation to find out what is wrong with you makes you forget you have not spoken to her since her son died.

"What is happening to me?" you ask the moment her head clears the water.

The woman in the water looks down her nose at you and flicks her tail so water lands on your threadbare shirt. Irritated, you brush the drops away. Her low-cut hair glistens in the sunlight, and naked eyebrows frame reddened eyes piercing you with disdain.

"So, you've forgotten how to even greet, talk less of coming to see me after my son's Death."

Shame prickles your skin and you temper your haste a little. "I'm sorry mama. But please, I really need your help."

You stretch out your arm to her, webbed fingers and all. The dotted scales are a shiny red and blue and complement your skin prettily like some kind of sick joke.

Her plump face goes through so many emotions; shock, revulsion, pity, and finally, Anger.

"I warned you," she says at last. "When you and my son started dating, I told the two of you that his magic might interact with that thing where your eye is supposed to be."

Her anger rolls onto you. How is it your fault that you lost your eye in the same accident that killed your parents and had to get an implant to survive? How would you have known at seven that you were going to fall in love with a mami wata and shouldn't get a technological implant that might react with his inherent magicity?

"Even you said there was a high chance of nothing happening. It's not like Tochi had magic!"

Tochi's mother raises a brow at your increased volume and you huff, folding your arms.

"Okay fine. Then what could be the cause of your hand looking like a frog's hand?" You pull your arm back into your hoodie. No matter your desperation, you cannot reveal exactly what you did. Doing so would reveal what you did that day, the day the grief of losing Tochi got so bad you nearly took your own life.

"I just need to know if you know what's happening to me, and if you can help." "How do you want me to know what you have done that has caused this? Eh, am I a sót now? What have you done, Sani?"

Her voice has risen and you tremble a little. At the sight, a little of the anger in her eyes gives way to pity, but you refuse to budge. She cannot know how you traded one mami wata's eternal life for the chance to come back and be with Tochi again.

Then she kisses her teeth and grabs your hand. "Wait, don't—"

You try to pull away from her wet grip but her long fingers are too strong. The second her hand touches where the gyara bone sits beneath your skin, she jerks back and all the blood leaves her fair face. She looks at you like . . . like . . .

Like you are the one that killed Tochi.

Your chest is heavy as you sprint away from the shore, ignoring her shouts for you to come back.

As soon as you get home, you run straight to the back of your house, where your workshop is. You can barely think straight. All you know is that you want the stupid hand and the bone in it gone.

The weight of your axe is familiar and already bloodied with one of your two misdeeds.

What's one more?

You heat the blade in the forge, waiting till it is red hot and glowing.

The blade comes down on your arm like an avenging angel, and you pass out in a haze of pain, screams, and whiteness.

When you come to, like a cruel joke, you still have an arm. But this time, there is no pretense of sparse scales and slightly webbed fingers. Your forearm is fully scaled and the gyara bone beats so fast you can feel it in your chest.

It is beautiful. It is grotesque.

A scream bursts out of the depths of your being, and you claw at your skin with your right hand until cold blood trickles out of small wounds. As you slump to the ground, wood chips digging into your buttocks, you know you have no other choice.

You must go to *him*.

And so, you go back to the river. But now, you go to meet someone Tochi warned you to never seek out, someone who should not exist, just like what you are becoming.

***

"So, a human knows enough about me to know my favorite song," the mami wata floating in front of you says, a sly smile dripping off his lips.

You struggle to not flinch as his fingers caress your cheeks affectionately. The gesture is a gross facsimile of the lingering touches Tochi used to leave you with before he transformed back into a mami wata and sank beneath the waves.

"Such a beautiful boy," he says, grasping your cheeks so tight their wet fingertips feel like claws.

Your restraint thins further and you struggle to not roll your eyes. "I know I'm not supposed to know about you, but someone I love told me about you and how you helped him get legs."

He gasps and his hands release your face to clap delightedly. "You're him! No wonder Tochi wanted to give up his life for you."

Your eyes travel over his trim torso and long dreadlocks, whose true length—as well as their aquatic half—is hidden beneath the water. His slanted eyes glow with a knowing light, and he licks his lips slowly.

Mami wata. Sót. Sea witch. There is no proper word for what he is, because he—a magic wielding mami wata—has not been allowed to exist by humans.

"Let me guess, you want to become like me."

The confidence he speaks with sparks a little old hope in you and you look away quickly, hoping he misses it. From his loud, mocking laughter, it is obvious he did not.

"I am not going to make you a mami wata."

You shake your head. "That's not what I came for."

You take off your hoodie with trembling hands and close your eyes. When there is no sound of splashing or even a gasp, you open your eyes to find him staring at you, barely contained anger contorting his features.

"What did you do?" His voice is a whisper.

Not trusting your tongue, you turn over your arm. The point of the transplant is now distended, your skin covered in scales and pulsing.

"Is that . . . ?"

You nod. Features you saw as pretty turn cold and distant.

175

"Why is it," he begins in a low voice. The water around you starts to ebb and flow faster, and you spread your arms in alarm.

"Why is it that humans cannot just be happy with what they have?"

His voice takes on a frightening gritty quality and the river responds in kind. "Wait, please—"

"Shut up! Your kind does not even allow mine to practice magic! Do you know what it took for me to learn everything I know?! If anyone important ever found out, I'll die without a trial.

"And you—you just wake up and *murder* a mermaid, steal their *bone, and put it inside yourself*, because what, you're heartbroken?!"

Their voice has hit a booming crescendo and the water is splashing against your chest now.

This is no dream. You can hear the sound of the water breaking on the river bank and threatening to break free of its borders. In desperation, you release the one secret you swore to never tell anyone, the true reason you want to reincarnate.

"It's my fault that he died!"

***

The day is still etched in your mind like a piece of pottery carving that will last forever.

The two of you had just stumbled out of a club, laughing, a little bit tipsy, and a lot delirious. Tochi tried to pull your keys from your hands.

"Are you crazy?" he asked. His gray eyes were wide and luminous in the yellow lights of the club. "You're obviously not driving."

More laughter spilled from you, even as your chest twinged with disappointment. You wanted to look responsible enough to not be too drunk to drive home for the man who'd taken a chance on a one-eyed orphan. But you could never say no to Tochi, and soon you were both walking the streets, making silly jokes and laughing at random strangers.

Then just before you turned the street to your house, you saw a scene in an opposite alley that chilled your blood so much you froze. A man had a hand up a woman's skirt, and she was wriggling like a salted worm, like she would rather be anywhere else.

176

NOT ALL YOUR BONES ARE YOURS

Heat flooded your body and cleared all the fogginess of the evening. The woman clawed at her attacker's back and his free arm snaked out to encircle her neck, cutting off her whimpers. Tochi gasped and you felt the vague sensation of his warm hand leaving yours.

Then a man and a woman turned the cover into the alleyway, giggling and touching each other all over. Your heart rate relaxed a little. You wouldn't have to cross the street after all. Then they spotted the other couple in the alleyway and did something that set your blood ablaze again.

They laughed, whistled, and walked away.

You'd seen enough. You ripped off your eyepatch, determined to obliterate the man where he stood.

You did not see Tochi sneaking up on the couple until it was too late, and he had a hole clean through his head where his eye should have been.

And just like that, you killed the only person who loved you unconditionally. You'd still ended up burning the man in the alley to ashes with your eye, but even that could not assuage your guilt over your mistake.

***

"I just want to be here when he comes back so that I can tell him I'm sorry," you whisper. "I can't live like this."

There is nothing but silence and you cannot bring yourself to open your eyes, because you fear you will see the same accusatory look you saw on Tochi's mother's face.

The bone beneath your skin feels like poison now. The bone that was meant to fix everything, feels like a cancer now.

"I will help you," the sót says.

Your eyes fly open in shock. His eyes are hard and unforgiving. "Thank—"

"But I expect something in return," he says, halting your spiel of gratitude. "Anything," you reply.

"No, not anything," he says, his eyes tracking you head to toe like you are the scummiest depths of the sea. "I want every single memory you ever shared with Tochi."

Your chest seizes and you forget how to breathe. You shake your head repeatedly without thinking. There is nothing left for you in this world but your memories of a mami wata who dared to love a man flawed and disfigured.

"I can't," you spit out. "I can't."

The sót raises one eyebrow and crosses his arms. "I hope you understand what is happening to you. Just because you stole what makes us special and put it inside you doesn't make you special; it just makes you a thief. And all thieves end up paying eventually, like you are now."

Your mouth opens to lash out in denial, but no words come out.

"I'm giving you one chance to choose right, or I'll just take the memories myself and tear that bone from your body and watch you die."

Then the sót grabs your head with both hands and your eye rolls back into your head. Images breeze past your inverted vision but you can decipher them despite their blurriness. The first conversation you had with Tochi after seeing him swimming with his friends every week. The sun glanced off the scales on his green and yellow tail that afternoon as he dove, and water rolled off his wide chest, creating crystal trails on his golden-brown skin.

Awkward about approaching him, your best friend had moved things along by pushing you over the edge of the canoe, and Tochi had to break away from his friends and save you. And when he'd smiled at you with the sunset lighting his dimples and tattooed, muscled arms, you swore to do all it took to make him smile again.

Another memory surfaces, this one less bright but no less powerful. An infection had gotten into your eye socket, and you lay bedridden with no help. Days later, Tochi walked into your house unsteadily on human legs he didn't have before.

The memories leave your head like they are being sucked through a vacuum as the sót removes their hands from your head.

You reach out in desperation and grab the hands. They are a lifeline, connecting you to memories that you are afraid will fade to mere wisps.

"Please," you cry out when they wrench away from you. "You can't take them away from me. They're all I have left of him. They're mine!"

"And I truly wonder how they even got made in the first place. How could Tochi ever choose to leave his family for someone like you?"

His words are a blow to your chest, and you come undone.

You stagger away from him, falling. They're right, and the realization of what you have become finally releases the tears you have been suppressing. Great heaving sobs rock your body, and you cannot breathe properly for the next few minutes.

You have become the very thing Tochi told you mami wata think humans are: greedy, opportunistic murderers.

"If I give them to you, what will happen?" you ask in between hiccups.

"You'll be surprised how much I can sell the memory of true love for. Oh, and I'll fix what the bone is doing to your body." His eyes bore into you, daring you to complain.

Many lives without memory of your great love?

Or, waiting for the bone to erode your body completely into an unrecognizable thing? one half of which made you want to kill yourself, forced to remember how you'd killed your lover, and worse still, how you became a person undeserving of his love?

A memory surfaces. You and Tochi are in the market, watching a groundnut vendor cheat his customers out of a handful of kernels. The two of you laugh at the nimble movements of his slim, dark fingers and the smirk on his full lips.

"If I die, I want you to find someone else to love you."

The abrupt comment had you whipping your head around to look at your boyfriend in shock. He gestured back to the vendor. His wife was in front of him, keeping their customers distracted with stories. As the man finished with one customer, she effortlessly switched to the next one, allowing her husband to continue his trickery. Their movements were smooth and choreographed by a lifetime of partnership and commitment.

"I want that for you, even if we break up or I die."

You wanted to protest that you would destroy anything that took him away from you. But then it was your turn to be swindled, and the strange conversation passed.

How did you keep that promise of destruction now, when you are the thing to be destroyed?

Your heart thuds painfully, and your tears slow. You know what to do, and it is what you should have done before you killed an innocent mami wata.

"I'll give you my memories."

The sót nods, their expression grim. He swims closer to you, his slender fingers reaching for your face, but you jerk away before they can make contact.

"But I want you to do something for me—please." You hastily tag on when his hostility returns.

This is the hard part, and you take a fortifying breath that feels lighter than any you have taken since Tochi died. "Take the bone out of me. I shouldn't have done what I did, both to that mami wata and T-Tochi."

The words are rushed. You do not want to give yourself time to think further and recant. Perhaps it is a coward's way out, choosing to live oblivious to how you'd killed your lover, and worse still, how you became a person undeserving of his love.

But you killed an innocent creature once, and you cannot continue to live with the potential to be that person again.

The mami wata swims closer to you and reaches for your head but you lean back before he can make contact.

"One more thing. If Tochi is reincarnated while you are still alive, can you save my memories and show them to him . . . everything? I don't want him to forget me. But-but I want him to choose to understand and love me, if he can."

The mami wata nods, and for the first time in days, your smile is real and bright, if small.

Then his fingers touch your temple, and everything dissolves in a haze of love and a pair of sparkling gray eyes.

THE YOLO WALLPAPER

SONYA VATOMSKY

ONE NIGHT MY WIFE came home and went to bed without saying anything. I figured she was tired or drunk or both, so I filled her water bottle and set our alarm for half an hour later than usual. She didn't get up at 9:30, though. She didn't get up at all.

'I'm not being funny but you need to stop with those void girlie books from TikTok,' I finally told her after I'd prepared and eaten dinner alone. She stared past me, blinking slowly.

Maybe it's burnout, I thought. I had recently listened to a podcast about this. Probably she needed a break. I joined her under the duvet, putting on highly rated Netflix shows she wouldn't pay attention to and ordering curries she wouldn't eat.

'What's wrong?' I asked, over and over. 'What can I do?'

My wife refused to answer these questions, though occasionally she squeezed my hand. Three squeezes in quick succession—like a stranger knocking on your door. On Monday I rang our GP and read him a list of concerns I'd written on the back of a Deliveroo receipt.

'Sounds like burnout,' he said. 'Get some sleep, drink some water, and make an appointment for blood work if there's no improvement.'

'How much sleep?' I asked. 'Precisely how much water?'

A month later, the blood work came back normal.

'There's nothing physically wrong here,' the GP said decisively. 'It could be depression. Is there a family history of mental illness?'

'I don't think so.' My wife's family didn't believe in mental illness, and they weren't the sort of people who experienced things in which they didn't believe.

'Are you depressed?' I asked her. My wife had a sleep mask over her eyes but I knew she was awake from the way she was breathing. She reached a pale hand out from under the duvet and scratched at her nose, then snatched the hand back. The gesture was vaguely reptilian. I picked the antidepressants up the next day.

'I'll get these too,' I told the pharmacist, setting down an assortment of supplements I had read about in a Facebook group dedicated to undiagnosed illnesses. A wild desperation bloomed through the knots in my stomach. I was open to anything and everything, so long as it kept my wife from continuing her metamorphosis.

Over the next weeks I tried herbs, crystals, a salt lamp, a SAD lamp, and a white noise machine that sounded like dying whales attempting covers of industrial albums from 1980s Berlin. I rubbed perfumed oils into every inch of my wife's body with every possible amount of pressure and begged her to drink things that were, even to me, increasingly questionable. I made spreadsheets. I applied for an increase to my credit limit. I took on extra bar shifts and a persistent odour of sour beer and grease.

The leeches arrived in an empty Vimto bottle, sickly thin and covered in gel. I didn't remember ordering them but the proof was in my email: two medium leeches, £28. I rinsed them in the sink and placed them onto my wife's left arm with a pair of blue plastic tongs. I waited. Google said that removing leeches before they were satiated meant one of their three jaws, each of which had a hundred teeth, could tear off and get stuck in the skin. When at last they detached from my wife and dropped onto the duvet like fat, milkdrunk babies, I scooped them into an ashtray and flushed them down the toilet.

'And how are we doing on the antidepressants?' the GP asked.

'She's still in bed,' I said. 'I don't think they're helping. I don't think she's depressed.'

'I'll increase the dose. Let's add some gabapentin for anxiety.'

I ended the call and screamed.

Next I tried reading horror novels like they were how-to manuals. I learned all the ways wives routinely became vampires, werewolves, birds, and fish; how their bodies regularly housed fungi, aliens, viruses, and demons. I reread fairytales about spells and curses where women, albeit generally virgins rather than wives, slept too deeply or too long.

I went to the library and made photocopies of passages describing not just a) survival but b) life in a modern metropolitan city, taping them around the bedroom for inspiration. I was willing to give up our Manchester apartment if the issue was mould or demons—though I hoped it wasn't demons because I was an atheist—but I didn't want to release a rabbit-wife into the forest. I didn't want to be married to a wasp. Facebook groups popped up in my feed like mushrooms once the algorithm figured out who it was dealing with. I joined them all, just in case.

My hair fell out from stress, clogging the drains and forming dreadful nests on the floor, while my wife's grew with abandon from new, surprising places she must have kept tweezed and waxed through our years together: long, dark fur along her upper lip, inside the creases of her elbows, around her six nipples. In time it was so thick she resembled a panther, her irises a cloudy yellow. This would have frightened me if I hadn't done my research— instead, I moved with precision, sliding a striped oven mitt over each paw so she couldn't scratch her face.

'I love you,' I told her. I went to the kitchen and cut open a bag of thawed rabbit meat, emptying it into an old yellow mixing bowl patterned with red flowers. I added four tablespoons of a raw food completer for cats and stirred everything with a long spoon. My wife sniffed at the bowl suspiciously, then buried her face inside.

A hot, wet stench spread throughout the bedroom. Trying not to gag, I nibbled at a half-eaten hamburger I'd rescued from the bin at work, imagining we were seated outside in Stevenson Square and having poached eggs on toasted sourdough. I fished my phone from my trouser pocket and took a photo.

Loving her rabbit! I posted to LYCANTHROPE FRIENDS AND FAMILY SUPPORT. *Your wife's coat is gorgeous*, someone commented. *u ever feed biscuits or only raw?* I typed *No biscuits!!!*, then deleted the exclamation marks and added a smiley face. *Cats are obligate carnivores*, another person had already added. A chunk of rabbit flew out of my wife's mouth and onto the carpet. Stretching out my foot, I pushed it towards the wellness graveyard under our bed: an unopened air purifier, two bottles of psyllium husk powder, a jade gua sha.

I liked Facebook because it gave me a sense of stability through observing people with even less of it. My feed was filled with desperate introductions. *Please tell me I'm not the only one going crazy about their wolf*, someone would write. *I am crying every day trying to figure out what's best for her. Nothing seems to help!! I am losing my mind.*

There would be dozens of replies. *U not the only one I am the same. i recommend holy water helps lot my daughter no shifts since May 2018.* Others would hijack the post with their own questions—*can u elaborate a bit on the supplement you are referring to?? I'm in Chorley PR6 Thanks*—and eventually the comments would get turned off.

ATTENTION #admin here kindly reminding members 'demonic possession' is NOT a Diagnosis but an UNSCIENTIFIC umbrella term for MANY different presentations of Lycanthropy or OTHER DISEASES!!! If you are new to the moon dance PLEASE read the Guides before posting or commenting.

My wife's parents, meanwhile, weren't concerned at all. They treated their daughter's condition like a new hobby she had picked up: something requiring a minor financial commitment and the pretence of caring about her progress. I called them every other weekend and thanked them for the money they were depositing into our bank account.

'Lymphatic massage?' I'd say. 'Yes, I'll definitely try that. Good shout.'

'Have you considered hiring a professional carer?' her father asked one week. They had just returned from a spa holiday in Karlovy Vary where they'd witnessed the restorative powers of old foreign women, specifically ones who pummelled you with alternating hot and cold water from a distance of three metres.

Impossible, I thought. I couldn't imagine anyone else looking after her the way I did. Would a professional carer go to the shops every morning to buy fresh crickets and mealworms? No. What I really needed was a professional me, someone to come in and live my life so I could focus on trimming the claws of my wife's eight legs with garden shears.

Instead I changed into my work clothes each afternoon and

walked across town to The Wailing Monkey. The floors there stuck to the soles of my shoes no matter how much I mopped and the faucets and drains were all ringed with a greyish pink mould. I sold cheap beer and prawn cocktail crisps and tried to keep my head down. One night the loneliness was insurmountable and I told a customer about my wife. He was waiting outside when my shift ended and waved a fistful of five-pound notes in my face. 'To watch you fuck her,' he said. I kept my socialising to Facebook after that.

Has anyone successfully used kiss me over the garden gate extract (persicaria orientale) to force a shift?

Hi everyone—just want to share my experience burning sage from Aldi

Werewolf_Nutrition_-_Feed_Werewolves_Like_Wolves.pdf

BOTH MY DAUGHTERS ARE WORMS URGENT #ADMIN

Anyone else misdiagnosed with depression/anxiety before lycanthropy???

u need holy water NOT SAGE if ur sister is a demon ffs

Can someone please add Caz Copperpot to the September Memorial Post

DO NOT share food lists from other groups to this group YOU WILL BE BANNED

Pic of my mum Lucy the Lion for the algorithm

But we weren't unhappy, for the most part. My wife enjoyed old Soviet cartoons with singing animals: *The Musicians of Bremen, Cheburashka, Vinni Pux*. I played prog-rock records, put on silly outfits, and danced for her. Sometimes we shared a bowl of freeze-dried chicken treats and her claws scraped against my fingers as we reached for the chalky cubes at the same time. On her fortieth birthday I spent hours blowing up multi-coloured balloons and let her pop them all, the velvet bows in her fur bouncing as she roared with pleasure.

The end of my wife's illness confuses me as much as the beginning. There is no reason, no one thing I can point to and go, 'ah, well, that explains it.' I was on the toilet when a series of sounds came from the bedroom: soft moans, rustling fabric, a grotesque squelch like a hand thrust into a jar of mayonnaise. I opened the door and stumbled out without wiping.

Our bed had been stripped, the pillows and linens thrown across the room. In the centre of the mattress was a speckled brown egg the size of a large grapefruit. I carried it to the kitchen and placed it gently in the fridge, rearranging two pickle jars and a pot of expired yoghurt so that it wouldn't roll out. My wife I discovered on the floor, ripping a packet of biscuits open with her very human teeth.

'I missed you,' I said, helping her up. 'I missed you so much.'

'I didn't go anywhere,' she laughed. Her face was covered in crumbs. 'Did you go somewhere, Katya?'

2023 was a hard year. That's what I tell friends when they corner me at dinner parties.

'For us too,' they say. They're not having sex anymore or they're having it with the wrong person or they're working too much or not enough. 'What happened to you?' they ask.

'Oh,' I say. 'Something like that.'

We keep the egg as a memento, packing it carefully in an old shoebox when we move to a bigger apartment and then, much later, to a terraced house outside the city where we have a garden and a little black cat. After my wife dies I put the egg in a pot and boil it but it tastes strange—almost like nothing at all.

GRAVITATIONAL PULL

SUSAN L. LIN

IN ONE OF my earliest memories, my sister Lulu lies facedown on the living room sofa while our mother leans over her prone body, liberally applying a topical medication behind her ears. The skin there is puffy and raw, an open wound.

"Your *zǐzǐ* pointed at the moon, and look what happened," our mother says to me, though her gaze never strays from the task at hand. "Now you will know never to do the same."

Lulu whimpers into the seat cushion, and when she tilts her head to peer up at me, there are tears in her eyes. My older sister is the toughest person I know, so I can only imagine how much the treatment must sting.

"I know, I know," our mother whispers, soothing Lulu with a comforting hand on her back. "I should have warned you sooner. That's why we won't make the same mistake with Lana. Right, Lana?" With those last words, she finally looks my way.

I am brimming with questions I can't yet articulate. Grownup questions about malevolence and intent. Scientific questions about the universe and our place in it. Instead of asking what I can't, I grant her a timid nod. "No pointing. Not ever."

"Good. You're my good girl, Lana." But her eyes have drifted off me again. She continues rubbing Lulu's back as she says my name, whispering it into my sister's bloodied ear.

That night, I stare daggers at the moon, which is waxing crescent beyond my bedroom window. The thin sliver of light looks harmless, like a clipped toenail glowing up there in the sky. Despite my promise to my mother, some of my limbs remain insubordinate and rebellious. They have minds of their own. They want me to raise my left hand. They want me to point up at the cosmos beyond in unguarded wonder. Thankfully, my right hand knows better. I use it to pin my left wrist to my stomach, keeping all eight fingers out of the moon's field of vision. There, in its blind spot, I'll be safe.

***

Years later, I discovered from my eighth grade science textbook that the same moon was also responsible for the formation of tides in oceans all over the world. This new nugget of information immediately piqued my interest. Our mother had never mentioned bodies of water before! I read on, hungry to find out more. Essentially, I learned, the moon's gravitational pull generates a force strong enough to distort and elongate the shape of the Earth. This change is so minuscule that it would remain undetected without special instruments. But our oceans are more sensitive. We can see the effect of that slight shift in mass every time the beach tides roll in and out.

This was fascinating stuff, but what I really wanted to know about were the scientific attributes that allowed our satellite moon to cause us bodily harm. From what little I knew in those days, I assumed invisible light rays or sound waves must be to blame— something none of us could see with the naked eye. Unfortunately, once I read past that section in the book, the text had moved on to a dull analysis of the sun's effect on global weather patterns.

No. That couldn't be the end of it! Not when I had been so close to solving the greatest mystery of my childhood.

I reread the page several times. The moon, the ocean, the distortion . . . blah blah blah. Paragraph after paragraph about the moon's effect on our shorelines, but not a single word about its effect on little girls' ears.

When the school bus deposited me back home that afternoon, the house was empty. Good. I dumped my backpack on my bed and marched into the master bathroom. I still remembered that Lulu's old medication came in a little tube, like the kind you might find in a fancy watercolor set. The label revealed a series of interlocking circles in a various sizes, printed in gray and turquoise ink. It had to still be around here somewhere. Our mother never threw anything away.

GRAVITATIONAL PULL

The medicine cabinet was cluttered with small containers: rubbing alcohol, hydrogen peroxide, green oil, antihistamine cream, ibuprofen, Tiger Balm, petroleum jelly, cotton swabs, bandages. No moon relief ointment, or whatever that mysterious salve was called. I searched in every drawer and cabinet, but I couldn't find the little tube from my memory anywhere.

Looking back now, that was the day my curiosity about the moon became a full-blown obsession. For the rest of the school year, I spent weekend afternoons at the library, poring over every relevant book I could find listed in the card catalog. I learned many facts about the moon, like how it's surrounded by a permanent cloud of comet dust. Or how water can't survive on the surface in liquid form due to solar radiation exposure. I regularly stalked the aisles of nearby pharmacies, hoping to one day stumble upon familiar packaging on over-the-counter shelves.

Years passed in the interim. I never did encounter what I was looking for.

***

Before I knew it, high school was over. My grades weren't terrible either, considering the circumstances. In college, I settled on a geology major after losing interest in several of the other hard sciences. I often spent hours in cramped basement laboratories, examining rock samples for unusual physical characteristics. Our entire cohort was so far removed from the outside world that I sometimes wondered whether the stairwell that led back to the ground floor would one day deposit us in the path of a sweeping tornado, or an alien invasion, or a zombie apocalypse. Like maybe the world could end while we were down there, and we wouldn't even know it.

But the world never ended. And whenever I emerged from the labs in the evenings, the moon was still there. Its menacing existence remained a constant in my life through the blur of work that followed. My senior thesis, in which I analyzed the mineral composition of meteorites found in the nearby desert. My personal statement for graduate school applications, in which I found myself pulled back down to more Earthly concerns.

By then, I'd dismissed many of my mother's inexplicable stories as superstitions with no basis in reality. That business with

Lulu's ears once upon a time was no exception. Why teach your child to wash behind her ears when you can give her a lifelong complex about the moon instead? I was over it. But as the living conditions of our planet deteriorated before my eyes, I found my attention wandering back toward the stars. The sight of the moon now comforted me, no matter what shape I found it in on any given night. Chasing that fleeting feeling of security is what eventually got me where I am today.

***

Fifty years have passed since Neil Armstrong first left his footprints on the surface of the moon. In all that time, no woman from any country on Earth has ever followed him. But two years ago, NASA announced that I would be one of the first. Now, decades later, we are finally returning to the moon.

A month before my launch date, a box is waiting on the doorstep when I return home from a long day of training. The annual Mid-Autumn Festival is also nigh, and each year Lulu and I exchange surprise packages to celebrate. When I tear open the cardboard flaps, I'm not surprised to find a commemorative tin swaddled in bubble wrap.

Lulu has outdone herself this time. The metal container is illustrated with white rabbits gazing at the night sky against a matte burgundy-and-gold backdrop. A black notecard is secured to the lid, "Congrats!" written in silver looping script. Lulu has always had perfect penmanship.

The mooncakes nestled inside are my favorite kind: a chewy Cantonese-style crust filled with white lotus seed paste and a salted egg yolk in the center. I waste no time retrieving a knife from the kitchen to cut one of the glossy pastries into quarters. After taking a gigantic bite from the slice with the largest piece of yolk, I swear I can hear Beethoven's famous sonata playing in the heavens. I'm about to call Lulu to thank her when I notice that the other three mooncakes in the box don't appear to share the same filling. According to the Chinese characters stamped on top, one contains red bean paste while another is stuffed with candied fruit. Both common, ordinary ingredients.

I don't recognize the characters on the final one though. That comes as no surprise, of course; even after years of lessons, my

190

language skills have remained elementary-level at best. I frown, looking around for an insert that might include translations, but I don't see one. With my free hand, I try lifting the plastic tray up out of the tin, along with the remaining cakes. Maybe there's something underneath . . . ?

That's when I stop mid-chew, nearly choking on a sharp, involuntary gulp of air. Because there *is* something hiding underneath the tray. But it isn't a helpful slip of paper detailing the contents of the box. It's a Polaroid. More specifically, it's a Polaroid of *me*.

I pick up the square photograph to get a better look. I can't remember the last time I posed for an instant film camera, and sure enough, no aspect of this image rings a bell. It's overexposed and my facial features lack clarity, but the person in that picture is unmistakably me. Those are my glasses. That is my hairline. What I don't recognize is the top I'm wearing. I'm certain I don't own that top. Even so, it looks suspiciously like a shirt with a sailor collar I wore frequently as a toddler—a hand-me-down from Lulu, as most of my childhood clothing was. It can't be the very same garment though. That's impossible. I don't exactly shop in the little girls' section anymore. But the chilling fact that I'm holding a photograph of myself in a perplexing outfit I have no memory of is not even the most troubling part.

In this picture, I have a toothy grin plastered on my face, and I am looking directly at whoever is behind the camera.

In this picture, I have my arm stretched out in front of me, and I am pointing at whoever is behind the camera.

In this picture, I cannot see my ears, because someone or some*thing* has scribbled over the space where they should be with a bright red magic marker.

✳✳✳

I call Lulu.

The other end of the line trills and trills. But just as I'm convinced I'll have to leave an unhinged voicemail, she answers. "Lana! I'm so glad you called."

"Thanks for the mooncakes, Lu," I say, unsure how to broach the subject. "You know I love the ones with the yolks inside."

There's a long silence, during which I wonder if she now regrets

191

orchestrating such a sick joke right before my mission. Finally, "Oh Lana, I swear I didn't forget this year. I've just been swamped with work. I was going to order them this weekend. Really. We still have two more weeks, after all."

"Wait. You mean you haven't sent them yet?"

"Like I said, I've been busy." Lulu sounds annoyed now. Defensive. "And I'm going to make sure they ship by Saturday. I know you have to enter quarantine at the end of the month. I have the date circled on my calendar." Her voice softens. "Congrats again, by the way. I'm so proud. I was just thinking last night about that weird phase you went through when we were younger. I was legitimately worried for a while there. You were really fixated on that moon in an unhealthy way. But you must be so excited now."

That was the problem with Lulu. She never understood that it wasn't a phase. That my so-called fixation had never waned. *I* never understood how she could so easily brush off a formative incident that should've affected her more than it affected me. "Thanks," I tell her, "I am excited, but that's not what I meant. I did get a box of mooncakes in the mail today. I thought they were from you, but I guess not." I scrutinize the accompanying black card in my hand more closely, hoping it might hold a clue I'd previously missed. No signature, no identifying marks of any kind.

"Oh, maybe a colleague then, someone from the program? That's sweet of them. Aren't you the only Asian person assigned to the mission?"

"As far as I know." But I can't think straight. "Listen, Lulu, do you still remember that time when we were kids and your ears got really infected?" We'd never talked about it as adults. For all I knew she had forgotten the ordeal entirely, however inconceivable that seemed.

"Yeah, I think I had an allergic reaction to my new shampoo, and of course I made it worse by constantly picking at the flaking skin. You know how I was back then." I can almost see her rolling her eyes from hundreds of miles away. "Anyway, you live and you learn, right?"

"Sure, but don't you remember what *Mā* said to us afterwards?"

"Uhhh . . . Not specifically, no. I just remember whatever cream the doctor told her to buy stung like hell when she slathered it on. Obviously it worked though!"

I want to press her further, but she says something about taking the kids out to dinner before excusing herself and ending the call.

Talking to Lulu usually makes me feel better. But that conversation didn't answer any of my questions. If anything, it only raised more. I could always go directly to the source and call our mother, but that would be an even more futile exercise. I can already hear her exclaiming in Taiwanese Hokkien: "I never told you that!" That has always been one of her favorite sentences, and it's sure to be her response now. I endured years of therapy before realizing that I wasn't the crazy one with the selective memory.

I refuse to be the crazy one now. Not when I'm so close to fulfilling all the dreams I'd worked for years to achieve.

***

On the eve of liftoff, I remain in quarantine near the launch site. The moon is a few nights short of full, but it's so round and bright that the light emanating off it peeks into my room, even with the curtains drawn. I feel that itch again. I feel that insubordinate, rebellious part of my body waking up again. It's the part that wants to point right at the moon and shout, "In only a matter of days, we'll be there! We'll actually be *standing* on the moon! Isn't that incredible?"

Still, an unpleasant, nagging feeling claws at the back of my mind. I still don't know who sent those mooncakes. Everyone I know has denied any involvement. Nevertheless, the tin was sealed, so I ended up finishing off every last crumb. Lulu's frustrating phone call left me ravenous. And even though I couldn't quite place the taste of the mystery flavor, it proved to be the most delectable treat of them all.

I'm not afraid anymore. I haven't been for a long time.

I don't yet realize that maybe I should be.

From where I'm standing now, I can't see the future. I can't see what will happen in a few days when we safely land our spacecraft on the moon's cratered surface. I can't see the vast blackness that surrounds me when I disembark from the vehicle. It'll be there though, when I become the first woman to ever walk on the moon. I'll feel a huge weight lift off my shoulders when it finally happens.

But then I'll notice one of my fellow astronauts waving her

arms wildly in my direction. The expression on her face will suggest extreme distress. She'll mouth words I cannot hear and I will panic with the split-second fear that I've gone deaf. That I've somehow misplaced my ears and lost my ability to hear. But then she'll gesture to the remote on my suit that controls our communications device, and I'll recall that in the excitement I forgot to activate it. By then, everyone will be crowded around me, concerned looks on their faces. "Your suit," she'll say, and the words coming through my headset couldn't be clearer. "Lana, you're bleeding." And that's when I'll finally witness the early stages of my undoing: tiny droplets of blood suspended inside my helmet, floating red before my eyes.

THE MAN WHO COLLECTED LIGOTTI

Erik McHatton

The Performer

DURING THE THROES of my most recent bout of melancholia I took to walking around the city, several miles per day after work. Truthfully, I can tell you that I took no pleasure in these daily jaunts, as my persistent malady will not allow such things, I merely sought to shorten the length of time between my return home each afternoon from my job at the office, to that time in the evening when I could finally permit myself the luxury of that little death called sleep.

It was on one of these pleasureless strolls that I happened upon a small cafe tucked away at the end of one of the many refuse-filled alleys that have multiplied in number throughout the city in recent years. The signage was plain, and bore only the name "Cafe," and hung over a door so paint-stripped as to be almost bare. I remember thinking to myself that this edifice must assuredly have been for an establishment that would perfectly mirror my pervasive mood.

Upon entering the establishment called simply, "Cafe," I found myself to be completely correct. The scarce tables, with their mismatched chairs, the threadbare and faded couches, the sparse and beleaguered lights and waitstaff, the ramshackle stage at the far end covered over with uneven curtains, the blacked out windows—all of these things gave the impression that I had entered some secret place in my own mind.

I was welcomed by not being welcomed. I found a seat, was ignored by the staff, and left after a suitable amount of time having not spoken to another person at all. But even though I took part in no traditional conversation, there was another kind of conversation happening, one I was definitely a part of, along with the rest of the small congregation gathered that day in "Cafe."

It happened in the spaces between deep sighs, and muffled sobs, in the nervous shuffle of feet, and in the rustle of collars during quick nervous glances. It was a conversation only the loneliest can have, and it was about the same thing lonely people always talk about, whether they mean to or not.

This establishment called "Cafe" became a favorite destination of mine, for in no other place could there be found a larger contingent of people who seemed to share the same malady which afflicts me so tenaciously. The face of every person that haunts the cafe called "Cafe" is an almost perfect match to the one that awaits me every time I make the mistake of looking into a mirror. I suppose it is possible I kept going back because I felt the need for company in my misery, but I suspect I just wanted to be assured that I wasn't the only person in the world who so pervasively didn't care.

So regular became my visits to the cafe that I discovered that every Friday there was held, on the ramshackle stage, a series of performances from the regular patrons of "Cafe." Invariably, on Fridays, at some nebulous time in the evening, one of the patrons would get up from their seat and shuffle their way up to the stage, demarking the beginning of the performances, at which time they would listlessly execute some artistic act of varying quality, before handing the stage off to the next person. And so on, and so forth.

One soul, a man with small, ovoid glasses, has an ancient dummy held over from a long-forgotten age of that much maligned pursuit known as ventriloquism, and he uses this nameless wooden compatriot, with its faded, chipped face, to tell dark limericks that make little to no sense to the ear. One woman warbles funereal songs while shuffling back and forth across the stage with dirty bare feet, and still another merely sits on a stool, vacillating between raucous laughter and uncontrollable sobs.

Each performer who took the ramshackle stage on Fridays, upon finishing their act, looked to me as if the activity gave them some measure of peace, a break in the listless gray storm in which we all reside. Something inside me was stirred by this prospect, and so it was that I came to join these strange performers, reading each Friday the stories of an author I had only recently discovered, and who I have come to understand shares deeply our collective pain.

I found a few of this author's books in boxes in my attic, left behind by a former tenant of my home. So taken was I by the writing therein that I found I had something to look forward to each time my hand passed into a box and found yet another cover bearing his name. Only someone with a profound understanding of the affliction shared by myself and the patrons of "Cafe" could possibly write such bleak and truthful tales. I knew that if I attended the Friday performances carrying one of these books from which to read, that the crowd would appreciate them just as I have, inasmuch as any of us have the capacity to still do such a thing.

So it was that I set about sharing the tales of this forlorn teller, and soon my weeks became nothing but blurs between Fridays at the cafe called "Cafe," which were the only days that now contained any semblance of living to me. When I read, I rarely looked into the crowd, as it was always filled with the same faces, and those faces never betrayed anything more than apathy, so it was easy for me to overlook the presence of the watching man for a considerable amount of time. When I did finally notice him—sitting at my table, his lamp-like eyes reflecting back at me—so unnerved was I that I cut off the story about a man obsessed with a cassette tape, thus depriving my audience of the crucial twist from which the story derives its power.

By the time I'd made my way off the stage and back to my seat, the man was gone. Upon inquiry I was informed by one of the waitstaff that the watching man had been attending my readings for weeks, somehow managing to arrive just in time for my turn on the stage, sitting down at my table, and leaving once I'd finished.

I had no idea what to make of this, so I put it out of my mind lest it aggravate my already worsening condition, and would subsequently forget about the watching man during the blurry week that followed my discovery of him.

But there he was, as if only to remind me, waiting at my table upon the completion of my reading the following Friday.

He rose as I neared the table and doffed the round hat he wore. I mumbled a greeting, asked him what I could do for him. In response, he simply reached into his coat and produced a book bearing the author's name, one I was unfamiliar with. He smiled as I stared at it, agog.

Returning the book to his inside coat pocket, he turned abruptly and made for the cafe door. Upon reaching it, he beckoned me with a swoop of his right hand without looking back, pushed the door open with the cane he held in his left, and walked through.

I could do nothing but follow.

The Paranoiac

There is a man—one of tall and spindly stature, wearing a round hat and brown overcoat, carrying a thin, black cane with a silver cap—who has followed me nearly all my life.

At the start, designs and patterns were his province. I first noticed him as a toddler, lurking in the gauzy, imprisoning mesh of my playpen. His form was unmistakable, and as I traced it with my pudgy, pink fingers over and over, burning his outline into my mind, I learned, inch by inch, to fear him; his meshy eyes staring, his uncaned hand reaching.

So disturbed was I by him that my parents were forced to throw the playpen out, as I could no longer bear to be inside it after. I would scream if they brought me near it, if it was mentioned, if they dared to walk me by the room in which it resided, regardless of a closed door, and when my father took it to the curb to be collected, I stood on the sofa and watched through the front window, just to be sure. When I found it removed the next day, I believed it meant I had escaped him, that I had won.

Unfortunately, this was not so.

The man continued to linger across the years of my childhood. He lurked in scattered shadows, in the patterns of furniture, skulked in the weave of our carpets. He reached down from our water stained ceiling, out from between the ever present wrinkles of my clothes, wavered in the pungent, sticky smoke of my father's hand rolled cigarettes, and hid in the persistent rash beneath my arms. He even roamed the greenish, blackish mold that propagated along the walls of our basement, where my mother would banish me whenever she grew tired of listening to me go on and on.

Outside of our home, he lived in whorls of tree bark, checkered flannel, plumes of spark and ash, in avian murmurations splashed across the sky; reeds of grass, mud puddles, brickwork, piles of garbage, the medium didn't seem to matter, only the message. He was coming, and there was nothing I could do to stop it.

His ever presence resulted in a purvading anxiety, a clinging cloud, whose causal nature produced countless calamities; accidents of distraction, frustrations injurious, and inevitable. Once, I was severely punished for cutting him from the chestnut locks of a classmate, and there he was afterward, purpled in the bruising left behind by my beating, defiant, as if nothing else should have been expected.

But the worst, by far, were those times when I found him cloaked between starbursts tattooed upon the backs of my eyelids, tightly closed in futile attempts to banish him.

There was nowhere where he wasn't.

Over time, as my mind gradually took on a less literal bent, I found my opinion of the man relaxed. After all, he was only an outline in form, not tangible beyond the varying lines that approximated him, and by my teenage years I came to believe that he was at worst a trick of the mind, a leftover trauma, carried over from that first encounter into every one that followed. It became amusing to me that I should have allowed myself to be bedeviled by such a small trick for so great a time. Eventually, I would laugh out loud at the man whenever I saw him, forcing him from my mind's darkest, most fearful places, and into the light of absurd frivolities. In doing so I reduced him, bit by bit, into a joke.

This, he could not abide, and shortly after my fourteenth birthday made this fact abundantly clear by modifying the way he appeared to me, taking shape in full color, with full features, and doing so upon a billboard situated along a stretch of highway navigated by my morning bus to school.

Time slowed the first time I saw him in this new manifestation. His dirt-brown coat whipped behind him. The silver top of his cane gleamed. The urine yellow nails of his reaching hand were cracked, and his eyes were pinpricks glinting from the shadow cast by his hat's wide brim. A wry smile sneered up one side of his face mocking me, as if to say: "How funny am I now, you wrong headed child?"

The apoplectic fit I had in response to this unvoiced question was an answer in and of itself, for while it contained howls and screams, there was absolutely no laughter in it.

After that, I became a distraction to my fellow students, as the man took to appearing only while I was among them. In class, he would stand in the margins of textbooks, in the background of school flyers, on posters in the hallways, in murals covering their walls. Sometimes, I would walk down a corridor and see him in some fashion only to round a corner and see him again, waiting for me, as if he were walking me to class, which of course he was. And when I would arrive, I would find that, naturally, he had beaten me there, creeping somewhere within my eyeline.

I threw the books he squatted in, tore down the posters, defaced his murals, and soon became a "problem student," expelled for my aberrant behavior. This was his plan, to return me to the isolation of my home, where he could have me all to himself.

My parents, who had little patience for me as it was, were furious, and relegated me, permanently, to the basement of our home, forcing me to finish my education by schooling myself from books they sometimes left at the bottom of the basement stairs, along with my meals.

And of course, in every book, there was the man, sneering in supposed victory.

I came to believe that I was simply insane, paranoid to the point of delusion, the man merely a manifestation of this rampant derangement. He had to be, for the alternative was too much to bear. So I ignored him, refusing to so much as glance at him when he popped around the edges of paragraphs, or profaned an illustration. I treated him much as the eyes do the nose, and by the arrival of my eighteenth birthday, at which time I found myself unceremoniously ejected from my childhood home, I'd tricked myself into believing he did not exist.

I became a derelict, thrown atop the tangled pile of other browned and ragged leavings that increasingly choked the streets of our town. I became another of the specters ignored by those still blessed to travel between their daily distractions. And in one of the hunched and faded edifices that grow like fungus across our formerly fair city, those places abandoned and no longer populated by the distracted, one in which I and many others of my new ken had come to find shelter, he found me.

And I found him, changed again.

As I had graduated to adulthood, transformed from homed to unhomed, he had graduated as well, from the second dimension to the third, transformed himself into a tangible, touchable being, leaned up against the far interior wall of the moldy building inside of which I'd come to lay my head by night.

He looked at me across a sea of other derelicts, propped on his cane, reaching, and over a din of moans and sobs I heard with my ears, for the first time, his voice; soft and colored with rasp. And what he said was the very thing I'd always imagined him saying, the whisper that infected me so long ago with his presence.

He said, "I am coming."

And then, he pushed off that interior wall of that inferior home, stepped carefully across the rotten floor, between the rotten things that populated it, and came for me.

And for the first time in my life, he was welcomed.

The Dreamer

Silent liquidity, formless smoke and ephemera; a coalescence each night as I lay my head upon my pillow, the result of which is a locality that can only exist in the darkest of dreamscapes.

It smells of must and rot, has rows and corridors filled with shelves bursting with faded impressions, is populated by broken machines and gadgets, puppets, dummies, dolls, and mannikins, all of them crammed between books teeming with lost antiquity.

I have walked it up and down, climbed ladders interminable into heights of darkness unyielding, and I have never found an end. Such is the way of dream places, and if this dream place were like other dream places I would not deign to speak of it, but this dream place is more real than those others, lit not just by sputtering, unseen candles, but with a definite sureness of being. This place exists. It is out there, somewhere, and I believe that I am close to being swallowed up, digested by it, my fate to be filed onto one of its endless shelves, collected amongst its trappings.

I know it to be a place for the lost, the weak and the wounded.

For you see, I myself am lost, I am weak, I have been wounded. I remain so. This place knows this. It sought me out, as it seeks out all things irreparable, feeds upon them, sucks them dry of their cracks and sharp edges, until they are nothing more than twisted, soft curves fading into entropy.

Its shelves are covered in strange dust, which yields not to the touch. Its floors are layered with dirt and grime that sticks to the sole. Its ladders are filled with cracks, and crawl with woodlice, making each step up an exercise in fateful temptation. Though they never break, the fear that they will persists, and this fear nourishes it. It hungers for this fear just as much as it does despair, as it does loneliness. It drains and drains, bloats itself upon those most hateful of emotions, reducing the collected into ultimate stillness.

It has a strong, deterministic will, which it wields with careful discrimination, and along with this will it also bears a face, a face with eyes that watched you, a nose that sniffed you out, ears that heard your cries. This face rests upon a head, one that decided upon you, wished to bring you to it, and this head rests upon shoulders that carried you, arms that deposited you. It has legs and feet as well, ones that walked away immediately after.

In aggregate, a man.

You see, there is a proprietor of this place, felt, but unseen. Seen or not, however, he lingers there, his ubiety leaving an impression upon every inch of the space. He can be felt upon the pages of the books I try to peruse, but can never read. He can be smelt in the red fungal bloom bursting from their pages. He can be heard in echoed footsteps that seem to be, but cannot be, my own. When I climb the ladders, he is there behind me, but should I look to catch him climbing, only wisps of smoke-like darkness waft between the rungs. He rests in the dull glinting of the broken machines, in the whine of the dead gadgets as they fruitlessly struggle to come to life. He is in the dead, lifeless eyes of the dolls and the dummies, in the featureless facades of the broken mannikins.

He is there, but not there. He permeates.

I wish I could know this proprietor. I have called out so many times to him, rushed up and down the corridors professing this very wish, shaken the bookcases and ladders in sorrowful fury. But as I said, he does not answer. He merely brings me time and again to his dreamplace, taking slowly from me my darkness.

He does not wish to know me, I think, for I suppose I am to him as unimportant as any other thing he has collected for depletion. He only wishes to know the things inside of me that nourish him.

He probably believes that I am angry. He no doubt thinks that I wish to attack him in some way, even though to do so would be the height of futility, I'm sure. Maybe he thinks that I would beg for freedom from the fate he has visited upon me. Perhaps he believes that I will ask to join him, to assist him in his efforts in some way, as if I could ever do the things he does. I'm positive that of the multitudes that have come before me, all of them, in some fashion, have desired to interact with this man, but I doubt few if any of them sought the thing that I seek.

I wish for only one thing. I wish to offer him my sincere, and profound gratitude.

I spent my last evening in his dream place screaming this intention into the infinite. I told of all the hurtful things from which he is delivering me. I wept in appreciation of his efforts, held my hands above me in supplication, before tearing at my skin to offer that pain to him as well. I even made a space upon the shelves and climbed inside, curling myself into a ball, to show him just how natural I would find my eventual placement within his menagerie.

While he did not answer me directly, there was something, a slight touch upon my shoulder, no more than a whisper; there but for a moment, and then gone as quickly as it came. Afterward, I believe I heard soft footsteps moving away from me, and a click upon the wood floor accompanying them, like that of a cane. I am sure that he was with me, that I reached out to him and he briefly grabbed hold.

I believe my time is nigh.

Tonight, I return there, to show him again how much I desire his gift of consummation.

I lay my head upon my pillow. I close my eyes.

He is here.

The Collector

You spoke to me, sir, and I have listened. The lessons you imparted have not been in vain, for I have taken your wisdom and transformed it into action. You uncovered the truth of it—that gnawing, brooding, laughing, terrible thing behind every other thing—and you brought that knowledge to the world, tried to educate these fools. And how did they reward your good will? They all but ignored you.

But I did not.

I could find but one flaw in your design, and that flaw is that you delivered your wisdom to them, hoping that they would use it. I wouldn't have thought you to be such an optimist. No, these troglodytes would never, could never, do what needs to be done. They are caught up in the ruse, the trick, the "conspiracy." They are lost in the dream.

But I am awake, and when I am done with my work, my own "special plan," I will bring the Void to us.

I was first and foremost a seller and keeper of books; a collector, purveyor of things mysterious, and esoteric, and it was during the course of this perveyance that I stumbled upon your work.

Outside of this vocation, I was also a hobbyist, a fellow writer in fact, and it was this hobby that allowed me to understand the true nature of a writer. We—if you'll forgive the vulgar comparison of you and I—are conduits, prisms through which other, more strange truths and realities are projected. Only through us, and those like us, can certain things take shape in the world of humanity. Religions and the sciences, those idiocies that can only hope to do what we do, could never comprehend the truth or value of that which is our providence. We purposefully do what they do only by accident. We make the unreal, real. Not that I have to tell you that, of course, but it is important to me that you know that I know it, so that you'll see that I am in full possession of the facts, that I am not doing what I'm doing out of anything other than complete knowledge and understanding.

Esoterica, by its very nature, begats all manner of odd illuminations, so you can imagine that beyond the realms of academic and artistic literature lie whole continents of fantastic and even supernatural discourse, representing themselves not as fiction, but as actual fact, and in my efforts to aggregate the various knowledges I spent so many of my years meticulously gathering, I became frustrated, for there seemed no way for me to join it together into anything that could come close to sense. I could feel the truth in my bones, could see the puzzle depicting it laid out in pieces before me, but could not conceive of how to arrange them. I am not too proud to admit that, in the end, I reached the edge of complete madness trying to find that unifying thing that would make it all coagulate. And then, your work arrived on my doorstep, and pulled me back from the brink.

I became obsessed with it from my very first foray. I could see your vision immediately, and with each new tale I would dash back and forth between the shelves of my shop, corroborating and validating that which you so clearly defined. It was as if you put a key into the locked door that had been keeping my enlightenment at bay, and when the inky truth came flooding out, I was overtaken by the mania that followed.

I instructed every contact I'd accrued during my time as a bookkeeper to find and deliver to me anything you'd ever written. "If this man's name is on it, I want it" was the directive, and within a month I had it all in my possession. I consumed it, ravenously, my head not touching a pillow for days, until every word was transferred from the pages into my head.

Next, I made a great collage across the back wall in my back room, blasphemously tearing out pages and affixing them to it, pairing them with other pages from other books that validated their philosophies and assertions. My basic needs were ignored, nearly outright. That I was required to leave the room to relieve myself became the height of annoyance, and if my idiotic vanity had not prevented it, I may have done so right there, if only to not waste a single, precious moment in the pursuit of that which I could sense was just out of reach.

Then, it was finished. Standing before it I trembled, and as it slowly imparted upon me its great revelation, I collapsed into a ball of exultation and exhaustion. With your help, I had completed that which I'd been pursuing unknowingly my entire life: A fully formulated, and perfect, plan.

It was so simple. All I needed to do was what you had done so many times, what all writers do. I needed to conjure that which is unreal, bring it to life, and then do what I do best: collect it.

You see, the very essence of that which you dubbed "The Tsalal," and what I refer to simply as the Void, as you well know, stands behind and is incorporated into everything you've ever written. You saw past the illusion and stared into its eye. You beheld its shadow, and then cast that shadow upon each and every one of the little mirrors of yourself you "created" and called characters, imbuing them with a piece of that essence. Unfortunately, there was no way for me to collect that essence from those little yous, as they are too far removed from myself—and my own creative vision—to be of use.

But, there was another way.

I realized that all I needed to do was create my own Tiny Toms, ones I felt most strongly represented you. Much as you did, I would cast upon them the shadow of truth, and then—through various alchemical and arcane practices gleaned from my collection—force them out of the world of the unreal and into the world of the real to suffer in the ways in which you have suffered, and once that suffering hardened them into diamond like prisms, I would find and collect these tulpas in turn—The Performer, The Paranoiac, and The Dreamer—drawing from them that essence, and distilling it into a singular form, made up of only it.

Sadly, they were not enough. These homunculi were insufficient on their own. My talent and imagination proved inadequate. The thing I made from them was half-formed, embryonic, slithering in the pool in which I keep it, moaning and babbling incoherence, incapable of what I needed it to do. It required something *more*.

I puzzled over this for some time. How could I extract that which I needed if I could not use your characters, or my own? Truly, a frustrating conundrum. Then, one night—while stroking my malformed avatar as it warbled—I found myself engaging a book of interviews you'd given, hoping to glean some heretofore unrealized answer from your wisdom. And then, between the coos and the gurgles of my creation, it came to me.

I realized that I needed to collect a different sort of distillation. It occurred to me that not only do your characters carry the required essence, but also the readers and acolytes of the work you created by showing their struggles to the world. I was but one prism through which your vision was refracted. Your influence, niche though it may be, has created so many more prisms, equal to or even greater than my own.

So I went about collecting the most afflicted of your followers; the monk, the musician, the German, the academic, the journalist, and finally, the puppeteer. I drained them, one by one, of you; fed their distillate to my mewling abomination.

It was nearly enough. As you can plainly see, it is now almost fully formed, glutted on their contributions. But yet, still incomplete.

There is but one thing left to do.

None of them could reach the required purity. The essences I gleaned from them were too cloudy, too infected with the lie. To bring about the end of all this nonsense, my phylactery requires a refinement that can only be found in a singular person.

And now, here we are.

It was the puppeteer who led me to you, but do not blame him, he did not do so willingly. I tore the information from him before taking the rest of what I needed. He begged me to spare you. I couldn't make him understand.

As I did with him, I've tried tonight to make you see what's necessary, to accept it. This is the only way, you must believe me. Search your feelings, you know it to be true. For *my* work to be done, for *my* special plan to be enacted, I must fit this final piece. Look down there, into that pool at your feet, at that thing which has started to resemble you. Behold the labyrinthine blackness swarming behind its eyes, ready to burst out and consume us all. Be honest, don't you find it beautiful?

I suppose it doesn't matter.

I won't lie, it will hurt. It must. For what it's worth, I am genuinely sorry you will never get to see the thing our creation brings about when it finally howls its summoning and pulls your "Tsalal," my Void, screaming into the world. Don't you worry, though. I will greet it for the both of us.

Are you ready?

No?

Let's begin anyway.

Welcome, dear Tom, to The End.

TRAVELING SALESMAN

ZOE KAPLAN

Originally Published in *The Cosmic Background*

Editor's note: It's a sad thing to have to tell you a tragic story around the story we were originally going to give you.

Zoe Kaplan's "Traveling Salesman" won a Brave New Weird award this year. She wasn't there to receive it.

While reaching out to let her know the good news, we discovered that shortly after submitting her story to us, she passed away. She was 28, and a brilliant writer. She was a BNW nominee in 2022, a fact that took prominent billing in her bio, which only breaks our hearts even more. Because she believed in us, sent us more work, this year she won, and she's not here; and that's incredibly unfair.

Her original editor at *The Cosmic Background* kindly worked with us to ensure that you'll always be able to read her story; even if we don't have her permission to print it ourselves, we can lead you right to it.

And make no mistake, whether we can print it directly or not—Zoe Kaplan won.

BRAVE NEW WEIRDOS, CLASS OF 2024

[sarah] Cavar is the author of *Failure to Comply* (featherproof books, 2024) and *Differential Diagnosis* (Northwestern University Press, 2026). They are editor-in-chief of manywor(l)ds.place, and their work can be found in *Electric Lit, The Rumpus, Split Lip Magazine*, and elsewhere. Cavar holds a PhD in Cultural Studies from the University of California: Davis.

Ainsley Hawthorn, PhD, is an author and cultural historian who writes about forgotten events, curious folklore, and the surprising connections between past and present. Her articles and op-eds have appeared in *National Geographic, The Washington Post*, CBC, and *Psychology Today*, and her nonfiction anthology *Land of Many Shores: Perspectives from a Diverse Newfoundland and Labrador* was named one of *The Telegram*'s Top Ten NL Books of 2021.

Alex Woodroe (she/her) is a Romanian writer and editor of dark speculative fiction. She's the author of *Whisperwood*, and has several short stories published in venues like Horror Library and the Nosleep podcast. Alex lives in the heart of the Transylvanian region of Romania, and is the Editor in Chief of **Tenebrous Press**.

Angela Liu is a Chinese-American writer/poet from NYC who writes about intergenerational trauma and Weird things. She is a 2x Nebula Award finalist and has also been nominated for the Hugo, Astounding, Ignyte, and Rhysling Awards. She formerly researched mixed reality storytelling at Keio University in Japan. Her stories and poetry are published in *Strange Horizons, Clarkesworld, Uncanny, The Dark, Interzone Digital, Lightspeed,*

When she's not bumbling through a mystical realm, **Azure Arther** is a playwright, an author, a poet, and, occasionally, a dryad. Her short stories and poems have appeared in over two dozen publications, including *midnight & indigo, Small Wonders*, and *Rogue Agent*. She is an editor for Augur Literary Society and has been a resident artist or scholarship recipient for numerous organizations.

Emma Burnett is a researcher and writer. She has had stories in *Nature:Futures, Mythaxis, Northern Gravy, Radon, Flash Fiction Online, Apex, Utopia, MetaStellar, Milk Candy Review, Roi Fainéant, JAKE*, and more. Her favourite story this month is "The Loneliness of the Long-Distance Teleporter" by M.J. Pettit in Flash Fiction Online.

Hailing from a haunted seaside town in Massachusetts, **Emmett Nahil** is the author of novel *From the Belly* (Tenebrous Press, 2024) and graphic novel *Let Me Out* (Oni Press, 2023). His obsession with horror and speculative fiction has taken his writing to *Nightmare Magazine, The Molotov Cocktail*, and elsewhere. In his other life, Emmett is the Narrative Director and co-founder of Perfect Garbage Studios.

Erik McHatton's passion for horror literature began in grade school and can be credited to an early fascination with the "Terrific Triples" horror collections of Helen Hoke. He has been published several times in print and online publications such as *CHM Magazine, Vastarien, Tales to Terrify*, and *Lovecraftiana*. His first fiction collection, *Straw World and Other Echoes from the Void*, will be published in 2025 by Undertaker Books. He lives in Kentucky with his beautiful wife and kids.

F. J. Bergmann is the poetry editor of *Mobius: The Journal of Social Change*. She lives in Wisconsin and fantasizes about tragedies on or near exoplanets. Her work has appeared in *Abyss & Apex, Analog, Asimov's SF,* and elsewhere in the alphabet. She has competed at National Poetry Slam and is a Grand Master of the Science Fiction & Fantasy Poetry Association. She likes to ride horses. She is pretty sure she'd like to ride unicorns, if only they'd cooperate. She thinks imagination can compensate for anything.

Hannah Greer's work has been featured in *Solarpunk Magazine, PseudoPod, Radon Journal*, and elsewhere. She is a first reader for *Fusion Fragment*, hoards books, and competes in combat sports. She resides in North Carolina with her partner, a trio of cats, a small flock of pigeons, and several geckos.

Ira Rat works and lives in Ames, IA. He runs Filthy Loot Press.

K.A. Wiggins (Kaie) is an award-winning Canadian speculative fiction author whose quietly subversive works explore the tangled webs of society, environment, and identity through intricate, dreamlike tales of monsters and magic.

Kay Vaindal is an environmental scientist and fiction writer who lives in Baltimore. Her favorite smells are sagebrush, dog paws, corn chip smell, and dimethyl sulfide. Her fiction has appeared in *Seize the Press, the Drabblecast*, and many anthologies.

Leo Oliveira hails from Ontario, Canada, where he studied psychology and creative writing. He nurses a soft spot for rats, prehistory, and flawed queer characters. His work has appeared or is forthcoming in *Radon Journal, Fusion Fragment*, and *Heartlines Spec*, (among others). His work has also been nominated for the PEN/Robert J. Dau Short Story Prize for Emerging Writers and Best Horror of the Year.

M. L. Krishnan originally hails from the coastal shores of Tamil Nadu, India. She has been awarded Fellowships and Residencies from Tin House, MacDowell, Millay Arts, and the Clarion West Writers Workshop. Her stories and essays have appeared, or are forthcoming in *Strange Horizons*, *Black Warrior Review*, *Diabolical Plots* and elsewhere. Her work has been anthologized in *The Year's Best Dark Fantasy & Horror, Afterlives: The Year's Best Death Fiction, Wigleaf Top 50* and more.

Matt Blairstone (he/him) is a writer, editor, artist, indie comics creator and the publisher/founder of **Tenebrous Press**. He lives in Portland, Oregon. Ghosts believe in him.

Matthew Mitchell is a fiction and comics writer from the Ozarks. His award-winning novella *Chaindevils* was published by Weirdpunk Books, and his short fiction is collected in *Release the

Horse from Filthy Loot Press. Matthew's comics have appeared in *Heavy Metal Magazine* and he is co-editor of the *Horrorium* comics anthology.

Plangdi Neple is a Nigerian writer and editor whose dark and fantastical tales have appeared in magazines such as *Anathema, Omenana,* and *FIYAH.* A lover of the weird and unnatural, his works draw inspiration from Nigerian myth, folklore and tradition. He is a co-recipient of the Milford 2024 Bursary and a Voodoonauts 2024 Fellow.

Samir Sirk Morató is a scientist, artist, and flesh heap. Some of their published and forthcoming work can be found in *Strange Horizons, Cosmic Horror Monthly, Nightmare,* and *khōréō.*

Shantell Powell is a two-spirit elder goth and swamp hag who grew up on the land and off the grid all over Canada in an apocalyptic cult. An alum of the Banff Centre for Arts and Creativity, The Writers' Studio at SFU, Vancouver Manuscript Intensive, the LGBTQ+ Novel Immersive at GrubStreet, Roots Wounds Words, and LET(s) Lead Academy at Yale. When she's not writing or making things, she wrangles chinchillas or gets filthy in the woods.

Sharang Biswas is an NYC-based writer, artist, and game designer. He has won IndieCade, ENNIE, and IGDN awards for his games and has showcased interactive works at galleries, museums, and festivals including Pioneer Works in Brooklyn, the Institute of Contemporary Art in Philadelphia, and the Museum of the Moving Image in Queens. His stories have been selected for two editions of *We're Here: The Best Queer Speculative Fiction;* his first book *The Iron Below Remembers* is out now from Neon Hemlock Press.

SJ Townend has dark fiction published in Eerie River Publishing, Vastarien, Ghost Orchid Press, *Dark Matter Magazine* and more. Her first horror collection, *Sick Girl Screams,* introduced by Robert Shearman, is out now (Brigid's Gate Press) and her second horror collection, *Your Final Sunset,* is coming—for you—in 2025 (Sley House Press). She's currently working on a third. Some (most) of her stories are inspired by the disgusting things her two wild children do.

Sonya Vatomsky is the author of poetry collection *Salt Is For Curing* and two poetry chapbooks. Their fiction has been shortlisted for the PFD Queer Fiction Prize and their nonfiction has appeared in The New York Times, Rolling Stone, and Smithsonian Magazine. Sonya was born in the Soviet Union and lives in Northern England.

Susan L. Lin is a Taiwanese American storyteller who hails from southeast Texas and holds an MFA in Writing from California College of the Arts. Her novella *Goodbye to the Ocean* won the 2022 Etchings Press novella prize, and her literary/visual art has appeared in nearly a hundred publications. She loves to dance.

Tehnuka (she/they) calls on all of us to use our wonderful, unique minds and/or bodies in whatever ways we can to refuse and resist the genocide of Palestinian people and the colonisation of Palestine. Resist with every breath and deed until Palestine is free—until we are all free.

Tiffany Michelle Brown is a Los Angeles-based writer who once had a conversation with a ghost over a pumpkin beer. She is the author of *How Lovely to Be a Woman: Stories and Poems* and co-host of the Horror in the Margins podcast. Her stories and poetry have been featured in publications by Ominous Thrill, Tenebrous Press, Black Spot Books, Death Knell Press, and the NoSleep Podcast.

Tim Pratt (genderfluid, any pronouns) is the author of more than 30 novels, most recently multiverse/space opera adventure *The Knife and the Serpent*. She's a Hugo Award winner for short fiction, and has been a finalist for Nebula, World Fantasy, Sturgeon, Philip K. Dick, Mythopoeic, Stoker, and other awards.

Zoe Kaplan (she/her) has been making up stories for as long as she can remember. She has a Bachelor's in creative writing from Appalachian State University and no less than four different swords. Her work has appeared in *Tree and Stone* Magazine, *Hidden Realms*, and the *Horror Library* anthology series, among many others. Her story "The Test" was nominated for the 2022 Brave New Weird award. She is a winner of the 2024 Brave New Weird award for "Travelling Salesman".

BRAVE NEW WEIRD– NOMINATED STORIES, 2024

(Author—Title—Original Publication/Publisher)

Aleksandra Ugelstad Elnæs—Spolia—Egaeus Press

Alex Fox—The City of Cities, Inverted; A Shadow Cast By Many Hands—*Myriad* (Hexagon)

Ann LeBlanc—Memories Held Against a Hungry Mouth—Three Lobed Burning Eye

Avra Margariti—Unbirthday Means You Wish Yourself Unborn—Seize the Press

Briar Ripley Page—Birth Of a Sucker—*It Was All a Dream 2* (Hungry Shadow Press)

Calla Eris Orion—Kiss of a Toad—manywor(l)ds.place

Casey Lawrence—Ten Things I Have Learned About Human Skin: A Presentation—*SKIN: An anthology of dark fiction* (Bag of Bones Press)

Dane Erbach—Something Else—*Mythaxis Magazine*

David Corse—The Amassing Man—House of Gamut

E.G. Condé—Sibilance—Interzone

E.M. Linden—Mangrove Daughter—Kaleidotrope

Elad Haber—End of Line—*Even Cozier Cosmic* (Underland Press)

Elana Gomel—Mother Black Hole—*If I Die Before I Wake* (Sinister Smile Press)

Eleanna Castroianni—Zarghána—*Uncanny Magazine*

Emma E. Murray—An Angel of God—*Vastarien* (Grimscribe Press)

Faith Allington—Teacakes for Foxes—*Broken Antler Magazine*

Guan Un—Painted Surfaces—*Nightmare Magazine*

Jack Klausner—Cardboard Faces—ergot.

Jack Lennon—The Scottish Welfare Fund Application Form—*God's Cruel Joke Literary Magazine*

James Cato—Wonders of a Plastic Ocean—Hexagon

Jes Malitoris—The House of Coiled Earth—*The Crawling Moon: Queer Tales of Inescapable Dread* (Neon Hemlock)

Jess Elizabeth Reed—The Belly—*MYRIAD* (Hexagon)

K. A. Roy—Welcome to Rebirth Grove—Malarkey Books

Kelsea Yu—Creature—Kaleidotrope

Lena Ng—The Halloween Horror Show—*Ghoulish Tales* (Ghoulish Books)

Leslie What—Wayback—khōréō

Lor Gislason—fumes—Weirdpunk Books

Lucas Yao-Bendimerad—So Dramatic—*The Horror Zine*

Madalena Daleziou—Hauntless House—*Inner Worlds*

Nayt Rundquist—Flashes of Neverwhen—*Genrepunk Magazine*

O F Cieri—The Tragedy Brotherhood—Weirdpunk Books

Raluca Balasa—Cogs in the (War) Machine—*Fraidy Cat Quarterly Volume 2*

Ryan T. Jenkins—The Potato Problem—*Hearth & Coffin Literary Journal*

Timaeus Bloom—Memorabilia—*Cosmic Horror Monthly*

BRAVEST, NEWEST, WEIRDEST

Additional Winners For This Year in New Weird Fiction

Editor's note: Each year, this section makes me curse because of how long it takes to put together, and each year, I look forward to it and get so much out of it. There's no continuity; categories come and go, I do as I please, because frankly, all we want is to showcase a snapshot of the true New Weird in this moment in time, and sometimes, that looks a little chaotic.

But also: there's only so much we can possibly view, review, and get through alone. It breaks my heart that I wasn't able to include a music category. I just could not have done it justice. As it stands, I know I missed many, many great things. I can't promise you anything other than this: what's here is fun and worthy and amazing, and you should pay attention to it.

And if you're a rabid fanatic of games, or comics, or music, or YA Weird, or anything else, and have time you want to volunteer? Drop us a line. Maybe we can work together and expand this section. The rewards are numerous; just be warned that they're all fictional.

Without further waffle; here are our BNW-nominated and BNW-winning works of this year!

xoxo
Alex

Winners in bold

NOVEL/LA
***The Head*—Robyn Braun—Enfield & Wizenty**
Failure to Comply—[Sarah Cavar]—Featherproof Books
Skull Slime Tentacle Witch War—Rick Claypool—Anxiety Press
The Siege of Burning Grass—Premee Mohamed—Solaris

COLLECTION

***Love Skull*—Emma Alice Johnson—Weirdpunk Books**

The Nightmare Box and Other Stories—Cynthia Gomez—Cursed
  Morsels Press

A Study in Ugliness & Outras Histórias—H. Pueyo—Lethe Press

Your Utopia—Bora Chung, Anton Hur (Translator)—Algonquin
  Books

SEQUEL

***The Sunforge (The Endsong)*—Sascha Stronach—Saga
  Press**

(Note: truly sorry that we did not wise up to the first of this series
in time for the first BNW; incredibly excited that we get to give it a
win now. Consider this an endorsement of the series as a whole
and go read it immediately. Yes, I made a sequel category just for
this book. Fight me. After you read it!)

COMIC

***The Sickness*—Jenna Cha, Lonnie Nadler & more—
  Uncivilized Books**

Tomorrow You Don't Know Me—raven lyn clemens—self

Zombie Funeral Services—Zephygaru , Mo.I—webtoons

Vengeance Is For The Living—Keenan Marshall Keller, Alex
  Delaney—Floating World

MOVIE

I Saw the TV Glow

Pater Noster and the Mission of Light

Sometimes I Think About Dying

All You Need is Death (and a special mention to this soundtrack;
  care of Ian Lynch)

GAMES

***The Exit 8*—Developer: KOTAKE CREATE Publisher:
  PLAYISM**

Animal Well—Developer: Billy Basso Publisher: Bigmode

Lorelei and the Laser Eyes—Developer: Simogo Publisher:
  Annapurna Interactive

Still Wakes the Deep—Developer: The Chinese Room Publisher:
  Secret Mode

ANTHOLOGY

***Through the Night Like a Snake: Latin American Horror Stories*—Sarah Coolidge—Two Lines Press**

Feral Architecture: Ballardian Horror—Sam Richards—Weirdpunk Books

The Crawling Moon: Queer Tales of Inescapable Dread—Dave Ring—Neon Hemlock

Escalators to Hell: Shopping Mall Horrors—Jennifer Jeanne McArdle and Michael W. Phillips Jr.—From Beyond Press

MAGAZINE

***Flash Fiction Online, Issue 133, The Weird Horror Issue*—Avra Margariti & Eugenia Triantafyllou (Guest Editors)—Rebecca Halsey (Editor-in-Chief)—Flash Fiction Online**

Fraidy Cat Quarterly: Volume 2—Robert Helfst, ed.—Fraidy Cat Press

Old Moon Quarterly, Issue 7—Caitlyn Emily Wilcox, ed.—Old Moon Publishing

Hexagon Magazine Issue 18/Fall 2024—JW Stebner, ed.—Hexagon Speculative Fiction Magazine

ACKNOWLEDGEMENT OF COPYRIGHT

"Mad Studies" originally appeared in *khōréō* Magazine.

"Big Cats of Newfoundland" originally appeared in *Cryptids from the Rock,* eds. Ellen Curtis & Erin Vance (Engen Books).

"A Contract of Ink and Skin" originally appeared in *Uncanny* Magazine.

"Reciprocity" originally appeared in *Aurealis* Magazine.

"Plastic-eating fungus caused doomsday[2][3]" originally appeared in *Nature* Journal.

"Vining" originally appeared in *The Book of Queer Saints, Volume 2* (Medusa Haus Press).

"The Man Who Collected Ligotti" originally appeared in *Cosmic Horror Monthly.*

"The Museum of Etymology" originally appeared in *Star*Line.*

"To Be Human" originally appeared in *PseudoPod.*

"Soft" originally appeared in *"hairs."* (Filthy Loot Press).

"The Tangle (Did Not Kill Kitsault)" originally appeared in *Strange Horizons* Magazine.

"Pig House" originally appeared in *Seize the Press.*

"They Remember Faces" originally appeared in *Radon* Journal.

"Measurements Expressed as Units of Separation" originally appeared in *The Crawling Moon: Queer Tales of Inescapable Dread* (Neon Hemlock).

"Knight Rumors" originally appeared in *Profane Altars: Weird Sword & Sorcery*, Sam Richards, ed. (Weirdpunk Books).

"Not All Your Bones Are Yours" originally appeared in *FIYAH* Literary Magazine.

"EGREGORE" originally appeared in *ergot.*

"The Snow Hath No Queen" originally appeared in *Metastellar.*

"Waiting for Jonah" originally appeared in Nightmare Magazine.

"I Have Seen Seven Bad Things" originally appeared in *TOO BAD, YOU DIE* (Infested Publishing).

"The Yolo Wallpaper" originally appeared in Witch Craft Magazine.

"Gravitational Pull" originally appeared on taiwaneseamerican.org.

"You Can Leave Your Helmet On" originally appeared in Interstellar Flight Magazine, April 2024.

"Full Immersion" originally appeared in *Tales of Sley House 2024* (Sley House Publishing).

"The Liminal Space Dating Agency" originally appeared on the author's Patreon.

CONTENT WARNINGS

Being a work of mature Horror, a degree of violence, gore, sex and/or death is to be expected. For more specific concerns, please check the list of stories below for specific potential triggers suggested by the publisher and by the authors themselves:

The Tangle (Did Not Kill Kitsault): Animal cruelty/death, racism, sexism/gender discrimination

Mad Studies: Animal death, institutionalization

Pig House: Attempted self-induced abortion (discussed)

Waiting for Jonah: Animal death (off page), homophobia

They Remember Faces: Cannibalism, child/animal abuse, suicide

The Man Who Collected Ligotti: Child abuse, anxiety, depression, kidnapping, stalking, torture

Grab another Tenebrous title!

Grab another Tenebrous title!

TENEBROUS

PRESS

Home of New Weird Horror, New Weird Dark Fiction, Oddities, Abnormalities and All Manner of Eccentricities You Never Knew You Needed More Than Oxygen

FIND OUT MORE:

www.tenebrouspress.com

@TenebrousPress on social media

HAIL THE TENEBROUS CULT